The Two-Sided Set-Up

Eileen Haavik McIntire

𝒜manita Books
Columbia, MD

The Two-Sided Set-Up

Copyright © 2018 by Eileen Haavik McIntire

Publisher: Amanita Books, Columbia, MD 21045. 410-290-7058. sumcross@aol.com

Author Websites: www.ehmcintire.com, www.secretpanels.net

LCCN: 2018936827

ISBN 978-0-9991565-2-0

Acknowledgements

The inspiration for this book comes from my husband, Dr. Roger McIntire, a psychologist who writes books for parents. His suggestions are positive and affirming. He asks parents to find something they can praise about their children and to let their children know they like them. He adds that other people won't treat your children any better than you do.

So what would an abused daughter of an alcoholic find in the world? What kind of friends would she make? What kind of people would she attract? That's how my story begins.

This book was also inspired by nostalgia for the three years I spent living on a boat and traveling the Intracoastal Waterway from Annapolis to Key West.

I also want to thank the usual suspects who provide encouragement, critiques, and suggestions. These include Marilyn Magee, cozy mystery author Millie Mack, Janis Wilson, editor Chase Nottingham, and readers Dr. Tom Fowler and Warren Schmidt, who are also authors.

This is a work of fiction. Any resemblance to a particular person or place is purely coincidental. I aspire to be accurate in my facts, but any errors are strictly my own.

Eileen Haavik McIntire

Chapter 1

I nibbled a peanut butter sandwich on my boat in peace, gazing at the budding trees mirrored in the placid water of this quiet cove. I was alone. No one to harass me, try to control me, tell me what to do. I could think and act like my own person, an adult woman, employed and competent.

Still, I felt as if I were only partly there. The rest of me, the self I hid, remained as a raw disconnect in my apartment. The boat was my real home, the place where I felt strong and capable. Here in this serene cove, perhaps I could pull myself together and ponder my mistakes.

Last night in my apartment in town, I woke up startled by a strange noise. A glance at the illuminated dial on the nightstand clock showed me it was one-fifteen. I lay in bed, held my breath, and listened. I heard the odd noise again—a soft rustling along the wood floor. Would a mouse sound like that?

I couldn't see Ryan in the dark and extended my foot to touch him under the pile of tousled blankets. Was he awake? Maybe he'd heard it, too.

"Ryan," I whispered. "Wake up."

No warm body responded to my touch. He wasn't there.

I sat up, peering into the darkness. Could that rustling sound be Ryan? Coming back from the bathroom or the kitchen? I clicked on the lamp and blinked as my eyes focused. Then I stared open-mouthed in shock.

Today, even though bright sunlight revived my spirit as I sat on the boat in this serenity, I shivered as I remembered what I saw last night.

On the floor, wearing black from head to toe, his face smeared with some kind of black goop, a man crawled toward me. His teeth were clamped down hard on a long, narrow knife, sharp and lethal-looking. He could kill with it, and Ryan looked like a killer.

I retreated instinctively to the blank-faced stolidity I showed when confronted. *Never let him see your fear.* My heart beat so loud he must hear it, and I wanted to shrink back against the headboard, but that's what he wanted. My terror. I had faced terror before. I wouldn't succumb now. I asked in as strong a voice as I could muster, "What are you doing?" Whatever happened, he would not cow me.

He stopped in mid-crawl and stared up at me. A puzzled expression crossed his face.

His puzzlement gave me courage. "Ryan, Ryan, wake up! It's me, Melanie, your friend."

I pulled the blanket up to my chin and hid my shaking hands under it. I had to keep talking. *Get him talking.*

"What's the matter, Ryan?" I asked, keeping my voice calm and confident. *Drop the knife, Ryan. Drop the knife.* "What's the matter?" I asked again.

His glassy eyes changed to gradual recognition. I could see the present return as the past slid into the background.

He shook his head. His body quivered. The knife clattered on the floor. He recoiled at the noise, but then gazed blankly at me. "Where am I?"

My boat rocked in the wake of a large yacht heading out to Long Island Sound. Since I was alone, I indulged in a shudder as I remembered the sight of him, shrouded in black, a knife in his teeth. What if I hadn't woken up? Would he have stabbed me? Would I be dead now?

I met Ryan three months before through an online dating site. I am wary of close relationships, but we hit it off, both of us hiding who we were. We put down similar preferences on the dating questionnaire. My photo showed me to be attractive enough—not a turn-off but not a beauty queen, either. It was all innocuous stuff, no-risk items that didn't require trust, which I don't have. Walking on the beach, watching the sunset, reading poetry.

He seemed nice enough at first, and we were both about the same age, late twenties. We'd only just started sleeping together, but I was beginning to notice an edginess in him that made me uncomfortable. It was time to move on. His actions last night made it imperative.

I took another sip of my morning coffee. I had lived through the night, but I didn't feel at all guilty about taking this day off to pull myself together. A solitary day of R&R on my boat felt good. My own special kind of rest and relaxation. Alone. I liked being alone. No fights. No quarrels. No threatening talk. No facade. Being by myself was good, but the events of the night before haunted me.

Thank goodness he dropped the knife, and I could breathe again, telling myself to remain in control but act sympathetic, behave like a friend. "You must have had a terrible dream or something," I said, softening my voice and easing slowly out of bed on the opposite side, keeping my movements smooth and steady, controlled but non-threatening. He could pick up the knife in an instant. I stepped around to the foot of the bed, then sat down on the covers and patted the place next to me. "Sit here." *Act like nothing's wrong. Don't look at the knife.* I had to force my eyes off it.

"You're safe now," I said. *No sudden moves.* I slowly reached for him, hoping to distract him from that knife. "You're safe with me."

"Oh, my god," Ryan whispered, crawling over the knife. As he reached the bed, he pulled himself up to sit beside me. He covered his face with his hands. "I don't know what happens to me." He turned to me, the black makeup smeared on his hands, tears leaving streaks in the goop on his face.

I put my arms around him, hugged him close and away from the knife. "You're safe now," I repeated in a calm and soothing voice. "Everything's okay." The black goop smeared onto my new pink nightgown. It didn't matter. After this, I'd never want to wear it again.

He buried his head in my shoulder. "It was Afghanistan, you know. They sent me home. Complete breakdown. PTSD they called it."

I looked down at him, the fear giving way to pity. "Are you getting treatment?"

"Sure." Ryan sighed. "I'm sorry." He wiped his face on a corner of the blanket and noticed the black stain it left. His body jerked as his head came up. His eyes gazed from one wall to the next.

"I should go." He shuddered and shook his head. "I'm sorry about this. Look, I'll clean up and change and be out of your hair." He gave me a weak smile, but then his body slumped. He stared at the wall in front of us. I held his hand, afraid to move, unwilling to speak for fear my words might cause him to reach for the knife. It lay glittering on the floor in front of us.

"Something comes over me, and I do weird things," he said, not looking at me. "Can't help it." He rubbed his face with his hands. "I'm so sorry I put you through this."

"It's okay. I understand." I stood and gently pulled him up. "Go on in and take a shower, then come into the kitchen. I'll fix breakfast." I longed to get away from him, to escape and run away to my boat.

I watched Ryan limp into the bathroom, head bowed, and shut the door. My arms and legs trembled with relief. For a moment, I remained sitting on the bed, listening to him stumble across the room and then turn on the shower.

I grabbed the knife and hid it in a drawer under my underwear. As sorry as I felt for the man, seeing him in that black outfit scared the wits out of me. I never wanted to go through that experience again.

While he showered, I threw on jeans and a T-shirt and ran a comb through my brown hair, cut short the way I remembered my mother's. Then I walked into the kitchen of my tiny one-bedroom apartment. The clock said one-forty-five. The most terrifying half hour I'd spent in my life. I took all the other knives out of the drawer, put them in a bag, and stowed them under the sink.

The shower should calm him. Neither one of us was going to bed after this. What should I do? I didn't want anything to set him off. Was he dangerous or just disturbed? Would he have used the knife if I hadn't woken up?

I wanted him to go.

I had to be careful. Making him breakfast would distract him and keep me at a distance. After that, he would have to get ready for work, and I could send him on his way. I hoped the best for him but never wanted to see him again.

I put on the coffee and got out the granola and yogurt. He liked that kind of breakfast, so I'd stocked up. I pulled out a bowl of blueberries, too, and broke three eggs into a bowl for an omelet. Then I sat down to wait for him.

After I'd gotten rid of Ryan, I tried to get more sleep. Impossible. I watched the sun rise and then called the office, leaving a message. I took a cab through the noise and congestion of New York City to the train station and bought a ticket for the commuter train to Norwalk, Connecticut. Two minutes later, my phone vibrated with a call coming in. I looked at the ID panel. My friend Amy. She found out I was staying home today. She'd needle me until she found out why. I felt too dispirited and tired to cope with Amy's sympathy. I didn't answer the phone, and I didn't call her back.

At Norwalk, I got off the train and hiked two miles to the marina on the Norwalk River. I needed to walk to shake off the emotional hangover from last night. The warm day, soft breeze redolent of spring flowers, and blooming daffodils, bright yellow in the sun, brought energy to my step even though I'd slept little last night. I hoped I could get to my boat unrecognized. The dock master and other boaters all knew me, but I didn't want their comments or advice, no matter how well meant. I didn't want to talk to anyone, but it was a vain hope.

"Taking a day off, are you?" asked the dock master, ready to stop me for a chat. I waved, but hearing his voice, two fishermen checking their tackle in an open boat, glanced up at me.

"Fishing's not too good today," said one. "We just came back.

Didn't catch a thing."

Their good-hearted cheer momentarily broke through my re-solve. "Too bad," I said. "Maybe I'll try my luck."

I stepped out on the dock, then paused a moment, gazing in fondness at the beat-up trawler before me. R&R. Refuge and retreat. An expensive necessity that none of my friends knew about. This was private, an escape that was mine alone. The one good thing my father taught me.

I leaped onboard. I had a luxury so many women longed for—a room of my own. A secret place just for me, and one I planned to keep, no matter what other mistakes I made.

No one, not Ryan, not my friends, not my boss, no one could find me here. I could be myself. A real person and not the strong, competent, in control fake I presented to the world.

I grew up on the water and always had access to some kind of boat I could row or paddle or sail. In my early years, when the family was intact and functioning, my father worked as a ship-yard carpenter, and we'd lived close to the water. He liked to fish, and so did I. That was about the only thing we had in common.

Of course, we had a boat, and when my father wasn't using it, which was most of the time, I could take it out. Later, when my father's drinking was out of control, and my mother left, the boat got me away from the house and his rage to the peace of the river.

The watercraft changed as I grew. First, a sturdy rowboat, then a canoe. Then a glossy speedboat with outboard motor, but all those boats belonged to my dad, so using them depended on following his arbitrary rules and schedule.

The boat I now owned, the one I scrimped and saved for, was mine alone. It was built with a fiberglass hull and inboard diesel engine. Before I bought it, I ordered it hauled out of the water and inspected thoroughly. I'd heard my father laugh too many times at the "landlubbers" who'd bought a boat with big dreams only to find the hull was rotten or the motor worn out.

A marina was the land of broken dreams, he said, but my boat was tight and in good shape, even though it looked well-used. It featured a tiny head—bathroom to landlubbers, minuscule galley, two bunks, and an enclosed wheelhouse with windows all around, but what I loved most was the roomy open cockpit at the stern. My "back porch." With a deck chair and a small table, it made a comfortable place to sit outside.

So how long had my relationship with Ryan lasted? Three months. Almost a record. I knew he was in the service and suffered from PTSD. He was one of the walking wounded, like myself in a way, which drew me to him. Panic attacks plagued me, and I suffered from debilitating nightmares, waking up screaming, "Don't hit me!" They terrified me. No telling what they'd do to anyone else who witnessed them. That's why I hardly ever let any man I dated spend the night. Ryan had been an exception. So while I was afraid my nightmares would frighten him, the horrors he was living with terrified me.

Chalk it up to another bad choice. I always seem to select the wrong kind of men, the cauldrons waiting to explode, the losers, the crazies, the disturbed men like Ryan. In one way or another, all the men I date are like Ryan.

It was times like this when I needed my boat. I could take it out, find a quiet place on the river, and anchor. Sometimes I'd drop a line in the water, and if I caught a fish, I might let it go, or if I felt like it, I might clean it for supper. If I were particularly morose, I'd see myself in that fish. Caught. An unwilling victim bearing her throat for the fatal slash.

Just stepping aboard made me feel better. I breathed in the salty smell of seaweed, gazed out at the sun sparkles on the river, and heard the gulls overhead screeching in their search for fish. I started the engine, checked the fuel supply, untied the lines, and backed out of the slip. I was in control and at peace.

I loved being on the water, and I loved boats. I needed boats. Taking mine out on the river was the best medicine for the horror of the night before. I hoped never to live through another one like that, but my track record was poor.

Why did I home in on the losers and the lost? My friend Amy at work met someone online, and they'd been together six years. He even had a good job, too, and everyone liked him.

Something was wrong with my internal selection mechanism, probably because with no positive role models for either men or relationships in my life—except Amy's of course—I'd never learned to discriminate. Maybe I was never meant to have a good relationship. Only a fake one that matched my fake self.

Next time I'd be more careful.

Chapter 2

I gave Amy and my boss Norma an edited version of my last stand with Ryan. Even with that, they were shocked.

"I would have been terrified," said Amy. "I never met anyone like that. Most of the men I dated before I met Charles," her eyes softened, "were mostly nice people."

Yeah, I felt like saying, but that's you, not me.

"I'm glad you got away okay," added Norma. "I guess a girl really has to be careful who she picks to go out with."

"But how do you know?" I asked.

"Oh, you'll know," said Amy, nodding her head.

Amy might know, but I wouldn't. After Ryan, I was in no hurry to find a boyfriend. I'd just make another poor choice, so three months passed without a date—a long dry spell for me—but I wasn't looking. Online dating sites had given me Ryan and a couple of other bad experiences. New York's bar scene didn't interest me and would only bring on another disaster. Museum exhibits and classes never netted anyone new in my life—not that I was looking.

I only had to review my dating history to realize that something inside me needed to change before I got involved with anyone else. I didn't know what that was, and even if I did, how would I change it? I was banking on time or experience or maturity. Maybe something would happen. Meanwhile, I enjoyed the alone time and spending weekends on my boat.

One day Norma stopped at my desk. "How about joining me and Tom for the evening?" she asked. "We have three tickets for a charity fundraiser in downtown Manhattan." I knew they were both on influential boards in the city.

I had nothing else to do. "Sure," I said. "Might be fun." Norma and her husband Tom were good company, and Norma always stopped short of giving me advice, which I appreciated.

I didn't expect much from the evening. My hair is brunette, straight and short and standard issue as are my blue eyes. Nothing stands out about me, not even my personality, which I've never heard described as "bubbly." People either tell me they appreciate my calm competence or say I have a chip on my shoulder. Amy calls me a "good sport" and appreciates my snarky sense of humor, so maybe that's a positive asset, but no one will mistake me for someone with money. I avoid mentioning I'm an account-ant since most people's eyes glaze over at the word.

I walked into the hotel ballroom with Norma and Tom and felt glad I'd changed into a plain black cocktail dress. Men were in tuxes and women wore dresses they probably bought at Neiman Marcus. Most of them had contributed thousands to the cause. That included Norma and Tom.

I didn't have that kind of money, but I toyed with a fleeting thought I might meet someone with a good job and money for a change—not that he'd give me a second glance, but then I proba-bly wouldn't give him a second glance either. Given my track record, I'd home in on the freeloader instead.

As the evening wore on with idle chitchat, I happened to turn and notice a tall, dark-haired man in a black formal jacket and black slacks staring at me. He smiled and lifted his glass in my direction with cocked head and a raised eyebrow. I started to turn away, but then he walked over and introduced himself.

"Hunter McCann," he said with a sweet smile. "Haven't noticed you before at one of these affairs." He twirled his glass and gestured at the people around us.

"I'm Melanie Fletcher," I stammered. "It's my first time..." I could feel myself blushing at the possible double entendre. "That is, I haven't been here before." The man's eyes were too close together, and his nose was crooked, but his blue eyes were striking. He looked smooth as if he wore a tuxedo to take out the garbage, and in the formal outfit, he was quite a handsome man. I pulled myself together. "Do you come to these events often?"

Hunter kept the smile. His eyes twinkled. "Of course. I am happy to support charities like this one. I also volunteer to help with the fundraising." I attributed his stiff words to nervousness. He had a faint New Jersey accent. He seemed like a nice man.

He glanced at the glass I held. "Let me refresh your drink." He took it and my arm and steered me to the cash bar. I glanced around the room. Most of the guests were older, in their fifties and sixties, I guessed. And most of them were coupled up. Hunter probably wanted to talk to someone unattached. He couldn't think I had money, but he must have a lot.

We spent the next half hour chatting. I liked him. He even asked about me. I told him I was an orphan because, after all, I feel like one. He was quite well-mannered. When he glanced at his watch and said he had important business to attend to, I hid my disappointment, recognizing a brush-off.

"I've so enjoyed talking with you," he added. "Can we continue this tomorrow evening over dinner?"

Not a brush-off then. I maintained a cool exterior, but my

spirits soared. I liked this man, and I thought we hit it off. I looked up at him and smiled. Maybe I'd met a genuinely good person for a change. You can't do better than meet someone at a charity event. That guarantees a nice person, doesn't it?

Later, in the cab on our way home, I noticed Norma grinning at me. "You seem to have made a conquest," she said.

I smiled down at my hands. "Do you know him?" I asked. "His name's Hunter McCann."

"Hunter? McCann?" She shook her head, pursing her lips. "Can't say I've met him."

"Oh, but dear," her husband broke in, "you meet so many people you can't remember them all."

She nodded. "You're right, m'dear." She winked at me. "Glad you had a good time, Melanie."

I smiled. "I did. Thanks for inviting me." Maybe I'd broken the spell of bad dates.

As the weeks wore on, I began seeing more of Hunter and counted myself lucky. Hunter told me about all the charities he supported, which spoke well for him. He seemed to be well-off, so his business must be successful. He said he was a lawyer, but he aimed to be an artist and printer. Then he'd modestly added, "I won't make much money at it."

I liked his modesty. Most men talked incessantly about them-selves, but he acted as if he were more interested in me. I tried to find out about his art, but he dodged my questions. I let it go, silently appreciating his reticence. I could find out more later as we grew to know each other better. Anyway, other people seemed to like him, and he was always smiling.

Our courtship continued for six months. I asked him about his childhood.

He hesitated. "It was rough. Broken home."

I sympathized—I knew how that was. The revelation gave him the wounded quality that drew me closer to him.

"What about your family?" he asked.

I didn't hesitate. "Only child. My parents are dead," I said. *They are dead to me.*

"Do you have any brothers or sisters?" I asked.

He didn't respond, but one day that question was unexpectedly answered when I ran into Hunter on the street in downtown Manhattan. He was walking with a tall, attractive blonde and was surprised to see me.

"This is my sister Anne," he said, "in town on business."

I couldn't see any resemblance, but with the bleached blonde hair and heavy makeup, why would I?

Later, I asked Hunter about her and if he had any other siblings. He shook his head. "I was only able to catch a few minutes with Anne during her busy schedule. No time to get her together with you." The perpetual smile left his face for an instance. "She lives in Iowa now. I hardly ever see her."

The day after I met Anne, Hunter sent me a dozen red roses. I never received roses before from anyone. When he went out of town, he sent expensive boxes of candy. I protested these gifts, but they continued to come.

The only negatives I could come up with about him were the sprawling tattoo across his back and the questions he asked about my job and the company I worked for. I questioned him about the tattoo, but he shrugged it off as a youthful mistake. Anyway, tattoos are the thing nowadays, and naturally he'd be interested in my employer since he is also in business. Besides, it was a pleasure to talk with someone who liked to hear about what I do.

If he were disappointed that I'm a mere accountant rather than a charitable heiress, he never let on. He still sent me candy and an occasional bouquet. His smile when he saw me was constant.

When we started sleeping together, I worried about how he'd react to my nightmares. I tried to explain them to him, but he brushed my concerns aside.

"We all have nightmares, Mellie," he said. "Even me—and I get some doozies." I let this problem slide with the hope I'd grown out of them.

I asked Amy what she thought of Hunter.

"He seems all right," she said, which seemed like high praise since she tends to be critical of the men I date.

Norma and Tom didn't volunteer any feelings about him one way or the other.

One day, Tom dropped by the office. "I hear you have a new beau," he said.

"I do," I said.

"Who is he and how did you meet him?" Tom asked, being friendly. "What does he do?" The usual questions anyone might ask.

I asked myself, what did he do for a living? I didn't know.

My life became a whirlwind. I felt like the wake behind a powerboat, following Hunter, *supporting* him, in whatever he wanted to do. In truth, I was afraid to do otherwise. The thought briefly surfaced that he wouldn't let me do otherwise, but I squelched it. After all, he was in love with me and I with him. We were getting to know one another. Doing what he wanted to do was simple enough, and I convinced myself that we liked to do the same things. Besides, he brought me roses and gave me the kind of love I'd always longed for. I was lucky to be with such a sophisticated, interesting man, a man who always smiled.

Life was wonderful on the whole, even though I continued to suffer panic attacks in tight spaces where I had limited control. They were irritating, but I could deal with them by taking deep breaths and walking fast.

I started buying flowers. Had an expensive stylist cut my hair. Shopped for more feminine suits. I was very much in love.

I listened to the song in my heart, but I couldn't miss the reserved way Norma and Tom reacted when I told them about Hunter's most recent gift to me, an expensive brooch, but whatever their concerns, they kept them to themselves.

One evening, Norma stopped by my desk. "Tom and I would like to have you and Hunter over for dinner. This Friday okay?"

I made a quick call to Hunter. He agreed, and I was thrilled to show Hunter off to a couple who not only were my employers but were also close friends. I told Hunter it was dressy casual. I wanted him to look good, which he always did without any prompting from me, and I dressed carefully myself in a sky-blue dress that set off my eyes and complexion.

The evening came, but Hunter arrived at my apartment late. While I was fretting about the time, the phone rang.

At first I couldn't understand what Norma was saying. Something was terribly wrong. I asked her to take a deep breath and slow down. I sat on the couch and listened. In between great sobs, she gasped, "Tom's been shot! I'm at the hospital, but he's dead."

"What?" I said, not grasping what she was saying.

"He was shot. Killed in the alley by our condo building."

I couldn't believe it.

Norma was still talking, her voice harsh and angry. "The condo bellman glimpsed a man wearing a hoodie. Can't describe him. Could have been anyone."

In shock, I turned to Hunter. "The dinner party tonight is canceled. Tom's been shot, killed." For once in our relationship so far, I gave an order. "You've got to leave. I need to go to her."

He started to protest, but then saw my face and headed for the door. He had to be gone before a panic attack set in. I would control it walking to Norma's, and Norma needed a friend right now.

I spent the night and following week with Norma, holding her hand as she made the final arrangements, talked to the police, and watched the news reports about the murder. She insisted on watching those reports, looking for a clue to why or who. They suggested Tom's involvement in contested city planning and zoning decisions might have been the motive, but it was all speculation.

Norma did not appear in the office all the following week. I did what I could to help at the office and stopped by the condo to offer Norma condolences and support. I felt sick at such a callous taking of the life of a man I liked and admired. I sent flowers to the funeral, held her hand during the memorial service, and later wrote Norma a heartfelt note.

Hunter was such a blessing during those sad times. Supportive and loving and strong. Two weeks after the tragedy, on our way back to my apartment after dinner, he reached for my hand.

"Marry me," he said.

I turned to him in surprise. "This is so sudden," I said, "and it's too soon after Tom's death."

"But Tom's death showed me how we can't put off living," Hunter said. "We have to seize the moment. We could be gone tomorrow."

I hesitated, not ready for his proposal. "I thought we might live together first," I said tentatively, "get to know each other better."

"Absolutely not." He sat beside me, nuzzling my ear. "I want you for myself," he said along with the kisses. "I love you," he whispered. "I want us to be together forever."

I felt flattered. This almost-handsome, modest man with the crooked nose and beautiful blue eyes loved me and for myself alone. I was madly in love with him, too. I was so lucky to have met such a good man. Maybe I had grown beyond my bad choices. I threw aside my doubts and misgivings. It did not take much persuasion for me to say yes. I still worried about how he'd react to my nightmares, but I hadn't experienced any since we started dating. Maybe being with him cured whatever caused them. I hoped so.

But even as I said yes and watched Hunter with an even bigger smile than usual put a diamond solitaire on my finger, I kept that one important piece of myself secret. My boat. Some things even my husband didn't need to know. Things that meant escape if I needed it. Guaranteed alone time. I'd learned growing up how fast family and friends can turn ugly, and I did not intend to waste my life stuck in an untenable situation. Back in the dark recesses of my mind, I didn't quite trust the situation I found myself in, or if I am brutally honest with myself, Hunter. What could he possibly expect from me? Meanwhile, as I had learned early in life, I went along with what he wanted, afraid to lose him in a confrontation. That night I had the worst panic attack I'd ever experienced. I hid in the bathroom, breathing into a paper bag, until I could control myself.

Three days later after a long kiss, Hunter whispered in my ear.

"Let's fly to Las Vegas and get married tomorrow!"

"Las Vegas?" I asked, feeling a twinge of panic. "Now? But what about my job? My friends. They'll want to throw us a party to celebrate." It was too soon. I needed time to adjust. Would Hunter wait?

Hunter nuzzled my ear. "We can do those chores when we get back."

Hunter wouldn't wait, and I wanted Hunter. The more I thought about flying to Las Vegas, the more romantic and spontaneous it seemed. I didn't have to be a stodgy accountant. For once in my life, I could do something exciting and crazy. "Let me call my office and my friend Amy. You should call your family and friends, too."

"I'll make the plane and hotel reservations. We can leave tomorrow morning."

I looked at him. "What about your family and friends?" I asked. "What about your sister?"

"I'll call them later." He was already on the phone, calling the airlines.

"I'd like to meet your parents and friends."

"Why? You're marrying me, not them. Plenty of time to meet them later." His tone said there would be no more discussion. How easily I bent to his will. Calm, competent, in control, but pliable.

It didn't occur to me that maybe he had no friends.

In the face of his demands, I squelched who I was. He didn't know he was marrying the facade. I never let him or anyone see who I really was. I didn't want to lose this man who seemed to accept and love me. I could take off the next few days. Nothing was pressing. Hunter owned his own business and could take off whenever he wanted. I idly wondered what kind of income he earned. He spent lavishly on me, and I'd met him at a charity fundraiser that he supported. He must be doing all right. It would be a good marriage.

When I called Amy, I was momentarily upset at my best friend's negative reaction. "What do you really know about this man?" she asked.

"He's a good man," I answered. "I know he is. I'm sorry you can't see that."

Amy persisted. "Why do you think he wants to marry you so soon? And in such a hurry?"

"Why not? We're in love and have no reason to wait." Her reaction disturbed me, but I put it down to jealousy. Her boyfriend and Hunter didn't hit it off. Hunter made him look like a gawky teenager.

"Norma would love to be in on it, too," Amy added. "But it's so close to her husband's death. It seems too soon."

Hunter and I flew to Las Vegas and were married in a chapel there, then stayed an extra two days for a honeymoon. The second night, after a wonderful evening and too much wine, I mentioned my boat.

"Boat? You have a boat?" Hunter stared at me in astonishment. "What kind of boat? Where?"

Something about the way he asked those questions made me hedge. "It's only a small boat. I keep it in Connecticut."

"Only a small boat. I get it." He laughed. The laugh took an ugly twist, but maybe that was the wine. He must have drunk too much. I knew what happened then. Thank goodness Hunter didn't usually drink at all.

"A rowboat. Or maybe a canoe." He tossed his napkin on the

table. "We can sell it off real quick," he said. "You won't be going up to Connecticut anymore."

Not going to Connecticut ever again? I kept my face blank. The thought chilled me, but I didn't want an argument. I felt disappointed that his only thought was to sell my boat. He didn't understand at all, and he certainly didn't ask what the boat meant to me or where I went with it or why I owned one in the first place. I was not going to sell it, and I already felt I would be needing a refuge from life with Hunter. That was the last time I said anything to him about my boat.

After we disembarked the plane in New York, we picked up Hunter's black minivan in the airport parking lot. As we drove, the repetitive clattering of a loose strip of chrome on the van lulled me into a doze. I didn't suspect a thing until we crossed the Verrazano Narrows Bridge into New Jersey. I sat up and looked around in puzzlement.

"Where are we going?" I asked. "I'm tired and want to get home."

"You'll see," said Hunter. He closed his mouth, stared straight ahead, and refused to say any more about where he was taking us. I was too tired for this, but I didn't want an argument. I sat back to wait and see.

Eventually, he turned into the driveway of a large house on a shaded residential street lined with sycamore trees. As the car slowed, I sat up and anxiously looked around

"Where are we?" I asked.

Hunter turned to me and smiled as if I would be pleased. "Your new home." He got out of the van and opened my door. I stayed in the van, absorbing this statement. We'd just come back from our honeymoon. I felt tired and now close to tears at this unexpected and unwelcome surprise.

For the first time in our relationship, I resisted. I didn't want to move away from my friends and my job. "I do not want to live here," I said. "I know my New York apartment is tiny and cramped, but we could get a larger one."

"Come on, honey. Give it a try," he said, the smile never leaving his face. "You'll learn to love it here."

I refused to move and kept my eyes straight ahead. I did not want to look at Hunter's house. "Why didn't you tell me about this place? My job is in New York. I don't want to be buried away from everyone."

"I work in New Jersey, and we'll live here." His voice made it a command. "Now get out of the van and come into the house with me. You'll love it." He sighed as if he were making a huge concession. "I promise." The smile remained. "All right. If you don't like it after awhile, we can always move back, but give it a trial first, okay?"

What happened to the loving, attentive man I'd married? Reluctantly, I slid out of the van and walked with head bowed behind Hunter to the front door. He opened it and turned around. Ignoring my protests, he roughly lifted me, carried me through the doorway, and with a smile, dropped me in the foyer.

Hunter had ignored my protests and hurt my back when he dropped me. I hid the pain and anger, but the eagerness and excitement I'd felt when we'd left for Las Vegas was now weighed down by the gray pall of dread.

Chapter 3

While Hunter acted as if he expected me to love his "surprise," my spirits drooped. I rubbed my back, frowned at the marble floor of the foyer, and stepped into the living room. I ignored Hunter as I folded my arms and surveyed the area. It was furnished like a model home, generic and bland, but also slightly pretentious. Compared to my New York apartment, it had palatial dimensions. "Very impressive," I said, not impressed. "And I do not want to live here."

"Only because it's all so new to you," said Hunter. "Loosen up. Try something new."

"I do not want to stay here. I hate this house."

Hunter turned cold. "You will live here," he said through gritted teeth and walked out. I heard him start the van and drive away. It scared me. We'd only been married a few days. I loved him, and he loved me. I knew he did. Maybe his heart was set on this place being our new home. I glanced around the living room. The furniture looked new, and the rooms were quite large. This house was supposed to be a big surprise for me. I suppose he really did think I would like it, like settling here with him. And I had rejected his gift and him as well.

When he returned, I apologized and begged forgiveness. He smiled and waved aside my apology.

"I guess it was too much of a change all at once," he said. "I should have realized that. I'm sorry."

I decided that living in Hunter's New Jersey place made sense. I had never visited Hunter's office, but it was close by, he said, and he spent a lot of time visiting the court house and clients. I didn't know anything about his profession, so I believed what he told me.

I finally decided that Hunter did fancy himself an artist and printmaker and used the basement as his studio. When I asked if I could see his work, he dismissed my interest with a curt, "I'm not ready to show anything yet, and," he added with his ever-present smile, "the basement is off-limits to you. You are never to go down there."

The curt tone hurt my feelings, but I hid my reaction and held back the tears. He didn't notice. Anyway, whether he went down to the basement or came up, he always locked the door behind him. It was made of steel and secured not by the usual bedroom or bathroom lock, easily opened without a key, but by a heavy-duty padlock. I suppose he was sensitive and didn't want me to see his unfinished work. I could understand that.

For me, the commute became long and tedious, but it meant escape from the increasing gloom at home. Hunter suggested I quit my job and stay home, and it certainly was an option if I felt too pressured by the commute, or we had children, but I loved my job and didn't relish the idea of being kept at home like a prisoner. I suppose the job kept down the panic attacks, which emanated from a feeling of being trapped. Besides, I didn't want to be totally dependent on someone else. Even besotted with love for my husband and my new life, I still wanted to earn my own income and live my own life.

Hunter needed to understand that. He seemed to feel the same way about his own activities and independence. I could be useful helping Hunter in his business, keeping his books or cleaning brushes or organizing his artist's supplies, but he refused my help.

One day as I ate lunch in a coffee shop with Norma, I happened to mention how Hunter and I met. "At that charity fundraiser last year." Seeing Norma's blank face, I added, "You know. I was there with you and Tom."

"I remember now," said Norma. "Was he active in the organization?"

I bit into my sandwich, remembering those sweet days. "He's one of their donors and spokespersons."

Norma shook her head. "Really? I didn't know that. Never saw him at any other function they held."

My stomach turned over. Had I gotten it wrong? "You're sure?" I tried to think how I could have misunderstood what he said.

"Not unless they're keeping him a secret." Norma winked at me. "Counterproductive for a spokesperson, though."

"But then why . . .?"

Norma brushed my question aside with a laugh. "Maybe he just wanted to impress you."

I couldn't eat any more of my sandwich. I could hardly wait to get back to the office. Once situated at my desk, I called the charity and asked to speak to the development director.

"Development. Ginger Ahern speaking." The voice was brisk and cold.

I introduced myself. "I was at the fundraiser you held about seven or so months ago and met Hunter McCann. He said he was one of your fundraisers and spokespeople."

"Hunter McCann? Name's not familiar. Hmmm. One moment, please, while I look."

I waited, gripping the phone, my mouth dry.

The woman came back. "I'm sorry. I don't see his name on our list. Could you mean Brice MacAtee?"

I swallowed. "His name is Hunter McCann."

"Not on my list of invitees and spokespeople. Perhaps he works for some other charitable organization here in New York."

"Thank you." I hung up, feeling numb. There must be some mistake. How could I have misunderstood him? I couldn't ask Hunter about it. He had grown so critical of me. He would be sure to accuse me of spying on him. Which I was. My marriage to Hunter was becoming a nightmare.

The next unsettling incident happened the following week. I stayed home one day for a doctor's appointment. Most of the time, I got home from work too late for the mail, but this time, I retrieved it. I shuffled through the stack and came across a personal letter addressed to a Ms. Corinne McCann. Hunter's mother? A sister? But his sister's name was Anne. He never wanted to talk about his family, and I didn't press. I put the letter aside to ask him about it later.

Which was a big mistake. Hunter blew up, accusing me of spying on him, poking my nose into places it didn't belong. Then with his gentle smile, he slapped me across the face. "Don't ever snoop in my things again," he said.

I couldn't believe what had happened. Had I been so very wrong to pick up the mail and ask him about it? He immediately apologized and was sweet and loving the rest of the evening.

Was Hunter right? I shouldn't interfere in his business, but as his wife, I could be, should be, a help and support to him in whatever he did.

In the back of my mind, the thought surfaced that I should be able to expect the same help and support from him. I longed to see what he did in the basement. And who was Corinne?

At the office next day, I googled the name. Although a number of Corinne McCanns were listed, none of them stood out as a possible recipient of the letter. What did the letter say? I had only seen the envelope. There was no mistake about the address. It was Hunter's, all right.

I pleaded a headache and left the office early. I knew Hunter was out making deliveries and sales calls today. I wanted to return home before he did and find that letter. What time would he get home? I didn't know. I was relieved to find his van not in the driveway. I rushed into Hunter's office. He always kept the door closed and told me to stay out. Of course I was curious, but it was just an office with desk and chair and two file cabinets. I rummaged through the waste basket. The letter was crumpled into a tiny ball and pushed to the bottom. Hunter didn't think I'd have the gall to search for it after his dressing down.

I spread out the paper and read. The letter was signed "Mom," and she was asking Corinne to write to her. Not asking but begging, wanting to know if all was well, if Corinne needed help. A letter from people who loved Corinne and hadn't heard from her for a long time.

I sat down, feeling sick. Who was Corinne? Her mom asked how Hunter was, as if he were close to her, as if asking about her daughter's husband. I searched the waste basket for the envelope, found it, and scribbled down the return address. Then I wadded up the letter and the envelope and hid them under the other papers in the waste basket.

I had to get out of there. Hunter would suspect something if he found me home so early. I fled, walking a mile to the local library and hiding out in a remote alcove.

That night, Hunter came home in a foul mood. I could tell he'd been drinking. Then he raged at me, tossed a cup on the floor, and crushed it with his foot because I hadn't fixed dinner. He grabbed my arm and threw me against the wall. I crawled away, hid in the locked bathroom, and cried.

After awhile, full of apologies, he sweet-talked me out of the bathroom as he also justified himself. He loved me so much, he said, as he always did after he'd hit me. I felt ashamed of my own behavior, regressing to a little girl, afraid, weak, sniveling, and accommodating. I began to hate his constant smile, always there whether he hit me, loved me, ridiculed me, or merely spoke to me.

The next day in my office, I wrote Corinne's mother a letter, asking her to respond only to my office address in New York.

After mailing the letter, the days dragged on. I disgusted myself by fawning over Hunter to avoid being hit but also to lull any suspicions he might have. I should have left him; anyone I might ask about Hunter's abusive behavior would tell me to leave. I knew I should leave, so I didn't tell anyone about it. I still felt the abuse was partly my fault. I had gone into this marriage with golden dreams, and he did love me. I knew he did. Was I the kind of person who ran away at the least bit of trouble? Like my mom?

Yes, I was. I'd done it before. I'd fled from an abusive home—both physically and verbally abusive. I was too young then to cope with it or fight it, so I grew a shell around me so hard no one could crack it. Now I needed to learn a better way to deal with what was happening, not just hide or run away from it. I knew I could bring my marriage around to the loving place it had once been. I simply needed to learn how to help Hunter and not annoy him. My mother deserted our family when it got tough at home, but I was not my mother. I was stronger and smarter. I could find a better way.

The fact that the charity hadn't heard of Hunter and his anger at my reading his letter could have reasonable explanations if we could talk about it. Only I didn't know how to bring up difficult subjects without causing a fight. Until I learned how, I was going to leave difficult questions alone.

Also, I was curious. Who was Corinne? Each day at work, I hoped for an answer from Corinne's mother. With my office address for a response, Hunter would never know, but the thought of what the letter might say made my stomach queasy. I harbored so many questions. Had Corinne been Hunter's wife? Were they divorced, or did she leave? Was Hunter a bigamist? How long had he owned this house? Corinne's mom wrote to her daughter at this address; therefore, she must have lived here. Where was she now? There must be a reasonable explanation.

Now that the luster of my relationship with Hunter had faded, I was astounded at how little I knew about him. Who was he? I listened for any clues he might drop in conversation. A couple of days later, I took the risk of asking him. "I should get to know your family," I said. "We've been married four months now, and I've never met them. Tell me about them."

He got up and walked toward me. I tightened my body, not knowing if I'd overstepped, and he was going to hit, but he wrapped his arms around me. "Aren't we enough for each other? I love you. We don't need anyone else." He kissed me and added, "I don't ask you about your family."

"All right," I said, my voice muffled in his sweater. That was the bargain I'd made early in our relationship. I wouldn't want to tell him about my family, and he didn't want to tell me about his. I guess it was an even exchange.

I didn't have many friends, either. I saw Amy and Norma only at work. No more after-hours socializing. Hunter expected me home. He didn't seem to have any friends and showed no interest in mine, so maybe that was also an even exchange.

Except that if I went missing, no one would write Hunter asking where I was. The idea scared and saddened me.

Feeling tentatively secure with his arms around me in a loving mood, I risked another question. "Do you think the letter to Corinne McCann was sent to the wrong address?"

"What letter?" Hunter asked, always smiling. "I don't know any Corinne McCann."

I tensed. Hunter lied. Why would he lie? I felt Hunter step back. I didn't dare look up at him face-to-face.

"Where did you hear about this Corinne?" I heard the threat in his voice and instinctively raised my arms to ward off the blow.

It came hard, knocking me to the carpet. "God damn it, woman! You've been reading my mail, haven't you?" He stood over me, ready to strike again. "Spying on me."

"No, no, I haven't," I whimpered, regressing to my little girl self as I slid my body away from him. "I just saw her name on the envelope is all. I swear!"

He kicked me. "Don't you ever snoop in my mail again. Do you understand?" He folded his arms, staring at me sprawled below him on the carpet. His eyes narrowed, the smile on his face at odds with his actions.

I nodded, tears streaming down my face and gasping for breath as a panic attack threatened.

Chapter 4

The next few days passed in a strained silence at home. I went through the motions of fixing dinner, tiptoeing through the entire evening, afraid of any notice that might provoke him. Part of me knew I should have left immediately after the first time he hit me, but I clung to the memory of our love for each other. Hunter had a right to his privacy, and I violated it. It was my fault.

Now I waited for the letter from Corinne's mother. The questions became so insistent in my mind that after a week, I donned an anonymous raincoat and umbrella and sneaked out of the house in the spring rain as if I were going to work early. At the bus stop shelter, I called my office and left a message saying I had a cold and sore throat and was staying home for the day.

I waited in the shelter for an hour, watching the house. I saw Hunter back out of the driveway, swing into the road, and cut off an oncoming car to speed to the Interstate. I observed the maneuver with a bitter smile. So typical of him—not going to let anyone go ahead. Then I walked back to the house and let myself in. I ran to the front window first and stared out to make sure he was gone. I hoped he wouldn't be back soon.

Rain dripped from the eaves. The daffodils along the drive dazzled yellow flowers against the bright spring green of the grass. Three teenagers waited for the school bus down the street. I stayed at the window, watching men and women emerge from their houses, get in their cars, and drive off. I changed out of my work clothes into jeans and T-shirt, made a cup of coffee, and whipped up a batch of cookies, cleaning everything up afterwards so there'd be no sign. Ten o'clock would be a good time to call on the neighbors. Hunter would never find out since he and the neighbors didn't talk to each other.

I wasn't sure which neighbors might be home during the day, but I started at the house next door on the right. I knocked and listened for movement. Nothing. No cars in the driveway.

I tried the house on the other side. No car in the driveway but one at the curb.

I heard shuffling inside, then a voice. "Who is it?"

"Hello," I called. "I'm Melanie McCann, your next door neighbor. I wanted to meet you. I've brought over some cookies."

The door opened. A tired-looking redhead stood there in jeans and flannel shirt. "I'm Alice. I was just straightening up after getting my husband off to work and driving the kids to school. Come on in. I'm ready for a cup of coffee."

The house was smaller than mine with faded and worn living room furniture. The rug was gray and stained. A child's table stood to the side with Legos stacked on top.

"Come on into the kitchen," Alice said. "What happened to your eye?"

I had covered the bruise with makeup and hoped it wouldn't be noticed. "Nothing," I said. "It's okay."

"Take a seat," she said, gesturing at the kitchen table. I sat, placing the cookies in the center.

Alice poured two cups of coffee and set out a container of

milk and a sugar bowl.

"Those look good. Mind if I have one?" asked Alice.

I waved my hand. "They're for you."

"I watched you move in. Hoped we'd get a chance to meet." Alice looked at me over her cup. "You work, don't you?"

I nodded. "Just took the day off."

Alice nodded. "Thought so."

I took a sip. "I was wondering. . ."

"Yes?" Alice looked up.

"I know Hunter used to be married, but I don't know anything about his first wife. Did you meet her?" I laughed. Just making conversation. Did the question sound too odd?

"Oh, yes, I met Corinne. Looked like you a lot. Oops. Sorry. I mean looks like you a lot. I don't know what happened to her."

"Really? She looked like me?" Were Corinne and I of a type?

"Gave me a start when I first saw you. From a distance, of course. Thought it was Corinne coming back. But, really, after that. . ." Alice stopped.

"After what?"

Alice bit her lip and stared at the table. "I don't want to gossip."

Pay dirt, I thought, hardly daring to breathe. "You're not gossiping," I encouraged. "I'm just interested, and I should know. . ."

"Weeellll," Alice began, "they didn't have the smoothest relationship, you know."

"Really?" I casually raised my cup to my lips, keeping my face bland.

"I heard a lot of yelling over there. Upset my kids, you know."

"Of course." Alice and her kids probably hear my cries, too. I felt uncomfortable.

"Then one day she was gone. Poof! Like that."

Poof like that. I couldn't help the shudder. What happened to Corinne?

Alice sat back, watching me. "Personally, I was glad. He beat her, you know. All of us on the street knew it. We're all hoping she's okay."

I acted shocked. "Beat her?"

Alice busied herself with pouring more sugar into her cup, only sneaking a look at me as she added, "Like he beats you, honey."

As I started to protest, Alice waved her hand. "Don't bother to deny it. You need to get out of there, and I mean fast."

I felt as if I'd been kicked in the stomach. The neighbors knew. Of course they did.

"Does he have a job someplace?" Alice asked.

"Sure. Why?"

"He's in and out all times of the day. Must work close to home, my guess."

I stood, reeling from one shock to another. In and out. He could come home any time. Had I left any signs indicating I'd stayed home this morning? "I have to leave," I said.

"Okay, honey. I just have one request."

I looked at Alice. "What?"

"Let me know you're all right." Alice sipped her coffee. "Oh, don't worry I'll tell anyone else. I won't. Only I'll feel better. I still wonder about Corinne. Where is she? Is she all right?"

Alice followed me to the door. I'd gotten more than I'd bargained for with this visit. "If I find out, I'll let you know," I said, walking with as much dignity as I possessed out the door and to my own house.

Hunter could come home at any time. I found myself listening for the familiar clatter of the loose chrome strip on his van, a sound I was learning to dread.

Chapter 5

I made sure the kitchen was in order, a habit I'd acquired to avoid Hunter's criticism. Then I stepped into the front room, listening to the silence. I folded my arms and frowned at the expensive furniture and thick carpet. A marble counter separated this room from the cooking area with its "state of the art" appliances. We never used the dining room for dinner guests. It opened into the living room and was also expensively furnished and impressive with its mahogany table, upholstered chairs, china cabinet, and chandelier.

Beautifully decorated and as cold as the diamond on my finger. As cold as my heart, where once I loved with hope and anticipation. I hated everything in this house. I glanced in the mirror as I walked to the phone. Last night he hit me for the last time. My left eye and cheek and my arms showed the bruises. Alice spotted them immediately. No makeup job could hide them. I called my office and asked for Norma.

"What's up, sugar?" Norma asked, her voice tinged with sadness. She still mourned for Tom.

I choked and couldn't stop myself from bawling like a kid. I never let anyone see or hear me cry. "I'm sorry," I gasped.

"It's all right, sugar. I've seen it coming. Did he hit you again?"

I forced myself to stop crying. I hiccupped and managed to

say, "You know about it?"

"Honey, we all know. Just hadn't known how to approach you. You always got so prickly when we tried. We were waiting for you to ask for help."

I felt shocked and humiliated. Everyone knew Hunter hit me. She'd explained the strange looks the others gave me when I got to work. More confirmation the makeup hadn't done the job.

"I need to get out of here."

Norma's voice was calm and businesslike. "You do. I'm putting you on extended leave as of today. I'll hold your paycheck here until you tell me where to send it. You need to disappear for awhile because Hunter isn't going to like this, and he's a dangerous man. He's probably a stalker, and who knows what else? I like you, and you're a good worker. I don't want you to get hurt.

"Now, I'll tell you something else. We've all had enough of Hunter pestering you and the office with useless phone calls. He's been trying to get you to quit in embarrassment or fired because of the nuisance. If he succeeded, it would only be the first round."

"I didn't realize," I began, feeling as low as I could possibly get. Everyone knew Hunter was an abuser. Everyone felt sorry for me. He humiliated me in front of my friends and coworkers. They were all worried about me. How could I have thought I'd hidden the abuse and my unhappiness? *What a laugh.*

"Now look," Norma continued. "get out of the house. Hide out in a domestic violence shelter. They'll take care of you, help you find a new place, and protect you from the asshole you married."

I hesitated. Norma was right. I had to leave, but I refused to go to a shelter. My life with Hunter was brutal but ordered. "I'm getting out, and I'll find a safe place," I said. "I'll let you know where to send my paycheck and mail." But I'm not going to a shelter. I grew up in chaos and I've known abuse before. I've been set up for this. The realization struck me with the force of a fist. It shifted my past and my present into a coherent whole, but I was no longer a scared and weak little girl—and I should stop behaving like one. I had a game plan, and it was time to use it.

"Good. Just get out of his house." Norma paused and then added, "We can arrange for you to work remotely from wherever you happen to land. Take your laptop with you."

But I was already turning my plan into action. "I really appreciate all you're doing for me," I said.

"You're a good person, Melanie. You deserve better. Now get busy and keep in touch." Norma hung up.

I agreed with Norma about getting away from the house. Only I added my own caveat: On my terms. I needed to find out a few things first. What exactly was Hunter's business? He told me he was a lawyer who liked to do artwork on the side. Whatever he did down in the basement, it was not producing art. He used some kind of machinery—I'd heard it, but he never came up stained with paint colors. What could he be doing? That question ate at me since I'd first moved in. He derailed my questions then, and I didn't pursue the subject out of some distorted sense of protecting his privacy. I ought to know, and I was afraid to ask him.

I opened up my laptop at the kitchen table and did a google search. First I typed in Hunter's name. Nothing turned up. Then I entered the name of his business as I'd heard it when he called someone. HoMelCo Enterprises. Odd name for a law firm, but I thought he probably worked as the firm's lawyer. Google took me to a site selling Mexican identification cards and international driver's licenses. The site also advertised it sold identification cards of all kinds. There was a link to something called The Cotton Road, which turned out to be a site selling illegal drugs. How could he get away with such stuff? I could feel a panic attack beginning and cupped my hands over my mouth and nose, forcing me to breathe slowly and deeply. After a moment, it subsided.

I sat back astonished, chilled, and feeling sick. How could a private company sell government identification cards? I googled International Driver's License and came up with a number of sites selling them. In digging through the verbiage, I decided the international permit translated a person's driver's license into a number of different languages so foreign officials could read the translated version.

It sounded iffy. What about the Mexican ID cards? Only the Mexican government should be allowed to issue those, so why was Hunter offering them for sale?

I deleted the sites I'd visited from the cache and turned off the laptop. I sat at the table, staring at the wall and drumming my fingers for several minutes. I rose to peer out the window at the street and looked in both directions. There were no cars, so I still had time.

I walked into Hunter's office and scanned the walls and furniture, looking for some kind of video device. Seeing none, I stepped to his massive mahogany desk. The drawers were locked, but I found a key taped under the center one over the knee space. The key unlocked all of them.

I opened the center one first and rummaged through it, but I found nothing odd, the usual office supplies, pens, paper clips, staple remover and such. Then I tried the sides. The second one on the left took my breath away. I could feel my pulse hammering in my ears. Did I hear something? I ran to the front window and checked the street again. Still no cars.

In disbelief, I pulled out several sheets of blank Social Security cards, each sheet having two columns of five blank cards each, printed in blue ink and looking identical to my own Social Security card. Under those were five passports, each with a different name. A stack of laminated New Jersey driver's licenses in different names were shoved in back of the drawer. Several other passports and driver's licenses carried Hunter's photo. I didn't recognize any of the names, even the ones with Hunter's photo.

"Oh, my god," I whispered, sitting back in the chair. I felt suffocated, and my pulse pumped in my ears. "This can't be happening."

Hunter sold fake IDs, Social Security cards, passports, and who knew what else? The cards and passports could only be used for criminal activities. He was a crook bunked in with other criminals and drug dealers. He could have ties to the mafia, the Mexican cartel, terrorists. What else was he involved in? I thought of Tom's unexplained murder. Had he discovered what Hunter really did? I knew Tom was curious. I found it hard to breathe.

Why had Hunter married me? I was a liability to him. Did he think he could win me over to a life of crime? I shook my head at the melodrama. What did he want from me?

I opened the bottom drawer. It contained a number of legal documents. One of them, I read in shock, was my will, leaving everything to Hunter. Another legal-looking document was a life insurance policy drawn in my name, again with Hunter the beneficiary. I stared at my signature. It looked like mine, but I had never signed this document. I didn't even know about it. Underneath that was a life insurance policy drawn in his name, with me as the beneficiary. For a moment, it puzzled me. Was this a legitimate attempt to help in case one of us died? Then I realized that he probably arranged "his and her" policies to divert suspicion when he got rid of me and wanted to cash in on the policy.

What happened to Corinne? Were we living on her life insurance?

I glanced at the clock. Twelve noon. Would Hunter come home for lunch? I thought not, since there was no provision for lunch in the kitchen. Did he feel secure enough about the locks on his desk he didn't mind if I stayed home alone? I hadn't done it before, and he didn't know I played hooky today. If he had known, I'd bet he would find a reason to remain home, too.

My eyes turned toward the file cabinets. I walked to them and opened the top drawer. Rummaging through the documents, I realized they all related to legitimate house bills and such.

In the middle one, I pulled out a folder labeled "Tom Haggerty." Why would Hunter keep information on Tom Haggerty? I leafed through the papers. It contained notes about Tom's business, background information on both Norma and Tom, and a detailed hour-by-hour schedule of Tom's movements over several days. Hunter had been watching Tom.

Norma was right. I needed to get out of here and disappear. Now.

Once again, I chose a loser. Worse, a criminal and a murderer.

I was well aware of my dismal record of making terrible choices. This was the worst so far. Thank goodness, some inner sense of self-preservation had kept me from telling him much about the boat. I started to on our honeymoon, but he hadn't been interested, so that part never became his victim.

What I needed was something I could use for protection. I took out a sheet of blank Social Security cards and the fake passports. Then I rummaged through the other drawers again. That's when I found a slip of papers with numbers on it. I studied it. Could this be . . .?

I turned around and pushed aside the painting hanging on the wall. As I suspected, behind it was the safe. A trite idea, but Hunter lacked imagination. I knew about the safe since he'd mentioned it once. I tried the numbers and opened it.

I riffled through the documents and found a box of financial statements from the Cayman Islands. I hadn't known about this. Only one showed Hunter's name. I knew two names as those of well-known political figures. I recognized another name of a man under indictment for criminal activities. I also found the deed to the house. Hunter bought it seven years ago and paid cash. Who pays cash for a house?

I removed a handful of financial statements before closing and locking the safe and desk drawers. I retaped the key in the approximate same place I found it and straightened the desk, hoping it all looked as if it hadn't been touched.

I glanced at my watch. I could not be here when Hunter returned. I had no idea what his daily schedule was, but he could be back any moment. I grabbed the statements and other papers and raced into the bedroom to lay them on the bed. Then I ran into the spare room to retrieve a suitcase.

I returned to the bedroom and opened the suitcase on the bed. Breathing fast, fingers trembling at the audacity of what I was about to do, I put the papers in first, along with documents of my own, added a few clothes—jeans, shirts, and underwear—then toiletries and closed the suitcase. I spread out the clothes hanging in my closet so Hunter wouldn't notice anything missing. I didn't want him to suspect I'd left until I didn't come home tonight.

I felt the quiver of cold feet, but then I looked in the mirror at the bruises. He was not going to touch me—or smile at me—ever again.

I had hidden a tote bag filled with other necessary supplies in the back of my closet. For months, I was prepared to leave, even though some sick part of myself hung on, thinking it was all my fault, unwilling to accept I made another bad choice. Hunter would not believe I had the nerve to leave him. He'd expect me to come crawling back, and his conceit would buy me more time.

I retrieved the tote bag, took one last look around the house, and glanced at the basement door—I'd dearly love to see what he hid there, but the door was impregnable. Considering the fake documents I'd found, the machine I heard could very well be a printing press. I carried the suitcase to the front door, but then I heard the peculiar clattering of the loose chrome strip on Hunter's van as it turned into the driveway. Hunter! My heart turned over, beating so hard I was sure Hunter could hear it.

He mustn't find me here. Already he was getting out of the van. I heard its door slam.

I ran on tiptoes to the back door, lugging the suitcase and tote bag. I heard him walk to the house. He entered the front room as I slipped out. I waited outside for a moment, visualizing him casting his eyes around the living room. Then I heard him call my name. He knew I was home then. He must have called the office. I ran to Alice's house and hugged the back door as I tapped on it, trying to hide from Hunter and not make much noise. He might be searching the house for me.

"Come to the door. Come to the door," I whispered urgently. I glanced at my own house and saw a light go on upstairs. Did he suspect I'd been there? Going through his things? He was a suspicious man. Did I put everything away? His office looked the same as when he left it. Unless he counted my clothes in the closet or bureau drawers, he would have no clue I'd left him. I could have simply ducked out of the office for a few hours to go shopping in the city. Unless he spied me here, I was safe.

Alice's face appeared at the window. Then she pulled me into the kitchen.

"I'm taking your advice," I said. "Would you call me a cab?"

"Thank goodness." Alice didn't hesitate. She found a company in the local directory. "Come up the driveway and into the garage," she told the dispatcher. "We have an invalid here who can't walk very far." Alice winked at me as she gave the address and then hung up.

"You can get into the cab in the garage, so Hunter won't see you," she said, glancing at her watch. "It's early. He'll think you're still at work."

I smiled at Alice. "You seem to have a knack for this sort of thing. That was good thinking."

Alice grinned. "Yep. I should go into the business. Have to tell you I'm relieved to know you're getting out of there. My kids will be, too."

I looked down at my feet, feeling ashamed and humiliated. "I'm sorry. . ."

"Forget it," Alice said, squeezing my hand. "Could happen to any of us."

A few minutes later, a yellow vehicle turned into the driveway. Alice opened the garage door. The driver brought the cab into the garage, positioning the passenger side at the kitchen door. I slid in while the driver stowed my tote bag and suitcase in the trunk. As he backed out of the garage, I waved to Alice. I kept my head low and face averted from Hunter's house until we were out of the neighborhood.

Sneaking a last peek at the house as we passed by, I saw Hunter run to his van. What was he doing? Had he seen me? Seen the cab? Guessed what I was doing?

I watched him back out of the driveway and pull in behind us. Was he following me? I hyperventilated from panic. The cab driver drove on oblivious. The van followed us for three blocks. As we neared the train station, it veered off. He hadn't seen me! I fanned myself in relief.

I sat back, staring out at the people as we passed by. My grin widened and pride grew with each turn of the wheel distancing me from the oppression that had stifled and terrified me. I was out of his horrible house. I could feel my wings spreading.

"You okay, lady?" the taxi driver asked. "Train station's up ahead."

I took a deep breath. "Yes. Okay."

He pulled in front of the station. I looked for Hunter or his van before I paid the driver and stepped out but didn't see either. The driver took my suitcase and tote bag from the trunk and set them on the sidewalk.

Hunter must have gone on some emergency errand. Maybe it's how he spent his day, running from one little trip to the next. I didn't know.

There was no turning back now. If Hunter got the chance, he would kill me. I knew it the way you know the sun will come up.

Tom found out the hard way how Hunter would react. I was sure of it. Only now, because I was leaving him, could I recognize his cold, hard core. He saw me as nothing more than his property and a means to an end. When he was ready, he'd kill me for the insurance money, as he'd probably done with Corinne. He would not accept the implications leaving him would mean. He was wrong. I could defy him, I could live without him, and I had muscle.

Moreover, I knew he was engaged in illegal activities. I possessed incriminating documents. They were my only bargaining chips, but once I secured a divorce and felt safe from him and his cronies, I would schedule a private chat with the FBI.

Of course, what I should do was to turn the incriminating documents over to the FBI immediately and go into the witness protection program. It's what Norma would say. I shuddered. Might as well go to the domestic abuse shelter, which I refused to do unless Hunter found me, and I had no other options.

Before such a thing happened, I had something else I needed to do first. Something I might never be able to do if I became a ward of the FBI. Because the one thing I never ever wanted to do again was to make a mistake about a man.

Where I was going, Hunter would never find me. If he did, I would be a changed woman, one who no longer stood for anyone's abuse. I had those financial papers and fake IDs to hold over his head if he did find me and resorted to threats and intimidation. Once I was out of here, I'd hide those papers along with instructions for what to do if I disappeared or died . . . suddenly.

In the meantime, I needed to find out who Corinne was, why Hunter married me, and the reason I, Melanie Fletcher, always picked the losers and what I could do about it.

I walked into the station and directly into the women's rest room to change into jeans, flannel shirt, and blonde wig. I'd bought the wig years ago for a costume party. Now it came in handy. While in the lavatory, I stomped on my cell phone to crush it and threw it in the trash, so it couldn't send a GPS signal leading to my whereabouts. Next, I bought a ticket to New York. While I waited, I used my debit card to withdraw $2,000 from my bank account, one Hunter didn't know about. I guess from the beginning, I hadn't really trusted Hunter. In New York, I transferred to a local train to Norwalk. From there, I hired a ride to get to the dock where I kept my boat.

This escape had been an option for months, beginning with the first time he hit me. I originally hoped the abuse was a momentary aberration, a mistake I caused by forgetting how his work must stress him. When it didn't stop, and a look in the mirror revealed my bruised face and arms, I soon corrected the foolish notion. Abuse is abuse. No excuses.

I couldn't help being the kind of person I was. I knew my past record with men. Long ago, I vowed never to get trapped. Always have an option was my motto. After the first beating from Hunter, I began saving more of my paycheck and grocery allowance, and I pawned my jewelry, all but my wedding ring. It would be the next to go as soon as I find a reputable pawnshop.

Thank goodness Hunter hadn't been interested when I started to tell him about my boat. He might know I had some kind of boat in Connecticut, but Connecticut harbored hundreds of marinas, miles of waterfront, and thousands of boats.

Norma and Tom helped me buy the trawler and found a relatively inexpensive marina to keep it. At first I wanted the boat just to get away from the busy pace of New York City. Then it became a place to go if I were hounded by one of my unacceptable boyfriends. It was the perfect getaway vehicle, one Hunter would never dream of. I thought of everything.

Did Corinne escape from him and was she hiding, too? If she did get away, wouldn't she contact her mother? If so, her mother wouldn't have written Hunter. But she did. Something bad happened to Corinne. I needed to find out what.

Chapter 6

I traveled long days, paying in cash for fuel, food, and marina fees the few nights I didn't anchor out off the channel. I didn't want to leave a paper trail. Eight days later, under blue skies and calm weather, I steered my boat out of the Chesapeake Bay and into the Rappahannock River at the northern neck of tidewater Virginia. I settled back to navigate up the river.

The wide mouth of the waterway gradually narrowed. A half-hour later, I lifted my eyes from the navigation chart, corrected my course to avoid the sandbar on the port side, then picked up the binoculars and peered ahead at my destination, my new home, in fact. The Riverbend Marina. Had I really gotten away with it? A tiny feeling of glee bubbled inside, morphed into triumph. A perfect plan, well executed. The glee dissipated as I neared the marina, and the task I'd set for myself loomed ahead.

I ran the binoculars across the distant structures. Two docks, one of them T-shaped with the top of the T parallel to shore. Side by side on it were the gas and water pumps and a machine for pumping out marine heads. On solid ground behind the docks was a white building that probably served as the office and maybe the marina store. The graveled yard was barricaded from the water by a three-foot-high sea wall along the shore. No beach to be seen, even though the tide was low.

As I approached the docks, I saw a man of average height and build, hand on hip, leaning against the gas pump. I couldn't miss the white cowboy hat he wore. He was looking my way and seemed to be waiting for me. I saw no one else on the dock or outside the marina office. Several small powerboats along with a couple of day sailboats bobbed at their slips. A trawler and two derelicts were propped up on land. A Travelift hoist for lifting hulls out of the water hovered against the fence behind them. No one seemed to be aboard any of the boats. Of course not. It was midweek, early spring, and late in the afternoon. I'd timed my arrival just right. I knew nobody was living aboard here. Not this early in the spring. The man's hands signaled me to bring my trawler to the end of the gas dock.

I glanced behind me. No one followed me up this river. A flash of curly blonde hair reflected in my wheelhouse window startled me. The wig was too uncomfortable for constant wear, so on the trip south, I'd gone to a Hair Cuttery in a waterway town. Still, I found it hard to get used to blonde and curly when I'd been a straight-haired brunette all my life.

I took a deep breath and pulled back on the controls to slow the 26-foot trawler as I approached the main pier and gas dock. Not much wind or current here. I slid easily alongside.

"You Ms. Fletcher?" the man asked, hand out to take a line. His deeply tanned and rugged face, razer-cut brown hair, and tight jeans made me wary, especially when he winked at me as he caught the line. Some women might consider him good-looking, I supposed, but I wasn't interested.

I nodded, watching him with suspicion through narrowed eyes.

"I'm Stu, the dock master here." He didn't look at me as he pulled the boat forward. "We're gonna keep you here overnight and haul you out tomorrow."

"Fine," I said. Stu was now all business as if he regretted the wink. No funny stuff, which was just fine with me. He huffed as he moved. "Long as I'm here, I'll pump out the head and top off the water."

I helped him secure the boat to the dock. Keeping my voice and manner casual, I asked, "Anyone else around?"

"Boss'll be back later." He wiped his hands on his jeans. "You're his kid, ain'cha?"

"Yeah." I didn't elaborate. My dad may have claimed me, but I didn't know yet if I'd claim him. Probably not, and I wasn't asking for any favors, either.

I caught Stu staring at me, an odd expression on his face. What did that mean? "I'm okay, then," I said. "I'll take care of the head and the water. See you later." I waved him off and set about the chores. He ambled down the dock back to the marina office, stopping to light a cigarette when he stepped onto the gravel.

As I worked, I noticed that the place was neat and well-maintained. The gravel yard was clear of litter and debris, the marina office shone with fresh paint, and the high chain-link fence surrounding the property showed no signs of rust or sagging. Even the gas pump had been wiped off. I had forgotten my dad was a neat-freak. He liked things "shipshape."

Neat-freak or not, he was probably warming a seat in a bar right now. In my experience, that's what he did best.

For a moment, sad memories surfaced. And brutal ones. I clamped my jaw shut. Just let him try anything. I was a grown woman now, and no longer vulnerable to his rages and abuse. There were other marinas up and down the coast, but I had business to take care of here first.

One more thing to do. I stepped into the cabin and found a large towel, brought it out, and hung it down from the stern so it covered part of the transom. I'd botched the paint job I'd done to cover the boat's name. Now the bad paint job might raise the wrong kind of interest. I'd kept the boat's Connecticut registration numbers. I could explain the lack of a name but not missing registration numbers. Lucky I'd made it this far without running into a marine patrol asking questions.

I was facing a sea of unknowns, taking a trip back in time to revisit my past, but now I was an adult with an adult's perspective and strength. I needed to face and conquer the forces that made me the way I am. I had come home to learn how to make good choices and reject bad ones. I needed to find out if I was tough enough and smart enough to stand up and fight brutal husbands, abusive fathers, and whatever else got flung at me.

Chapter 7

I sat in the cockpit late that afternoon munching on a sandwich and enjoying the quiet. I savored a peace I hadn't felt for a long time. Hunter knew by now I wasn't coming back. He also knew I'd found his stash of fake Social Security cards and passports, and I'd stolen financial records out of his safe. Had he hounded Norma and the office for my address? Would he dare? He'd be afraid I'd turn him in, wouldn't he? He must be raging, but there was no one to kick around at his house. Not anymore.

What did he think I would do with the fake documents and financial records? Was he hiding himself? Waiting to see if the FBI raided his house? He must be connected to other criminals. Were they all searching for me?

My stomach felt queasy thinking of what the mafia might do to me. But if Hunter told them about the missing stuff, they might punish or kill him. He would probably keep silent about what I took to save his own skin. The more I thought about it, the more convinced I became Hunter wouldn't tell anyone about what I'd done. Still, he must be looking for me.

Little boat traffic maneuvered on this tributary of the Rappahannock, so I was safe. For now. Only an occasional fish splash broke the smooth surface and left ripples on the water. I supposed Stu was around somewhere. Maybe he was paid to stick around until my dad came home. I didn't envy him having his job. I idly wondered what my dad would say when we met, but the thought didn't upset me. I called him a couple of days before, telling him I was coming, and he had seemed reserved and noncommittal, not at all the raging bull I expected. It threw me off. Now I didn't quite know what to expect, but I'd been through his rages and abuse. I could handle what he dished out, and I rehearsed our meeting many times on this trip.

In most normal families, I supposed, a person in trouble could go back home for support and protection. Of course, it's the first place anyone would look if searching for that person. If mine had been a normal, loving family, I probably would have seen through Hunter from the beginning. I would never have married him. Just goes to show.

I told Hunter I was an orphan. He knew I'd gone through an unhappy home life growing up. He said his was the same. Passive mother. Abusive father. The similarities made me feel close to him. Now it seemed he might have made up an unhappy home life, knowing it would have the effect of bringing us close. How come I hadn't realized this ploy? He was like a fisherman, always changing the bait to see what worked, what didn't. Why didn't I recognize the manipulation? I finally needed to admit the reason was I didn't want to. I was too busy covering up my own feelings to analyze another's.

As I thought about my parents, an epiphany struck me. I suddenly understood in order to survive the marriage and avoid the abuse, my mother went passively along with her husband. What would she have been like married to a different kind of man? In fact, I followed the thought: What would I eventually turn into after another few years with Hunter?

My father moved around so much since I'd left home I often

lost track of him. I suspected he changed locations when he'd offended people so much they wouldn't tolerate him anymore. He'd bought this marina a couple of years ago and written me a brief note about it. I'd taken a risk when I sailed in here, but if he had moved on and there was a new owner, I would have stayed here anyway. I was paying my own way and didn't need to beg for anything from him or anybody else. But then I wouldn't be able to tackle the beast that set me up for bad choices.

For awhile, staying here should keep me safe from Hunter. My father was another thing entirely. He could intimidate and threaten his wife and child in a drunken fit, and he'd set me up for the Ryans and the Hunters of this world, but I was through with their kinds of brutish behavior. I was here as an adult to test myself against the force demeaning me when I was too young to protect myself.

I sat up as I saw a red pickup truck hurtle down the road and screech to a halt in front of the locked marina gate. A tall man with a neatly trimmed gray beard, stout with age and, no doubt, bad living, stomped over to the barricade, fussed with the lock for a moment, then opened the gate and swung it wide. He stalked back to the truck, drove it in, and parked it in front of the marina store and office. He stepped out of the pickup and stood beside it, staring at my boat. Stu leaned against the store, still smoking his cigarette and watching. A rusty old coffee can sat next to him, and he flicked ashes from his cigarette into it.

I ignored Stu and the other man's stare. Was he another employee? Business must be good then. Out of the corner of my eye, I saw the man hitch up his jeans and stride confidently toward me, his feet in heavy black shoes that clomped with each step. I stood up in the cockpit and waited for him.

When he got to the gas dock, he stopped, folded his arms, and frowned at me. "So you got here," he said. He was not acting friendly. "What did you do with your hair?"

I took a moment to reply. In my imagination, my father appeared as I remembered him. Tall, heavily overweight with a beer belly, bushy brown beard, and a can of Budweiser perpetually in his hand. Who was this stranger?

I stared at him and suddenly realized he was eyeing me as if judging a cow. He didn't look pleased at what he saw. I could feel my weak little girl self respond to the confrontation. I straightened my body to stand tall, folded my arms, and frowned at him. All right. I put on my stolid face. I didn't like him any more than he liked me.

"Got here awhile ago." I said it without emotion, ignoring the hair comment, but inside I was reeling from shock. This was my father? He didn't seem drunk. Back when I'd still lived with him and after my mom ran away, a fact I now understood, he'd be drunk by mid-afternoon. And ugly. Something must have happened today to keep him out of the bar.

"How long you planning to stay?" he asked in guarded tones.

"I don't know." How should I act with this man, this stranger? He'd lost a lot of weight and actually looked as if he'd been working out. "I'll pay the fees and expenses." I saw the hardness in his face and added, "In advance."

"Uh huh." He turned and walked back down the pier. "We'll talk about it tomorrow," he said. "I got somewhere to go tonight." He stepped off the pier onto the gravel. "I'll need your boat registration number and insurance papers," he threw over his shoulder. "If you're moving down here, you better see about getting your boat registered here."

"I want to be hauled out first thing tomorrow," I called after him. "Bottom needs work."

He threw me a wave and kept walking.

I couldn't figure out what just happened. My dad was different. Totally unlike the way I'd remembered him. I sat in the cockpit and puzzled over him. I had not expected a warm homecoming. Certainly not. Yet in most families, I reflected, there would have been hugs and kisses and smiles. I couldn't remember any time growing up when they were part of my family life, except once in a while from my mom, when she wasn't crying.

I thought of Hunter. What had I expected out of marriage with him? Love? Acceptance? Had they ever been there in our relationship? At first, maybe. Acceptance had been the real drawing card, and I had tried hard to live up to my own image of a good wife. I shook my head as I remembered my attempts to please a person who, after our marriage, would not be pleased. Nothing I did measured up to his increasingly rigid expectations until I secretly met his criticism with cynicism as it turned to brutality.

Thank god for Norma who countered my rationalizations with clear-eyed assessments and anger, and then boosted my self-esteem with a job that kept me in touch with the real world. Without her and my work, I would have succumbed.

I shivered and returned to the present. He said he had something to do tonight. Meet his buddies at a bar, my guess. He said I needed to register the boat in Virginia. Register. Drat. I'd have to check the Virginia boating laws. The state has to give you a couple of months. I could put it off.

Did I need a Plan B? I had expected a sloppy welcome from a drunk. Instead, I was confronted by a cold and sober stranger. Could my dad have changed so much in the ten years since I last saw him? Apparently he had.

Years ago, his adjustment to my mother's defection made him brutal, even though his drinking was the real cause. He became angry and bitter, hard to live with. I stood it long enough to get through college. Then I confronted him, and we said ugly things to each other. I moved to New York. I didn't tell him about Hunter until we'd been married for two months, and that was way more than long enough to be married to Hunter.

I expected my dad to be the same man I knew before, an alcoholic who would welcome me back with great sentimentality and struggle to remember my name. I thought I could easily wangle a place here, no questions asked, until it was safe to leave. I hoped I'd learn a better way to cope with men like my dad by having to deal with him every day. Dad had been small potatoes, though. Hunter was big time. I needed to grow a lot stronger before I could confront him and survive.

I heard a power boat chugging up the river. A houseboat high in the water. It was probably returning home after using up the fuel and water. I hurriedly stepped below to escape being seen and heard the engine noise fade away around a bend.

That night, sleep came in brief respites from disturbing memories as I stared at the paneled ceiling. I assumed no one at my dad's marina would question my presence here, but I didn't know how much he'd changed. Nothing was given anymore. What would we talk about in the morning?

Chapter 8

I woke early, ate a quick breakfast of cereal, and took a cup of tea out onto the dock. No one around yet. The place was quiet except for the gentle quacking of a duck on the river. I walked to the gate and latch, hefting the lock. Heavy duty, requiring a heavy-duty tool to break it. I tried the door of the marina store and office. Also locked. A sign hung on the door said the marina opened at seven-thirty a.m. unless advance arrangements were made.

My dad probably slept in the back rooms. I wondered how he kept them or if he did. The dad I'd known had been super neat. What was this new dad like? Did he make his bed? Wash the dishes? There must be a bathroom, but was there a kitchen? His name was Amos, and I decided to call him that. It gave us equal footing. He'd never been a real dad to me.

My aim was to make a simple business arrangement with Amos. That's all. I didn't like the sound of the "talk" we were supposed to have, but I would leave if I had to. I didn't want any complications, but I did want some protection if I needed it. I thought Amos, as unreliable as he had been and as controlling, might provide it. I was an adult now, and despite his and Hunter's efforts to prove me incapable, I was going to find out how to handle difficult situations. My husband. My dad.

As I thought about it, I realized the sober Amos might no

longer be the abusive brute he had once been when he was a drunk. Of course, I was no longer the vulnerable little kid, either. My heart was hardened against him, and he seemed suspicious of me and too ready to tell me what to do. I'll see what happens, I concluded. I can push back, and I can leave.

I returned to the boat and sipped my tea, looking out over the water and spotting an osprey sitting on its nest staring down at me. Tears sprang to my eyes at the fierce protectiveness of the bird. It reminded me of a different mother who did not protect but abandoned her offspring to a savage and out-of-control brute. Still, what could my mother have done against him? The bitter thought I'd pondered in tears as a child resurfaced. Why didn't she take me with her?

At seven-thirty, I heard a rattletrap bouncing down the road, stopping at the gate, and the crunching of shoes on the gravel walking to unlock the gate and swing it wide. Whoever it was drove the rattletrap in and parked. I turned my head to see Stu scramble out of an antique Chevy Impala with flaking paint in patches of tan, blue, and red. He threw a cigarette butt out toward the road as he walked to the marina office. He knocked on the door. My father opened it, gazed quickly across the yard and retreated inside. Stu followed him.

After awhile, Stu came out and stepped onto the dock. He spied me in the cockpit. "Y'all ready? Go on in and settle up. Amos is waiting for you. Then we can haul this thing out of the water." He walked back toward the store and lit a cigarette, but he stayed outside to smoke. At his feet was the same battered, rusty coffee can he used for butts.

I made a fresh cup of tea. With that in hand, I meandered to the marina office and walked in, unable to quell a feeling of dread. *I can always leave. Find somewhere else.*

The office was actually a small store with groceries, marine supplies, a freezer for bags of ice, and a refrigerator with a hand-printed sign listing various baits and prices. The walls were covered with cheap, light oak paneling, and a couple of bare light bulbs dangled overhead. Standing two feet from the side wall at the left was a tall six-foot-wide counter with a cash register on a shelf behind it. Against the wall at the back was a scarred wooden desk covered with neat piles of paper. The air smelled faintly of bacon grease and fresh fish.

"Go, Dad," I muttered to myself.

Amos came out of the back room, cup of coffee in hand. "So," he said, gazing at me with a stern look on his face. "You came back."

I took a step to the rear, weak, tongue-tied, and angry at myself. I still could not respond to such direct antagonism. I felt like retreating against a wall, arms in front to protect my body as I did when I was a child confronted with his unpredictable anger. I felt an insane urge to cry. I must not cry. Get a little backbone, I chastised myself. He can't do anything to you. If he tries, you walk away. Or call the police. I edged toward the door. This was a terrible idea. All those counseling sessions, all those self-talks, and you still can't stand up to him.

That thought galvanized me. I stepped away from the wall, took a deep breath, and stood straight, face composed, eyeing Amos with crossed arms. "I am only here to get my boat hauled out and the bottom painted." A little more than that, actually. "I've left Hunter and would like to stay here awhile. I'll get a job in town." How was he taking this so far? I couldn't discern any clues in Amos' face. "I have the money to pay all my expenses."

Amos contemplated me, a slight smile on his face. "Does he know where you are?"

I shuddered. "No." It was all I was going to say. Hunter had a murderous temper. He saw me as his property. He went after his enemies, and now I was his worst enemy.

"You see here," said Amos. "You go on back to your husband. A wife belongs with her husband." He frowned. "Or are you carrying on like your mother? You're going to turn out to be just like her, aren't you? A deserter just when things get tough. Like a rat on a sinking ship."

"You were a rotten ship," I said, anger gripping me. "I couldn't fight your drunken rages. Nobody could." I wanted to add, she should have taken me with her, but those words hurt too much to say. I wasn't going to give Amos the satisfaction.

"I was a rotten ship?" Amos stared at me as if digesting my words. Abruptly, he laughed and turned away. "Maybe so, but she still shoulda stayed, taken care of you," he said in a low voice.

"My mother did what she had to do," I added defiantly, not sure I heard him right.

"No. She belonged at home. She should have made a decent home for us. But she didn't. She took the coward's way out." Amos banged his fist on the counter.

"Yeah. Sure." I watched Mom run out of the house in tears more than once. She desperately needed to leave that terrible life. I didn't dare say those words aloud.

Instead, I folded my arms and said flatly, "Hunter beat me."

Amos pushed his lips out and narrowed his eyes. "Sometimes women need to know who's boss. Were you misbehavin'?"

"Excuse me?" I asked. I couldn't quite believe I'd heard him right. I felt my body tremble and took a deep breath. I was not going to let a panic attack take over.

"He had to have some reason to punish you."

I stared at him a moment. Of course he'd think that way. Nice to have it confirmed. "Hitting a person, anyone, is abusive. I won't stand for it." I paused, then said deliberately, hoping it hurt, "Neither did Mom, finally."

This is why I came back to this place. This is what I needed to fight, and I needed to win this fight. I was an adult now. I could make my own decisions. I could leave if I wanted to. Right now, I didn't want to. I needed to face this dragon and conquer its power over me.

After a moment of staring at him and feeling the force of his disapproval at me, I turned my back on him, walked to the counter, and pulled out my wallet. "I want my boat hauled," I said to the wall behind the counter. "I mean to stay onboard while I work on it. Don't know how long that will take. I know your rates, and I have cash. Do you want me to pay now?" I waited.

Amos walked around me to stand behind the counter. "You steal money from your husband?"

"I earn my own money," I said between clenched teeth. "And I bought that boat myself, too. I don't steal, and I don't beg. I want my boat hauled, so I can work on it."

"Are you kiddin'?" He snorted. "You're going to work on her? I'd sure like to see that," Amos said. "Okay. Five hundred to start. Cash, you said?" He opened a ledger in front of him and pulled out a receipt form.

I counted out the bills. "Now I'm going into town and put the rest into a checking account." I eyed him deliberately. "I don't keep much cash around." I knew he'd stolen the few pennies I'd saved as a child. Drinking money.

I watched him frown and his face fall. He looked hurt at the obvious insult, but that couldn't be, could it?

I picked up the receipt and walked out as Stu wandered in, taking off his cowboy hat as he stepped through the door.

"Put your cigarette out," Amos roared at him.

Chapter 9

An hour later, Stu was prepared to haul my trawler out of the water and prop it up on land. He steered the Travelift so the wheels on each side straddled a short inlet of deep water. Two slings suspended from the connecting bars on the machine dropped into the water. I steered into the inlet and over the slings. Stu maneuvered the slings to position them under my boat to cradle it while it was lifted out of the water. I held my breath. I'd seen larger boats than mine transferred onto dry land by similar machines, but it still seemed like a risky operation to me. I had a lot of money tied up in that boat.

I checked everything over carefully before I left Connecticut, and I experienced no trouble on the trip from Connecticut down to the Chesapeake Bay and on up the Rappahannock to my dad's marina. But the bottom needed scraping and a new paint job. The propeller needed work too.

I crossed my fingers that we wouldn't find some major problem to fix.

Stu maneuvered the hoist to bring my trawler into place among the three boats propped up on land. "Put it in the middle," I said. *Where it can't be seen.*

After Stu lowered the keel to rest on three logs, my dad came out of the office, walked over and helped Stu put sturdy wood buttresses in place to hold the boat upright and level.

"So you're planning to live onboard while you work on her?" Amos asked.

"I do," I said defiantly. "You got your deposit. While I'm fixing her up, I'll find work around here." I'll contact Norma, too, and see what I can do for her online.

"Summer season starting. Should be jobs." Amos squinted at me in the bright sunlight. "Course I don't hold with no wife leaving her husband like you've done."

"I'm supposed to take the abuse, is that it? Would you?" I folded my arms, frowning up at him. "Anyway, Hunter agreed I needed a breather," I lied. "He knows what I'm doing. It's all right with him." I rarely wrote to Amos, but in one letter to him during my marriage, I only told him about it and the move to New Jersey in cursory terms. After I left Hunter, I wrote Amos about putting into the marina. By that time, I knew not to give him the address of Hunter's house. Hunter was secretive, kept himself hard to find, and his home address secret—something else to be thankful for. I didn't want my dad trying to find him, trying to get us together again. That was not going to be my story.

It must not happen, or I would be as dead as Tom Haggerty.

I turned away from Amos and studied the hull, now exposing the algae and barnacles clinging to it. I'd have to scrape all that stuff off first. Clean it up. Look for cracks, wormholes, or other damage. Make sure it was okay. Paint it.

I also needed to find someone to paint a new name on the transom. I'd pondered it on the trip down but hadn't decided yet. I wanted something to indicate the south, not the north. Something like Little Peedee, a river in South Carolina. The name made me smile.

Stu finished propping up the boat and stood back. "I'll get a ladder so you can climb on and off." He wiped his hands on his jeans and took a drag on the cigarette hanging from his lips. "You can use the boaters' head and shower behind the office." He threw the butt into the battered coffee can on the ground, released the slings from under the boat, and secured them out of the way. "Save pumping out, you know." He started the motor on the Travelift and navigated it around the other boats to park it again alongside the fence.

I joined Stu as he walked back to the office, cigarette in one hand, butt can in the other. "So how far is town?" I asked.

"We're on the outskirts, but it's too early in the season for much happening," Stu said, smiling down at me, acting friendly. "Maybe half a mile." He pointed down the road. "That way."

"Thanks." I glanced at my watch. Only ten-thirty. "Think I'll walk into town. Check it out."

"Sure." Stu stepped to the office door, dropped his cigarette into the can and left it outside. "Come in here first. You'll need to be able to open the lock on the gate." He grinned and winked at me. "Case you stay out late."

That wink again. With that ruggedly handsome face, cowboy hat, and razer-cut hair, he looked like somebody's boyfriend. I hoped he wouldn't try coming on to me.

Amos made me sign for the key, but he couldn't lay down a curfew—anymore. I shook my head at the pettiness of it but toed the line. Control freak that he was, I suspected the only reason he gave me a key was because otherwise he'd have to open and close the gate every time I wanted to use it after hours. I also needed to work on not ticking him off. I took the key and walked out the gate, passing on my right the marina mailbox in the form of a large bass. Did Amos put that there? I wouldn't expect him to possess that kind of whimsy.

I headed for town. I needed cheap shore transportation. A bike. As I walked, I assessed the situation. Hunter had separated me from my friends and always made it hard for people to track him down, so if Amos had a notion to do that, he would soon feel frustrated and give up. No one I'd known up north except Norma knew I owned a boat or anything about my dad and family. Only Stu, Amos, and I knew where the boat was.

This marina was the last place Hunter or anyone up north would think I had gone. I certainly vented my feelings about Amos to my close friend Amy long enough, so Hunter couldn't get the marina's address out of her, even if she knew it which she did not. Anyway, Amos bought the marina after he retired, and I was long gone.

Hunter thought my parents were dead. He knew nothing about the marina or my interest in boats. I said nothing because he hadn't asked. If I hadn't found out he was a criminal, how long would I have stayed? Until then I was still working out how to behave the way he wanted his wife to behave. Now that I was away from the situation, I felt ashamed and sickened by my stupidity and complicity in his brutality toward me. Now I hoped my plan would let me stay alive.

And Hunter needed to make sure that didn't happen.

Chapter 10

The walk into town took only about ten minutes. It was on the main two-lane road down Virginia's Northern Neck and marked by two stoplights. Strip shopping malls lined each side of the street. On the far side of town away from the marina was the Food Lion grocery store.

On my first trek into town, I found a bike sales and rental place in a separate barn-like building before the first traffic light. I entered the store and saw a man about my age sitting in a chair at the front window reading a book. He rose and put the book down. I couldn't help glancing at the cover. A book of poetry. He wore a navy sweatshirt and jeans. Was he a student working here or the owner?

He peered down at me through round glasses with a thin wire frame. He was a good foot taller than I. "What can I help you with?"

"I need a used bike in good condition with multiple gears," I said, eyeing the rack of shiny two-wheelers lined up in front of the door. "Nothing fancy."

He followed my glance to the racks. "Those are new models. Expensive." He glanced at my T-shirt and jeans and walked to the back of the room to pull forward one of the bikes leaning against the wall. "Here's what you want." He bounced it on its tires. "Lightweight hybrid with all-terrain tires. Used but reconditioned." I peeked at the price. Reasonable. I could afford it.

"One thing about having so much flat country around," he said as he checked the tires and brakes, "is people like to pedal. They rent mostly if they're summer people. If you're buying, you musta moved here. Planning to stay?"

I pretended to inspect the tires as I considered my answer. What was I going to tell people that wouldn't raise questions or suspicion? This was a small town. If I lied, they'd soon know. I temporized. "Maybe. Depends on how cold it gets in the winter." I laughed. *All a joke.*

The man echoed my laugh. "Exactly what I thought when I moved here five years ago. Found I liked it. When this little shop came up for sale, I bought it." He walked to the cash register. "You'll like it here, too. Nice people." He filled out a sales slip. "I'm giving you a break on this one 'cause you're paying cash."

I noticed a card table set up in the back corner with a computer on it. Two piles of papers and a display of bicycle accessories flanked the computer. He counted out the change as he gave it to me and added his business card. "My name's Cal Brenner. Number's on the card. Let me know if you need help."

"Thank you." I shook his hand. "I'm Melanie Fletcher. Staying at the marina right now."

"Amos' place." Cal nodded. "Good man. Works hard."

I didn't comment. First time I'd ever heard anything positive about Amos. I tucked the card away in my purse. As I took the bike, I nodded at the computer. "Use that in your business?"

"Sure, but I'm a writer, too. Free-lance, and I'm working on a novel." He laughed ironically. "Good thing I've got the shop, or I wouldn't eat."

"Sounds like you have a fulfilling life," I said. "Enviable."

"I like it." He walked out of the store with me. "You have any trouble, you bring it back, y'hear?"

While I was in town, I bought a cell phone since I'd crushed the one I had in New York. I didn't want Hunter chasing me down through the phone's GPS. I didn't know how it worked, but I was taking no chances.

Then I tooled down the road back toward the marina. So Amos was a good man, worked hard. That was different. However, this foray into town had been worthwhile. I owned shore transportation. I'd met Cal Brenner, who might be useful if things got tough. Plus, I'd spotted a community bulletin board in his store.

I needed to decide how I was going to earn a living. Norma would let me work online, but I felt too unsettled for the kind of intense work she required. I sent her an email with my resignation and my regrets.

I had to get my head on straight before I went back to a real job. I could live on my savings for awhile and find low-key day-to-day jobs, nothing stressful and nothing that would require references Hunter might find out about.

I rode into the marina and walked the bike across the gravel to my boat. It was sandwiched between two propped-up wrecks waiting for the weekend when the owners could work on them. The marina's big business would come later in the spring and summer. I leaned my wheels against a sawhorse and made a mental note to get a lock and chain next trip into town. I walked into the marina office.

Stu sat in a chair tipped back on two legs. He swigged on a Coke. Amos fiddled with a pile of receipts. They both glanced my way when I entered.

I looked from Stu to Amos. "I need cleaning supplies for my hull, and a sign painter to put the name on the transom."

Amos frowned at me. "Now see here," he said, "you didn't steal that boat, did you? It's yours fair and square?"

"Of course it is. I told you before." How dare he? "I had a good job up in New York. I made money." I fought to keep the anger out of my voice. So typical of him to think I couldn't support myself, that I couldn't hold down a good job. How little he understood me. "I bought that boat myself with my own money, and I brought it down here myself."

Amos raised an eyebrow. "Some guy came nosing around while you were gone."

I froze. "What guy?" Hunter couldn't have found out about the boat so soon. No one knew where I'd gone. No one even knew I had a boat. Hunter thought my dad was dead and didn't know his name. This is the last place Hunter would think to look for me, wasn't it?

"Tough-looking dude," said Amos.

Not Hunter then. I smiled at the thought. Hunter was a sharp dresser, wearing either a business suit and tie or if he wanted to be casual, a fresh ironed polo shirt and jeans. He was the only person I'd ever known who insisted his jeans be pressed. Of course, that was supposed to be my job as his wife. I sent them to the cleaners.

"Not your type," added Stu. Then he grinned. "I don't think. He came to see me, so don't get your hopes up. Just wondered who you were, that's all."

Why would some local dude be asking about me? My voice quavered. "What did he want?"

Stu sat up. "No problem. He was curious about your boat—

and about you. He knew a woman was using it. Wanted to know who. Just local busybodies, that's all."

"You didn't tell him anything, did you?" I asked.

"N'uh." Stu pointed at Amos with his Coke. "Don't know about him."

I looked at Amos.

Amos grunted. "Don't tell no men 'bout my married daughter." He looked over at me. "What do you want me to say?"

"Nothing. Don't tell them anything." I turned to go. "And drop those supplies by my boat, okay/"

I stalked out. Who was the stranger? Why did he want to know about me and my boat? What happened to Amos? Could he really be trying to protect me? I immediately shook my head. No way. More likely, he was back into control mode. I needed him to shield me from intrusive questions, but I'd have to stay on guard against Amos as well as this inquisitive stranger. A quiver of fear raced down my spine.

Chapter 11

That evening at dusk, I sat outside in the cockpit, enjoying the balmy spring weather. I was eating a quick casserole I'd made of canned chicken and noodles, peas, and a chopped onion after heating it in the microwave. The boat was tethered to shore power, so the tiny refrigerator hummed, the microwave worked, and the two-burner hot plate was adequate. I'd boiled water for tea and, in deference to the warm weather, added ice cubes to it.

I heard a motor and looked out at the river to see the same houseboat chugging by, just as high in the water as before. I picked up binoculars and tracked the behemoth through them. I could see the dark outlines of several people inside the cabin and wondered idly who they were, where they were going, where they'd been.

I supposed the vessel belonged to one of the families upriver. Several gated communities were situated there, I knew. Most of their expensive homes were still vacant at this time of year. The houseboat would fit right in at one of the docks on the river, although it might be a bit déclassé among the high-end power craft snug in their expensive boat sheds.

It must belong to one of the year-around group.

I wondered if any of them needed help. Tomorrow I would put together a flyer and some notice cards, bike to the office supply store in town to get copies, and then zip around to stores in town to post them. I also needed to find a bank. I'd feel a lot safer once those financial statements were locked inside a safety deposit box, and someone I trusted knew what to do with them in case something happened to me. Something like being killed. The thought chilled me. What was Hunter doing now? Could he have contacted some of his crooked friends to look for me? How extensive was his criminal network? Who was that strange man who'd come around asking about me? Was he just a local bar buddy as Stu claimed? Did it mean Stu gossiped about me to his buddies in town? Or was the man connected to Hunter?

Amos said he wouldn't gossip to strange men about his daughter, but what if Hunter called and talked to him? He'd act like a deserted husband, and Amos would lap it up.

I felt a panic attack coming on and willed myself to breathe deeply and relax. No one knew I was here. It was a mantra I repeated. No one knew anything about my dad, and I'd told Hunter I was an orphan. No wonder Hunter zeroed in on me. An orphan meant no close relatives to ask questions if she disappeared. I remembered those life insurance policies.

How long would I have lived if I'd stayed with him in New Jersey? I thought of Corinne, the missing Corinne. She had a mother asking questions. Would the neighbors put two and two together now that I've disappeared, too? Alice would know I left Hunter willingly.

What had been Hunter's plan? To get rid of me, he'd need to insist we move first, away from the neighbors who knew Corinne and me. He hadn't made any such suggestion—at least not yet—but he wouldn't ask me, would he? He moved me out of New York without my consent, and he was working on getting me fired. Removing me away from anyone who knew me was the first step in abuse. I was forced to add "murder."

Alice said Corinne and I looked alike. Could Hunter have thought the neighbors might think I was Corinne? We didn't socialize, and no one saw me up close. Some of them might think Corinne had returned. Hunter didn't know about Alice and her sharp eyes.

I took a deep breath. Stay calm, I repeated to myself. I was safe for the time being. I'd done the right thing getting away from Hunter. Now I had to start a new life for myself. I spent the next hour jotting down jobs I thought I could do. Cleaning, pet sitting, house sitting, anything that didn't require a reference from up north.

Hunter's rages and threats couldn't hurt me here. As long as I kept a low profile, he might never find me. Meanwhile, I would get a lot of practice dealing with another brute, my dad, without being threatened with murder. I was buying time until I could safely turn Hunter and the papers over to the FBI.

I surveyed the marina. Stu had got into his rattletrap and gone home an hour ago. Amos had locked up the store and the gate. A light was turned on in the back rooms behind the office, but he'd told me earlier he was going out that night, and I'd seen him leave, all spruced up with a shine on those heavy clompers he wore. What did he do when he went out? He wasn't drinking any more.

Only the hulks of other boats propped up on land to be scrubbed and sanded and painted kept me company as the moon rose, the shadows grew, and the croaking of the spring peepers escalated to a deafening pitch.

Chapter 12

I woke up. What was that sound? I held my breath and listened. Gravel crunched as someone walked stealthily across the marina, a grating sound at every footfall. Someone was trying to step quietly, but the white pebbles covered every inch of the yard. The crunching footsteps came closer and stopped.

Thief? Who else would be inside the gate at this time of night? I glanced at my clock. The illuminated numbers said 3:00. Three a.m. I snuck out of bed and crept to the cockpit, then lifted myself up to peer over the gunwales into the darkness.

The waxing moonlight reflected off the white gravel and the white hulls, so I could make out the boats and equipment surrounding me. A dark shadow appeared at the foot of the ladder. It paused, and its head turned as if searching for . . . what? The intruder wore a hoodie, which kept his face hidden. I stared down at him, my heart pounding so loud it should have alerted the figure below. Then he put one hand on a rung of the ladder.

I had to stop him. I took a deep breath. "Get out," I yelled. "You're trespassing! I have a gun and won't hesitate to shoot!"

The shadow hesitated. Then the yard's spotlights came on. "Get out!" Amos yelled. "I've called the police!"

The shadow turned and ran toward the pier. I lost sight of him and then heard a boat motor sputter into life. Which way did it go? I couldn't see it in the darkness, and the chirping, buzzing, croaking sounds of the frogs and cicadas on the water mingled with the motor into a confusing chaos.

Amos walked to my boat and looked up at me. I was shaking and trying to control my breathing. I didn't need a panic attack. The intruder deliberately sought out my boat, and he was going to climb up the ladder. What would he have done then? What did he want?

"That one of your fellers? Come to call?" Amos asked scornfully.

"Of course not." How dare he think that. "One of your pals? Couldn't find his way home?"

"I don't have friends like that," Amos said. I could barely hear the next word. "Anymore."

"Sure. Like when?" I turned. "I've got to get some clothes on if the police are coming."

"I can hear the car now. Gotta unlock the gate." I heard Amos walk to the gate and unlock it as I pulled on jeans and a sweatshirt.

I stepped down the ladder and watched the police car drive in and park. The police officer was so tall he seemed to unfold as he got out of the car. He hitched up his slacks, pulled a flashlight out of his car, and walked to Amos, nodding at him and tipping his hat to me. "I'm Officer Pete Henschel," he said to me. He must already know Amos. "So what happened here?" He tucked the flashlight under his arm and pulled a notebook and pen out of his shirt pocket.

I spoke up. "A prowler. I heard him walking on the gravel. He woke me up." I stopped. I suddenly realized that I didn't want to say anything to indicate the man had been heading for my boat, maybe targeting me. Maybe he was after something else. Other boats were in the yard, some outfitted with expensive equipment. It didn't have to be all about me. Except, he had singled out my boat and started to climb my ladder. I shivered and wrapped my arms around myself.

The officer paused in his notes and peered at me under his hat.

"Got here by runabout," added Amos. "Skedaddled when I turned on the spotlights. Heard him start the motor but couldn't figure out which way he went in the dark, what with the frogs and all."

The officer scribbled some more. "Okay." He glanced at Amos. "You own this marina. Any reason why someone would sneak in here and try to climb into this boat?"

"It's my boat," I said. "I don't have anything anyone would want."

"Yeah. This here's my daughter." Amos pointed at my boat. "Staying on her boat. Just came in from up north a couple of days ago."

"I see." The officer glanced at me and turned back to Amos. "So you can't think of any reason why this guy was prowling around?"

"Absolutely not."

"Tools and anything else of value are all locked up," I said.

"Yep. We lock everything up," added Amos.

"There've been some break-ins up river in those fancy houses. Could be the same guys." The policeman glanced around the yard. "Might wanna get a dog. A barker. It'll help keep the prowlers and the crooks out." He closed his notebook and put it back in his pocket.

"I'll take a look around, see if I spot anything, but if he didn't take anything. . ." he shrugged. "Probably some kid."

"Thank you for coming," I said.

"You're welcome, ma'am." He tipped his hat. "You wanna check back on this, just ask for me." He gave Amos a card, turned on the flashlight and played it on the gravel as he walked around my boat and down towards the pier. I watched him but he didn't find anything. He returned to his car and drove out.

Amos closed and locked the gate. He turned to me. "Tomorrow we're gonna get ourselves a dog."

As I climbed the ladder into my boat, I reflected that it was the friendliest comment I'd heard from Amos since I arrived.

Chapter 13

I went back to bed and slept restlessly, waking frequently and listening for the crunch of gravel. Thank goodness I had none of my usual nightmares. That was strange.

The deputy was right. We needed a dog. The chain-link fence and locked gate weren't enough—not with open access to the water. Anyone with a dinghy could row it to the pier and get off, walk around the area at will, climb the ladder, assault me. A vision of Hunter crossed my mind, but he didn't like watercraft of any kind. His first thought when he heard about mine was to ridicule the idea and assume it was a rowboat he could sell. At least he hadn't mentioned it again, so he must have forgotten about it. Anything with oars was beneath his notice.

I woke and dressed early, preferring to sit in the cockpit where I could keep an eye on things. I sipped a cup of tea, nibbled on a piece of toast. No lights on in Amos' rooms. He usually didn't surface until seven. Stu would drive through the gate awhile later.

The sun rose, but it was still too early to burn off the low-lying mist that shrouded the river. The air felt cool. A couple of mallards paddled softly along the shore, a comforting sound punctuated by the occasional splash of a fish breaking the surface with a widening circle of ripples.

I'd forgotten the peacefulness of the river in early morning. I grew up on the water too many years ago, back when I still had a mother and a father, back when it felt safe to be a part of my family. It all eroded when my father started drinking. That was when I lost the safety of family and retreated to the peace of the river. My mother ran away to survive, but she didn't take me. I lacked a defense and couldn't run away. I was left to be a victim. That was when I changed and began looking for love in all the wrong places. I smiled at the thought,

It was inevitable that I'd meet someone like Hunter and fall madly in love. I was raised to take abuse.

I watched the lights come on in Amos' rooms. He no longer drank and the fact surprised me, but he was the same judgmental chauvinist he'd always been. I needed him to be that way, so I could learn what made men like him tick. I needed to develop the strength to recognize and overcome their power over me. It's why I was here.

I wondered where he went in the evenings. Could he possibly have a lady friend? I couldn't believe that.

Looking down the road, I saw the cloud of dust signaling the arrival of Stu's rattletrap. I hadn't quite figured him out yet. He seemed to work as an all-around handyman at the marina, but he called himself the dock master. He and Amos seemed to like each other. Except for Stu's cigarettes, they got along well, but where did he come from? How long had Amos known him? What did he want?

I watched Amos walk out of the office and to the gate. He unlocked it and let Stu in. Just for something to do, I guessed, since Stu carried his own key. Then Amos glanced at me and waved. "Come on in the office," he said, "when you're ready."

I looked at my watch. "In a bit," I said. I didn't want to seem eager, even if the invitation actually sounded friendly.

I took my time writing out cards offering my pet-sitting and house-cleaning services, keeping one eye on Amos and Stu puttering around the marina. When I saw Stu throw his cigarette butt into the old coffee can and meander down to the gas dock to help a fisherman fill his tank and Amos go into the office, I stepped down the ladder and followed him. What did he want to talk to me about? Was he going to try to bully me back to my husband? Tell me to leave? Whatever it was, it was going to be a test. I'd gotten through the first hurdle—showing up here. And the first confrontation. Let's see how well I handle this one.

When I entered the office, I let my eyes adjust to the dimmer light, then saw my dad sitting at his desk in back. He turned and waved, pushing another chair out with his foot. I took it as Amos leaned back and gazed at me, his arms resting on the chair arms.

"So," Amos said, "you think we oughta get a dog?"

I blinked, too surprised to respond at first. I thought of all the times he had reneged on promises he'd made. Last night he said we should get a guard animal, and he actually remembered that this morning. "A dog?" I stammered.

A grim smile hovered around Amos' lips. "Yeah. A dog."

"You get prowlers around here often?" I asked. I'd had a puppy once. A beagle named Caesar. He'd disappeared. I thought Amos had probably run him over in a drunken drive home.

He shrugged. "Not till you came."

"A pet would be nice," I said cautiously. "If we can take care of it here."

He squinted at me. "How long you planning to stay?"

I tried to figure out what he was really after. Was this a straight question with no agenda, or did he have some plan in mind? Finally I said, "I don't know. Depends on whether I find work in town."

"What are you looking for?"

"Right now, odd jobs." I was getting tired of this fencing. I stood. "I gotta go."

"I'll give you a job here," said Amos. "Looking after the store."

I glanced around the shop, keeping a blank face as I considered this new surprise. He was willing to help me out with a job? Or was this some gambit to control me. Maybe keep me here until he could bring Hunter down.

"No, thanks," I said, heading toward the door. I stopped halfway there. "We could get a rescue, a mutt with some German shepherd in it." After all, it did need to be a guard dog. I walked out, letting the door bang shut behind me.

I climbed back into the boat, picked up the cards, and glancing around the cabin, decided it was time to take care of the fake IDs and the financial statements. I retrieved a large and bulky manila envelope from the drawer under one of the bunks. I pulled out of the envelope three letters I had composed on my laptop and printed in a Staples Office Supply on the way south. The top letter said:

> **To be opened on my death:** This key unlocks a safety deposit box in my name at the Citizens Bank in Oldtown, Virginia. The box contains documents that show illegal offshore bank accounts held by Hunter McCann for himself and his clients as well as fake ID cards I found in his desk. If my death is suspicious, Hunter is responsible. He has threatened me many times. I left him to survive, but I have rea-

son to believe he murdered Tom Haggerty, New York City, and Corinne McCann at his home in New Jersey. He is a killer.

The name of the bank came from a quick Internet search. I signed and dated the letter. The second one was the same and would include the second safety deposit key. The third letter would omit the key since the letter would remain with the documents inside the safety deposit box.

I folded each of the first two letters, added a piece of cardboard and placed each inside a business-sized envelope.

I had plenty of time on the trip down the waterway to write the three letters. I picked up my bike and pedaled into town. Amos offered me a job. What was that all about? No way was I going to put myself under his control. *Been there. Done that.*

The bike shop was my first stop. Cal looked up from a tire he was fixing as I walked in. A teenaged African-American boy was watching him.

"Nothing wrong with the bike, is there?" Cal asked. He nodded at the teenager. "This is Greg. Helps out around the place."

"Hi, Greg." I waved as I walked to the message board. "Just posting my ad." I found an extra tack and pinned my card to the board and stopped to chat. "Looking for odd jobs. Pet-sitting, house-cleaning."

"Seems like you could do a whole lot better." Cal reached over for the air pump. "Get a real job. Not here, though. Need to find a bigger town."

"Did it. Got burned out. I want to take on a few no-stress jobs for awhile." I watched Cal pump up the tire. Did he buy my story?

Cal took the tire off the stand and laid it against the counter.

"Don't blame you," he said. "Sometimes it's good to take a break, if you can. Exactly what I did. I lucked into this shop. Love it."

Maybe he did buy the story.

I biked to the bank. The staff were friendly and eager to help. I opened a savings account and rented the safety deposit box, placing the manila envelope inside it along with the cover letter. I received two keys and inserted one into each of the other envelopes after writing, "To be opened in case of my death" on the outside. At the post office, I bought two large, stamped envelopes for each of the smaller ones with a key. I was mailing one to Norma but not yet. I needed to find a way to get it to Norma without revealing where it was mailed. For the time being, I hoped Cal would let me keep the other in his safe.

Chapter 14

I used my cell phone number and the name Sierra on the cards advertising my services, just in case, but how would anyone in New York know where I went? Why would Hunter in New Jersey even consider this tiny Virginia town? He didn't have the introspection, empathy or imagination to think I might want to rectify, justify, or understand my relationship with my father, even if Hunter knew Amos were alive. He'd be looking for me around New York, watching my friends and the old hangouts.

He might remember I owned a boat, but he assumed it was a rowboat. Connecticut was a large place to snoop around if he considered I might move there, but why would he?

I left cards in the Food Lion, the Subway, and at the mailboxes for an attractive condo on the outskirts of town. On the way back to the marina, I stopped again at the Bike Shop. Greg was stooped over a sleek racing bike fixing the handlebars. I walked to the table where Cal was sitting and watching me, his chin in his hand. I sat in a chair facing him.

"How's it going?" I asked.

He shrugged. "It's going. I'm on chapter fifteen."

"Wow," I said. "Pretty good. What kind of book?"

"Thriller." Cal sat back and put his hands behind his head. "At least, I hope it'll be a thriller for the people who read it."

"I could be one of your beta-readers." I smiled at him. "Give you a critique, you know, when you get it finished."

"Thanks. I'll hold you to the offer," Cal said. "What can I do for you?"

I laughed. "I do need a favor." I pulled one of the letters out of my backpack. "Can you lock this away for me?"

"What is it, a will? Leaving me your millions?" Cal grinned and took the envelope.

I shook my head, sharing his grin. "Nothing like that. It's just . . ." How could I say this without being melodramatic? "If something happens to me, I want people to know what to do. You know, last wills and stuff."

"I get it." Cal took the sealed packet and unlocked his desk drawer. "I'll lock it in here. Who should I give it to if something happens to you?"

"This is going to sound. . .weird, but I think. . .the FBI." I glanced at Greg, but he was taking the bike outside. I waited until he'd closed the door after him. "Not my father and not anyone else." I refused to mention my husband, but he was uppermost in my mind.

Cal whistled. "It's pretty serious, is it?" He stood watching me. "Are you running from something. . .or someone?"

I nodded. "I haven't done anything wrong. Please don't tell anyone about the letter. I'm sorry, but no one else must know about it. Unless something does happen to me." I suddenly realized what I was saying. I got up and placed a hand on his arm. "I know this sounds crazy. . ." I hesitated. "But it could mean your life. Some bad people are after me. They want what's in that letter."

"My life?" Cal sat back and frowned at me in disbelief.

I shook my head. "I shouldn't put you in danger. I'll find

someone else. Give me back the letter. I'm sorry. Should never have suggested it."

"Are you kidding?" Cal put it in the drawer and locked it. "Most exciting thing to happen to me since I moved here. Don't worry about it. I'll take care of it, and I swear I won't say anything to anyone." He winked at me and added, "But I get first rights to the story."

"Do you have a safe?" I asked. Anyone could open that drawer.

"Never needed one." Cal shrugged. "I do have a safe deposit box, and I'll put it in there first chance I get. Will that be okay?"

I nodded. "It would be much better."

Cal studied my anxious face. "This must be very important," he said softly.

Tears sprang to my eyes at Cal's understanding and support. I expected derision or intrusive questions, but he eagerly helped instead. I felt as if a burden had been lifted off my shoulders. I wiped the tears away quickly, not wanting Cal to see them, but he was watching me and noticed.

"Must be a relief, I guess, to get it off your mind," he said as he sat behind the computer again. He busied himself with shuffling papers, not looking at me. "Don't worry about it. It'll just be our little secret, okay?"

I nodded. "Okay." I waved at him as I walked out the door. Being a writer, Cal was probably intrigued by the mystery, but he still felt like a true friend. Absolutely not a boyfriend, though. I was through with that and already regretted my momentary weakness in front of him.

Biking was the ideal way to travel in the area. It was flat, probably built up from sediment to rise above the river that encroached along the roads and fields. I felt the breeze lifting my hair and enjoyed the scent of new flowers as I pedaled along. My heart felt light and happy. Such a change from the fear and turmoil I'd lived with in Hunter's house. Hunter's house. Not my house. It had never been our house.

I heard Stu's rattletrap coming up behind me. Too late and too close. He honked which startled me so much I lost control of the bike and fell over. My arm hit the mud hard, and the momentum rolled me into the middle of the road. Stu's car stopped an inch from my leg.

In a cloud of cigarette smoke, Stu slid out of the car, walked over to me, and extended a hand to help me get up.

"What the hell did you think you were doing?" I yelled at him.

He took off his hat and scratched his forehead. "I just wanted you to know I was coming up behind. Didn't think you'd jump like a scared rabbit. You ain't hurt, I don't think." His eyes roved over my body as if searching for broken limbs or bruises but lingering on my breasts. "Seem okay."

"I'm all right. You startled me, coming up close and honking the horn." I brushed myself off and picked up my bike. "Don't ever do that again." I examined my bike. "Looks okay, I guess."

"You should go back where you came from," Stu said, towering over me with folded arms.

"What?" Did I hear that right?

"You're making a big problem for Amos, you know," said Stu, putting his hands on his hips.

"How's that?" I asked as I mounted the bike. "I'm just one of the customers."

"You're a worry, just the same." Stu turned to walk back to

his car. "Yes, sir, you're a worry, all right."

"Can't help that. I'm going to wait here until you pass me," I said. I didn't trust him behind me. I glared at Stu's back as he opened his car door. He drove by a little too close.

"You need to go back where you came from," he said as he passed. He grinned at me as he gunned the motor, not even noticing the spray of mud and pebbles he threw my way.

"Damn fool," I muttered, watching his car disappear around a curve.

I bicycled down the road to the boatyard. At the gate, I saw Amos talking to a man in uniform. A plain black sedan was parked alongside the office. I hesitated, but they'd spotted me, and Amos waved. I didn't see any way to avoid meeting the guy.

"This here's the police," said Amos. "Chief Yost. Got some questions for you."

"Why would I know anything helpful to you, Sir?" I asked, trying to act pleasant instead of confrontational, which was how I felt after the run-in with Stu. "I just got here."

"Asking about the break-in you had," Chief Yost said. "Did you get any kind of look at the perp, ma'am?"

"He was in the shadows." I glanced at the sky, trying to remember any details. "It was dark. He was wearing a black or navy hoodie that covered his face. I couldn't make out anything about him that would be useful."

"Thought you might since you're out here in the yard. Exactly where was he when you saw him?"

I shivered, remembering the menacing figure at the base of my ladder. "Next to the ladder," I said.

Yost raised an eyebrow. "Next to the boat. How high up the ladder did his head go? What rung, would you say?"

I nodded. "Oh, I see. I think the top of his head barely came up to the second from the top rung." I walked to my boat and studied the height of the rungs. "That would make him not quite six feet tall. I only come up to about four inches above the fifth one, and I'm five feet and four inches."

Amos broke in. "I heard someone crunching around on the gravel. Got up to look. She yelled." He nodded at me.

"And I got rooms the other side of town," explained Stu, who'd walked over to join us.

"Does this kind of thing happen often?" I asked.

He looked me up and down. "This is a nice town. Not much trouble hereabouts, but we get tourists, people from the big city, kids. Even getting some gang action. We've had a rash of burglaries recently, but we'll get them." He turned and headed back towards his car. Keys jingled in his pocket. "Let us know if you find out anything," he said, tipping his hat to us.

Amos looked at me, a slight smile hovering around his lips. "Come on in the office. Got something to show you."

I followed him wondering what was up. Amos seemed almost. . .nice. That would take some getting used to.

He opened the gate leading behind the counter. Immediately a small squealing black and brown mass of fur ran out and circled me.

"A dog! You got a dog!" I knelt and gathered the wriggling, squealing bundle into my arms, holding him close and nuzzling his neck. "He's beautiful."

"He ain't purebred," said Amos, "and you'll have to house train him."

"I love him," I said, hugging the wriggling pup as he licked my face. I almost slipped and called Amos "Dad." "He'll be great around here. Give him a few months, and he'll be a terrific watchdog."

"He better be," said Amos, turning back to the papers on his desk. "So what are you going to call him?"

I stood watching the pup run circles around us and thought. Finally I said, "Peedee," I grinned at Amos, spelling it for him. "It'll sound like Petey, but we'll know it's Peedee."

Amos grunted.

Chapter 15

I took Peedee to the boat with me for the night. I made a bed for him out of an old blanket but relented and let him sleep at the foot of my bunk because I couldn't stand the whining. His restlessness in the new surroundings kept me awake much of the night, and several times, I braved the darkness to take him down to relieve himself on the gravel.

I still hadn't picked up any jobs but kept my cell phone handy. Amos had come through with a painter for the boat name. Simon Cook. I called him, and he answered with a cheerful British accent.

"Allo. Brightview Graphics here," he said, his voice overloud. In the background, I could hear a vacuum.

I winced at the volume and raised my voice. "I'm at the Riverbend Marina on River Road. I need a name put on my boat transom."

"I say, new boat, then?" Simon asked.

"Old boat. New name."

"Bad luck, what?" he said. "Changing the name of a boat, luv. You sure about this?"

"When can you come here and do it?" I hadn't expected questions. Just do the darned job, I thought.

"Let me check the calendar, luv."

I heard paper rustling, and Simon came back to the phone.

"Tomorrow morning, About ten?" he said. "What name do you want on your boat then?"

"Little Peedee." I waited for the comments.

"Oh, the Carolina river." He paused. "Scenic, don't you know? Pleased to paint that on a boat, bad luck or no."

"Fine," I said and closed out. I looked down at the pup. "You're Big Peedee, so you gotta grow."

The phone rang. I didn't recognize the caller, but I answered it.

"Is this the right number?" a female voice asked in a southern accent. "For cleaning services?"

I perked up. A job. "Yes, ma'am. When would you like me to come?"

"This afternoon if not sooner. The place is a mess."

"Let me check the calendar," I said. Didn't want to look needy. "Okay. I do have a three-hour block of time this afternoon. Would you give me your name and address, please?"

"Right. I'm Ann Summers, and I live in the gated community just off River Road toward the river. You know the one I mean? Belleview Estates, Number 132."

"All right, ma'am. I know where that is. I'll be there at one."

Ann Summers heaved a sigh of relief that even Peedee at my feet heard. He looked at me with head cocked. I smiled at him and scratched his ears, feeling good.

Then a problem occurred to me. I was using a fake name. "Uh, by the way," I said, fingers crossed, "can you pay in cash?"

Ann didn't hesitate. "Sure, honey. My housekeeper in Richmond prefers cash, too, but she just doesn't want her husband to get his hands on it. Hope you don't have the same problem."

"No, ma'am. Don't want to go to the bank more'n I have to."

I reached down to pet Peedee. I'd do a good job for Ann, so she would recommend me to the other residents of Belleview Estates. Jobs. Peedee. I just might stay here awhile.

I spent the rest of the morning scraping barnacles and algae off the hull and cleaning the stern. Then I painted the entire vertical stern a plain, smooth white. Plenty of time for it to dry before the sign painter arrived.

***

That afternoon, I bicycled up to Belleview Estates, a gated and landscaped community of McMansions. On one side of the street, the houses backed to the river. The guard at the gate brought out his clipboard, took my name and address, insisted on seeing my driver's license, and noted the name of the person I was visiting. He called Ann Summers for verification, which led to confusion since I forgot I'd used the name Sierra on the cards. "Sierra's my nickname," I explained, mentally kicking myself.

The guard returned my driver's license. "You're being pretty thorough," I observed. I'd been to communities like this before, and the guards there never asked for ID. They usually didn't even confirm with the resident being visited. At the most, they might take down a license tag number, since most people came by car.

"Yes, ma'am. We patrol this community regularly, but we've still had some break-ins. Can't be too careful."

He stepped aside to let me pass, and I bicycled down the curving road to No. 132, a three-story brick house with cupola on top and two white columns on each side of the entrance. A boxwood hedge lined the front of the house and each side of a walk to the road. The whole place looked pretentious and ultra colonial.

I rang the doorbell, thinking that with this set-up I should have charged more than thirty dollars an hour. Once I got established, I would.

I heard the tapping of heels approach, and the door opened. A slim, middle-aged woman wearing gray slacks and yellow sweater peered out at me. "You're Sierra? Y'all come on in," she said in a soft southern drawl. Her bright-red lipstick, light makeup, and short well-cut gray hair made her look youthful and active.

I walked into chaos. Chairs were overturned and tables swept clean. Broken pottery and shards of glass littered the carpet. Such destruction wasn't necessary for a break-in. The burglars must have had a fight. A vision of Amos heading out to some mysterious destination in the evenings flitted across my mind. Was he involved with the robbers?

"I wouldn't even have known about this for weeks, except that I just happened to come out here from Richmond." Ann glanced around in distaste. "Spend the winter there at my condo, you know. We live here the rest of the year."

"I guess the robbers thought they had a lot of time before you'd find out." I was appalled at the random destruction. If they'd been more subtle, took what they wanted and left, the theft might not have been discovered for weeks, if at all. Missing items would be put down to simple misplacement.

"The bedrooms are even worse," said Ann Summers. "They were pigs. I can't bear to look at this mess. Thank goodness I saw your card. You'll find the vacuum cleaner in the hall closet and the cleaning materials on the shelves alongside the stairs to the basement."

"Fine," I said, looking around. "Don't worry about a thing, but with all this mess, it will probably take me four hours instead of three."

"Whatever. Just make these two floors presentable. Nobody goes up to the third floor." Ann picked up her purse. "By the way, where do you live? I haven't noticed you around before."

"I live at the Riverbend Marina. Dad owns it." I hoped that would satisfy Ann enough, so she wouldn't ask for references.

She didn't. "Fine, then. I've got your phone number. I'm going out. I'll be back in four hours or so." She took another look around, shuddered, and went out the kitchen door to the garage.

I heard the car door open and walked to the window to watch it leave. A BMW. Then I set to work, but first I climbed the stairs to the third floor, which was barren of furniture in all four rooms. I couldn't resist finding the door to the cupola and exploring the little room at the top. From there, I could see the dock for this house on the river below me. Raising my eyes, I could look over the trees to the river and the marina. When I turned in the other direction, I had a clear view of the fronts of the other houses across the street and the woods beyond.

Once the furniture had been set back in place and the debris picked up, I ran a vacuum over the rugs, cleaned the bathrooms, and straightened up the kitchen. The four hours passed. I was working on the final touches when I heard Ann's car enter the garage.

I put the vacuum cleaner away as she entered and looked around.

"Well," she said. She walked into the living room and surveyed it, hands on hips. "This is more like it."

"Did you make a list of what was stolen?" I asked.

"They took mostly electronic stuff. A computer, microwave, TV, a couple of radios." She laughed. "I don't keep my silver here or my jewelry. Why did they have to vandalize the house?

For the life of me, I don't understand such viciousness." She sat on the couch and motioned for me to sit. I took an armchair.

"Too bad," I said. "With a guard at the gate, you'd think this place would be secure."

"They patrol at night, too," Ann added. She opened her purse. "I think you said cash."

I nodded. I took the cash but paused as I turned to leave. "Serial numbers would help. The police check pawn shops, you know. The local police probably collaborate with the Richmond and D.C. cops on that."

"I've already talked to the local police, but I'm going to have to search for any records of serial numbers, and they would be back in Richmond."

"Too bad," I said.

"Yeah. C'est la vie. I'll call you again when I'm back for the summer," Ann said. "You did a good job. I'll tell my friends here." She walked to the door with me and waved as I got on my bike and tooled away.

When Ann went inside and closed the door, I turned left at the end of the driveway to bicycle away from the guardhouse. I wondered if the road dead-ended or circled or if there was another entrance. I bicycled that way for about half a mile, then the road terminated in a cul-de-sac of houses. Whoever came in would have to go out the same way. I turned back.

At the guard station, I stopped. "So is someone here all night?"

The guard leaned against the guard house and lit a cigarette. "We're here at the gate until midnight. Back at six a.m. We do have a security guard patrolling the road from midnight until six. Anyone wants to go in or out between those times has to push a button to call the guard on patrol. No big deal."

"Most of these houses don't seem to be occupied." I waved behind me.

"Yeah." He drew on the cigarette. "Summer places and people here travel a lot, have other places to live, go to Florida."

"The Summers house was robbed and vandalized. How'd that happen with you guarding the gate and a security guard on patrol?"

The guard threw the cigarette into a receptacle and stepped into the little house. "We know about the break-in, and we're looking into it. So are the police. Won't happen again."

I got on my bike. "See you." I pedaled back to the marina, not at all convinced that the robbers could be stopped from hitting some other house. With most of the houses locked up for the winter, who would know if it hadn't already happened?

Chapter 16

As I biked into the marina yard, I noticed Amos' pickup was gone. Stu parked his rattletrap in its usual place. I chained my bike to the fence halfway down the length of it from the gate and waved to Stu, eating an apple and leaning against a piling on the dock. I could hear the puppy squealing at me from the cockpit.

I laid one hand on the rung of the ladder when I noticed sawdust at the base of one of the buttresses holding my boat upright on land. I took a closer look. Then I ran my finger along the buttress. Halfway up I found a crack across its width. Examining it further, I realized it was too straight to be a fault in the wood. Someone sawed the buttress almost entirely through. Wouldn't take much for it to break once I started climbing the ladder. The boat would collapse over me. Goodbye, Melanie. I stepped away as chills raced down my spine. Whoever did it meant to kill me, and it couldn't have been Hunter. How did I make an enemy in this town when I'd just arrived? I looked at Stu and his apple.

"Hey, Stu," I yelled, waving at him. "Come over here."

He took a final bite and threw the core into the water. I watched him wipe his hands on his jeans and amble to me.

"What's up?" he asked, eyes roving around the yard taking in everything but me.

"Look at this." I pointed to the sawdust around the base of the buttress and moved my finger along the crack in the wood.

"Someone's been busy here. Who did this?"

Stu bent over for a closer view. He straightened and cast his eyes around the marina as if he could spot the culprit. "Real odd," he finally said. "Could have broke your boat."

"Right. It could have." He still wouldn't look at me. Did he think I would accuse him? Someone was out to kill me. I was lucky to spot the damage. Who would do such a malicious and potentially fatal act of vandalism? Against me. Could Amos have done this? He might have left, so he wouldn't see the result.

Stu? Why would he want to get rid of me? I couldn't figure him out, but why would either Stu or Amos want to hurt me? I meant nothing to Stu and tried to stay out of his way. There wasn't much love between my father and me, but even though he'd send me back to Hunter if he could, he wouldn't hurt me like this.

Someone else then. I glanced at Stu. "Who's been here?" Did anyone come in the yard while I was gone?"

Stu scratched his head. "Two locals came in for bait. Heard somebody else working on his boat in back there." He waved towards a wreck near the fence. "Course I been in the store most of the time. Gate was open."

"So you didn't see anyone messing around here?"

"No, ma'am. Soon as your Pa left, I went into the store to see to things, take care of the customers, you know. I was in there a long time. Real long time. Waiting for customers, you know. Taking care of them when they came in. After awhile, I came out to do a few things in the yard, but I sure didn't see anyone. How could I?"

I took a long look at Stu. That was the longest speech I'd ever heard from him. Was he lying? Why would he want to hurt me?

He couldn't be jealous, could he? Of what?

He said he was inside the store for a long time. Anyone could enter the yard and saw the wood. You couldn't see them doing it from inside or in front of the store or even from the docks. Who in this small town could possibly want to hurt me? Cal and his helper Greg were the only other people I knew, and why would they want to hurt me?

The only one who had any cause was Hunter, but he didn't know where I was.

If I really had a devious mind, I might think Ann hired me to clean her house to get me out of the way while someone snuck in and sawed the buttress. This idea was too farfetched even for me. She couldn't know Hunter or have any reason to kill or injure me, and she seemed like an honest, open, and kind person. Of course, that's what I thought Hunter was. And Ryan.

I put my hands on my hips and surveyed the yard. No one else was there now. I turned to Stu. "Okay. You might as well help me replace that wooden buttress with a good one."

Once that was done, I climbed into the cockpit and retrieved the pup. I held him in my arms and carried him down the steps to give him a walk. We were still running around the yard together when Amos returned, the back of his pickup filled with boating supplies.

I confronted him with the sawn-through buttress. "How could this happen?" I asked. "I was out most of the afternoon, and Stu says only a couple of guys came into the store to buy bait, but he was inside the store and wouldn't have seen anyone who came into the yard."

Amos scratched his head and looked from the wooden buttress to me. "I don't know who did this," he said, "but I'll get to the bottom of it. Nobody's going to hurt my girl, not on my watch." He clenched his jaw. "I'll call the police."

The police. Of course. I usually wasn't this dramatic, but I could have been badly hurt or killed. That made it a case of attempted murder. Really? I couldn't swallow that. Perhaps a joke.

"Good idea," I said.

"Might be fingerprints or something on that wood." Amos turned and walked to the office.

First a prowler and now this. I hadn't been here for more than a few days, and yet I had created enough of a problem that someone was out to get me. I didn't know I had that much power.

The police came by an hour later, but Officer Henschel wasn't excited about this "case." He took down notes and threw the two pieces of wood into the trunk of his car. "I'll check it out, but if nobody saw anything suspicious, we can't do much. Some kids with nothing better to do, probably."

"Kids!" Ridiculous. "Stu would have seen kids around here," I said, "and chased them out." Were kids blamed for everything that went wrong in this town?

"We'll look into it," he said as he walked around to the driver's door of the car. "He wouldn't see the sneaky ones with mischief on their mind." He heaved himself in the car and drove away.

I felt irritated at Henschel's lackadaisical attitude, but what could he do? The buttress halves were probably covered with the fingerprints of half the town. Footprints didn't show up on the gravel. Maybe there would be telltale sawdust on someone's shoes, but I didn't hold out much hope for that. Stu and Amos already walked all over the area.

Amos almost put his arm around me but stopped and let it drop to his side. "He'll be no help," he said.

I grabbed the puppy and carried him up the ladder to play in the cockpit. Then I found a towel and headed for the marina shower behind the store. "I'll feed you when I get back," I reassured the little guy. He better grow up fast, I thought. We need him to go to work.

Chapter 17

Nothing disturbed me that night. I was tired after my cleaning job and additionally stressed by the sawn-through buttress and the idea someone here might want to hurt me. I slept with the pup curled against my side, but he didn't wake, either.

The next morning, I walked Peedee a half mile along the road in both directions, noting the summer cottages and checking for any signs of a kid's vandalism. I didn't see any and returned to the marina to find Stu getting out of his car. Amos stood at the office door, looking as if he hadn't slept much.

"Morning," I said. I felt energized, and maybe I could even say I felt happy. The scent of lilac wafted along with the cool breeze, and I was ready for breakfast. I checked the buttresses before placing a foot on the ladder, but they were all in good shape.

After breakfast, I played with the dog and read, waiting for Simon Cook, the sign painter, to show up.

At precisely ten o'clock, a blue Subaru Forester drove into the yard and a tall, thin, older man got out. His blue overalls were stained with splotches of paint, and he wore a train engineer's black-and-white striped cap over a head of bushy white hair. He saw me looking at him from the cockpit and waved. "I say, are you Melanie Fletcher?" he called up to me.

"Yep, that's me." I stepped down the ladder and shook his

hand. It stuck to mine with some kind of adhesive, and I had to pull it away. "You're Simon Cook, I take it."

He nodded as he turned back to grab a tool box and a clipboard out of the trunk of the Subaru. "And, hallo, that's your trawler over there?" he asked, squinting as his eyes ran over the boat's lines, seeming to measure it.

"So what is the home port?" Simon asked as he removed a tape measure from the tool box. He looked up at me. "I'll require the registration number then. Certificate decal?"

"Oh." I'd had all that stuff for Connecticut. I needed to go through the process again for Virginia. I didn't want anything about the boat to say "New England." I lifted my shoulders. "Not yet."

"Since you've got it up on the ways, I guess you can hold off on that. I can come back and put the registration numbers on later. Give me the number when you get it. So what's your home port?"

Not this place. I thought a moment, trying to think of a town that wouldn't lead to this marina. What was near enough to be acceptable but far enough away to be safe?"

"You could make it Richmond," Simon said as he measured the transom area. "A lot of people from Richmond have summer homes here."

"Okay. Make it Richmond." It was maybe a hundred miles away. Should be okay for now.

"All right. Now did you want the name to be plain? I could add a shadow effect. A picture or logo?" He pulled a book out of the tool box. "Look through here. See if something strikes your fancy."

I glanced through the book. Some of the designs and names were quite clever. The typefaces ranged from ornate to simple, but I didn't want clever or ornate or noticeable. I wanted plain, so it wouldn't attract attention.

I looked up to see Simon watching me. "You do good work," I said. "Some of these are really striking."

"I try to be creative, what?" he said, slipping the tape measure back in the tool box. "So what would you like, then?"

"I'd like plain lettering, nothing fancy."

"This style, then." Simon showed me the plainest entry in the book.

I nodded.

"All right. Let me get the details and a fifty percent deposit, and I'll push on."

I looked back at the car. "I don't see any paints. Aren't you going to do it now?"

"Would that I could, Miss. I go back to the shop and cut the names out of vinyl." Simon carried the tool box and clipboard back to the car.

"Vinyl?"

"Yes, Miss. Most signs are done that way now." He handed me a form. "Much simpler, last longer, better all around. If you would fill out the form and give me a check, we'll be done for today."

"When will you be back with the sign?"

"In a couple of days." He got back in the car. "It'll be perfect, luv. Don't you worry, but you might as well go ahead and get her registered. Then I can finish the job." He winked at me. "Keep me, the marine patrol, and the Coast Guard happy, don't you know?" He waved as he drove out.

Chapter 18

After lunch, I biked to Cal's shop. I'd bought saddlebags for grocery store trips, but this time they were loaded with cleaning supplies. Cal only had an ancient vacuum, and the shop showed the lack of attention. The restroom had been disgusting. He could lose customers if they saw that mess.

Cal looked up from the counter as I walked in.

"I came over to clean your shop," I said. "Gratis. As a thank you for your help."

"Thank goodness you're here," he said. "I guess you could tell I need your expertise."

"You need a lot of my expertise." I walked over to the counter. "And I want to ask you about boat registration." Better to ask Cal than my Dad, who'd probably sidestep my question with a lecture on how I should go back to my husband. "How do I do that?"

"I've got a boat, and it's registered. You got the title? ID? Insurance?"

"Sure."

"Go to the Motor Vehicles Administration. They can take care of it there."

"Even if my ID is out of state?"

"Maybe you want to get a Virginia driver's license, too. Might as well. Have to do it eventually. I think they give you ninety days to replace an out-of-state one."

"Thanks." I picked up the bathroom cleanser, a rag, and a trash bag. Holding my breath, I walked into the restroom.

As I worked, I thought about what I needed to do to change my residency to Virginia. Getting a new driver's license appealed to me. Another step farther from Hunter. Registering the boat and getting the numbers on it would keep it from attracting the wrong kind of interest by the marine patrol and anyone else. One day, I'd have to get a car again. When I lived in New York City before Hunter, a car was a nuisance and a needless expense. In New York, I didn't need a car, but I did need a boat to escape the crowds. When I bought it, I hadn't known it would also take me away from a brutal husband and save my life.

My mind wandered to Amos. Where did he go at night dressed up with shined shoes? A burglar wouldn't need to look good, but a girlfriend might want him to. I couldn't see my dad with a girlfriend.

Cleaning Cal's store took me two hours. When he walked into the bathroom and whistled, I felt good. That was one thing about cleaning houses. You didn't need anyone else's approval. You could look around and see you'd done good work.

I hummed to myself as I bicycled back to the marina and walked into Amos' store to chat with him and play with Peedee.

Amos looked up from behind the counter. "How are things going?"

"Fine." I reached down to pet Peedee. "You got him house-trained yet?"

Amos grunted. "Your job."

I grinned. "Don't have a house."

He laughed, and I laughed with him, feeling good about the

unfamiliar easy banter between us. Maybe our relationship was improving.

"By the way," he said, keeping his eyes on the papers he was fiddling with. "Hunter called last night."

I froze. My stomach flipped. My pulse pounded in my ears. I swallowed. "What did you say?"

"Glad to have a chance to talk with your husband. Seems like a good guy. Looking forward to meeting him."

I looked up. "You didn't tell him. . ."

Amos stared down at the papers on his desk. I felt my stomach curdle.

"Tell me you didn't let him know I was here." Please say no, I prayed, but I already knew the answer.

"I'm sorry," Amos said in a low voice. "He caught me by surprise. Anyway, you need to keep talking with him. It's the only way to iron out your problems. You've got to tell him what you want. Not fair to just keep him hanging."

"Oh no," I started shaking. "He'll kill me." I knew too much, and he had a big carrot, the life insurance policy. "I don't want to keep him hanging. I want him to go away. Forever."

Amos narrowed his eyes as he looked at me. "He misses you and wants you back."

Keeping the fear and anger out of my voice, I asked again. "You didn't give him your address, did you?"

Amos glanced at me. "There's no reason why you can't talk things out, is there?"

I closed my eyes and made fists of my hands. "Did you give him your address?"

Amos didn't look at me. "Would I do such a thing?"

He'd sidestepped the question. Amos told him where I was.

"So he called last night." I made some quick calculations. Hunter could get here by this evening or any time now. He could have left last night.

"But how did he know to call you?" I never told Hunter anything about Amos and my life growing up. Hunter thought I was an orphan, didn't he? Could Amos have called him?

Amos shrugged. "Why wouldn't he?"

Chapter 19

Somehow—probably from Amos himself—Hunter found out where my father lived and called him. Hunter knew more about me than I'd told him. Despite what Amos said, I also knew he'd told Hunter I was living at the marina. Amos was a misguided old fool and an ex-drunk with his own axe to grind. I felt shaken and scared. My hideaway had not been safe for long.

Now I worried if Amos had worked out some other plan with Hunter. They'd want me to stick around until Hunter could win me back as Amos would say—or as I would say, attack or kidnap me.

I pulled three spoons out of a drawer in the galley, tied them loosely together with string and attached them to the ladder. Their clanging should warn me if anyone stepped on the rungs. I picked up the hand-held air horn and placed it within easy reach. Weak defenses, but all I could arrange at the moment.

I needed more protection, but meanwhile, with those precautions in place, I sat in the cockpit and tried to anticipate what Hunter might do after he got to the marina. I didn't think he'd show up in a rage. He knew a multitude of tricks to ingratiate himself with Amos. He'd act hurt by my defection. He'd try to win over his father-in-law by appearing cool and reasonable, while hurt and puzzled about why I would leave him and, as he'd present it to Amos, his cushy set-up, big house and all. He'd already started his campaign with the phone call, and Amos bought into it. So would Stu, most likely. Then what?

Hunter would next try to belittle and undermine me, so I'd feel weak enough to go back to him. Or he'd look for the first opportunity to get me away from the marina and nab me. Once I was under his control, he could make up any story he wanted while he took care of me. . .one way or another. He'd want to punish me first for leaving him. I'd seen him operate and knew enough about him to realize how ruthless he could be. Most of all, he'd want the papers I'd taken.

How could I protect myself? I had to tell him he would get those papers only after we were divorced, all claims had been severed, and I felt safe enough to relinquish them. I didn't know how I'd determine my safety. Still, he wouldn't dare kill me as long as my letters were out there somewhere like land mines. The documents themselves were in the safety deposit box. He needed them. If he got me alone and away, he'd torture me until I agreed to go with him to the bank and withdraw them.

Because he couldn't stand feeling bested by a woman and since I knew too much and was covered by a hefty life insurance policy that named him as beneficiary, he would kill me. No doubt he'd planned to do me in from the time we met.

It meant I needed to be extremely careful. He was a charming man, a killer in camouflage. He would twist my words and actions into a bid for sympathy and support. I would be able to trust no one.

I glanced at my watch. Two p.m. The thought of buying a gun passed through my mind, but guns were no good for self-protection. Not really. If Hunter knew I had a gun, he'd get a bigger one and use it first. To him, I was only property that had done the unthinkable—rejected his ownership.

Even if Hunter didn't have a gun, and I drew mine, he'd attack me while I was still debating whether to actually use it. If I used it and killed Hunter, the police might not believe my story of self-defense. Even their fellow officers had trouble with that.

In short, guns only spelled trouble.

It was still mid-afternoon and would be light outside for a long while yet. Hunter could show up at the marina any time now, but he'd probably have to take care of things in New Jersey first. I'd better count on him showing up by tomorrow.

I bicycled into town to a strip shopping mall. I'd noticed the martial arts school before. Now I thought I could use it. I locked my bike outside the school and walked in. A bald older Asian man was leading five teenaged boys through exercises in the middle of the floor. A younger man sat at a glass counter with shelves underneath displaying belts and various kinds of martial arts clothing. A range of tall and short awards were arrayed on a wall shelf behind him. He looked up and nodded at me.

"Class not over yet," he said.

"I'm not interested in that class." I picked up a schedule of classes and glanced through it. "This is what I want," I said, pointing to a line saying "Self Defense for Women."

He looked at me and nodded. "Very good class. Yes. Many women like it." He laughed. "Make them powerful. . .like me." He flexed a muscle, grinning.

"Good. That's what I want. How much?" I asked.

"Monday nights, seven to eight p.m. Ten sessions. One hundred fifty dollars." He pulled out a form and turned it around for me to read.

Monday nights. I could manage the money and the time, since

the days were getting longer. I didn't want to bicycle in the dark. "When does the next session begin?" I asked.

"Monday night. Every Monday night. You come. You learn. You practice. Become strong." He waggled his hand. "You start this Monday. One hundred fifty dollars."

I pushed my lips in and out as I thought. A lot of money, but the lessons would be useful and might save my life. Hunter probably would have arrived by next Monday, but it was about time I learned to protect myself—especially with the kind of people I got involved with.

"Okay," I said and filled out the form.

"Good. You not make mistake."

"I'll bring the money in next Monday." A week from now was too late for my first self-defense lesson. I opened my purse and drew fifty dollars out of my wallet. "Could you give me a lesson today? I have fifty dollars here to pay for it."

The instructor glanced at the bills in my hands, pursed his lips and his eyes darted from the boys on the mats to the clock on the wall before he nodded. "Okay, Miss. Class be over in ten minutes. We teach you then. I have break until six. You wait here."

I waited, watching the kids practice, but I learned nothing from their exercises and was wondering if I'd made the right decision. The boys were dismissed, and the instructor beckoned me to the center of the room. We spent forty-five minutes in which I learned some strategic moves to break a nose or jab a sharp elbow in the stomach and otherwise free myself from an attacker. It was all good, I decided, and happily paid the fifty dollars. He returned thirty of it. "Fifty dollars too much, Miss," he said. Small town living had its benefits.

From there, I dropped by the grocery store, then walked down the road to a stand-alone tawdry gun shop where I bought a canister of pepper spray.

An hour later, I biked back to the marina. It was almost dusk on a lovely spring day. If only I could enjoy it, I thought. I rounded a curve and screeched to a stop. Ahead, stopped in the middle of the road, was a black van. It looked like Hunter's. It hadn't taken him long to get down here. Why had he parked there? The road was narrow. He meant to grab me as I bicycled by or open the door and knock me down.

My heart hammered. My palms felt sweaty as if they'd slip off the handlebars. I couldn't go forward past the vehicle. I looked behind me. Could I make it back to Cal's before it caught up with me? It would have to turn around or back up fast. I didn't think I could pedal fast enough to beat the van to Cal's, but what could I do? I'd even be grateful for Stu's rattletrap right now. I'd rather Stu run me over any day than have Hunter catch me.

I glanced at the woods on each side. Multiflora rose shrubs, impenetrable masses of thorns, grew alongside. If I could get through them, I could disappear into the woods and pick up my bike later. Was there any way through the thorns?

Someone in the van honked the horn. An arm extended out of the window on the driver's side and waved me forward. It could actually be a disabled van for some local business, waiting for a mechanic. It could be, but I wasn't going to risk it. I searched for an opening in the barbed thickets and found an almost invisible trail. A deer trail. Deer didn't like going through thorny bushes, either.

I took another look at the arm waving at me. I couldn't go forward, and I couldn't go back. Taking a deep breath, I pulled out the canister of pepper spray, laid the bike down beside the road, and sprang through the bushes, fighting off the thorns and branches. A minute later, I raced through the woods on the faint deer trail to the shoreline. When I reached it, I paused to listen. No one was crashing through the woods after me. I walked along the river's edge to the marina, ready to shoot the pepper spray if needed.

I hoisted myself up on the seawall and spied Amos sitting on a bench under the oak tree at the side of the office. He held a Coke in one hand, while he played with the puppy. I passed him without a word to go to the gate and close it, snapping the padlock into place.

"Hey! What's the idea?" yelled Amos. "We got a business to run here."

Barely controlling my rage, I walked to him and said through gritted teeth, "Did you tell Hunter where you live?"

Amos watched me from the corner of his eye as he took another sip of Coke. "Yes, I did," he said.

I froze at the words. "You lied to me."

"It's for your own good." Amos bent to pet the dog. "Anyway, he found out where I live on his own. I didn't tell him."

"What did you tell him?" Amos was so cantankerous, he probably told him everything.

Amos glanced up at me. "What'd you want me to tell him?"

"Nothing. That's what I wanted you to tell him." I spat out the words. "Nothing."

Amos was quiet a few moments. "You know what I think?" he asked. "You're a married woman. What makes you think you can just desert a man like he was nothing, like he was dirt under your feet? You two need to talk your problems out, like me and your ma should have done."

"Seems to me you did all the talking. And the drinking." I remembered the fights they'd had. I was only a young child, closing my ears with my hands under the pillow. I'd heard Amos hit my mom. I'd heard her sobbing in the night. I hated those memories and put all my hatred into the glare I threw at Amos. "You were brutal to her."

"We could have made things better if she'd stuck around."

"For what? More beatings? More tongue-lashings? What kind of life did she have?"

"I'm not saying I was perfect," said Amos, staring at his feet.

"You certainly weren't then, and you aren't now. So you think I should have stuck it out with Hunter, a criminal who beat me. You think that's all right?" I seethed, wanting to throttle him. I leaned over Amos, still sitting on the bench, staring up at me. My hands knotted into fists. I pulled myself back. I was not going to behave like my dad. . . or Hunter.

"You're not putting him up, are you?" I asked through gritted teeth.

Amos shook his head. "There's a motel down the road. Can't crowd you that way."

"Did he say when he was coming in?" Was it really his van out on the road? I didn't see the driver.

"In a couple of days. He said he had to finish up some business first." Amos picked up the Coke and twisted the cap off.

How long would it take for Hunter to get here? "When did you last talk to him? Did he call again today? Is he here?"

"I told you. Talked to him last night. We had a good conversation. He seemed okay to me, like he wanted to do whatever you wanted him to if you'd go back to him. I think you're wrong about him, Mellie. Maybe he was tired. Maybe his job is full of stress. You can be hard to deal with sometimes."

"Sure. All my fault." That probably was Hunter on the road.

Amos frowned at me. "Now I didn't say it was your fault. I'm sure there was enough blame to go around."

I stared at the ground and pressed my fingertips against my temples. Amos was a stubborn old fool. I silently counted to ten before I spoke. "I am going to need protection," I said. "You or Stu need to be here when he's around. Don't give him a key to the gate." I saw Amos' expression. He still thought he knew best. He thought it was a lover's quarrel, and all we needed to do was sit down and talk out our problems. Patch things up. I couldn't trust him. Or Stu.

"I need you to promise not to give Hunter a key to the gate. I need to be able to trust that when the gate is locked, he can't get in."

I saw Amos studying me, ready to dismiss my fears, ready to help out "his side."

"I'm serious."

"All right. He doesn't get a key, even though I'll be here to protect you."

"No key. Tell Stu, too."

"All right." Amos took a swig of the Coke. "Anybody with a boat can get in, though, around by the dock."

"Rats." I hadn't thought about the river access. Hunter hadn't been around boats, though. Maybe not on his radar. I thought about my trawler. I might have to get out of here fast. "I'll paint the bottom tomorrow morning, so you can put the boat in the water when it dries. Simon can stick the name on there."

Amos scratched his head. "I don't know. . ."

"What?" I put my hands on my hips.

"If you're so serious about not wanting to talk to your husband," he said, "then seems to me you're making it easier for him if your boat is in the water."

"How do you mean?"

"If he got a boat, he could bring it in right next to you. Easy to board you then."

I stared at him, lips pressed together. Amos saw my expression. He shrugged. "I think you should talk it out on equal ground, that's all. Not equal if he can board your boat anytime."

Amos being fair? Trying to give me a break? Hard to believe, but he was right. Better to stay away from easy access by water. Up here, I was closer to Amos, if I could count on him to hear my cries for help. He'd respond, wouldn't he? He wouldn't let Hunter hit me in the marina, would he? Hunter would have to climb the ladder. I'd booby-trapped it, and Peedee would be onboard. He'd better earn his keep. I also carried pepper spray, and I'd love to break Hunter's nose with my self-defense skills.

"I need you to be here at night," I said. "You're out almost every night until after ten."

Amos frowned at me, pushing his lips in and out.

"Where do you go anyway? You're not out robbing houses, are you?"

"I go. . .dancing," he said.

"Dancing?" I stared at him. "Dancing?" I couldn't help giggling. Not burgling houses. Not seeing some girlfriend. Dancing.

"I don't see no reason to laugh," said Amos. "I like to dance."

I stopped giggling at the seriousness of his tone. My dad had changed. Not drinking. Dancing. Wonderful. At that moment, he seemed almost human. Despite my worries about Hunter, my heart felt lighter. Even so, I left a parting shot. "Go pick up my bike and my groceries. It's your fault I left them on the side of the road when I saw Hunter's van."

I walked back to the boat. Peedee followed me as he looked reproachfully back at Amos. Peedee was a good little guy.

Chapter 20

It was late afternoon, and the sun still shone high in the sky. I puttered around my boat, but I felt restless and too hungry to open a can. Afraid to ride my bike, I borrowed Amos' pickup to drive to the Coffee 'N' Cook Café for dinner. A good meal, for a change, rather than the canned soups I poured into a bowl and microwaved. A good iced tea, too. I felt I could splurge with the extra money I'd earned cleaning. I didn't mind eating alone, either. I kept an eye out for Hunter, but there was a restaurant and bar on the other side of his motel where he'd probably go. It was too early for him to eat dinner, anyway, as I well knew.

Since I had no one to talk with, I listened to the conversations around me. At the next table, three middle-aged guys sat with Officer Henschel. I kept my eyes down and face blank. I didn't want to be noticed or recognized. Other than the officer, I hadn't seen any of them before, which wasn't surprising, since I was new in town.

"Yep. Two more last night," said Henschel. "The big homes on the water in that development. Security patrol and everything."

"You don't say," said old freckle face.

"What'd they take?" asked the guy wearing a red ball cap.

"The same kind of stuff they always take. Electronics. TV, radios, cell phones, computers. Anything they can sell fast."

"How do you figure they get in?" asked the third, a hatless

white-haired man, deeply tanned with blue eyes. "They've got a
security patrol. Don't they put alarm systems in their houses?"

"Sure they do. Most of them—if they remember to turn them
on." The officer stared into his coffee cup. "We never see the
culprits, but we don't see much of the security patrol, either." The
other men snickered.

Out of the corner of my eye, I saw him lean forward and
glance around the room, quickly assessing and dismissing me. I
appeared absorbed in the menu.

Red ball cap picked up his coffee cup. "What? They break in
and steal before the security detail can get to them?"

Henschel nodded. "Yep. You know what I think?" He rapped
on the tabletop. "They've got a boat. We've got to get the marine
patrol on this."

"A boat, you think?" said ball cap.

The officer leaned back. "Security uses cars, and so do we.
Those crooks hold the boat to the dock in the rear of the house,
then two or three guys run up to the house, break in, take whatever they can get, run it to the boat, and disappear."

"I can see it," said freckle face. "So many coves and inlets
and boat ramps on the river."

"Boat sheds," added ball cap.

I thought about the houseboat I'd seen plying the river back
and forth. A lot of room in it, but it wasn't fast. It could go right
up to a bank, though, hide under trees and brush, maybe by a road
or a boat ramp, so it could be unloaded easily. I looked up as the
waitress hovered. I glanced at the menu and gave my order. I
could feel Henschel's eyes on me as I spoke. He'd probably
recognized me by now.

I pulled a book out of my backpack and pretended to read.

The four men paid their bill and headed out. The officer stopped by my table before following the others.

"Any more trouble out at the marina?"

I acted surprised as I looked up at him, "Why, Officer, uh, Henschel, isn't it? How are you?" I was all sweetness and charm.

"Just fine, ma'am." He tipped his hat. "Any more trouble?" he repeated.

"Not at all," I said.

He tipped his hat again as he left. I should have told him about the houseboat. Why didn't I? As he said, he patrolled by car. He'd miss the ordinary boating on the river. What about the marine patrol? Who were they? Would they notice the houseboat, or did they just keep their eyes on registration numbers and count the life preservers onboard?

I enjoyed the café-cooked hamburger and cole slaw and drove home before it became dark, keeping an eye out for Hunter's van. The gate was open, so I drove through. As I stepped down from the truck, Amos walked out of the office.

"The pup okay?" I asked

"Sure," said Amos. Peedee pushed open the office door and ran out yapping joyously around me.

"Good."

Amos handed me a letter. "For you," he said. "One of your admirers?"

"Don't have any," I said. The letter was addressed in printed letters as if to disguise them. It looked like a movie ransom note.

I opened the envelope with a quiver in my stomach and read the message, also printed in crude capital letters. "GET OUT OF TOWN NOW AFORE SOMETHING HAPPENS TO YOU, YOUR BOAT, OR YOUR DOG."

I showed it to Amos. "Who sent this?" I looked at the envelope. Local postmark. Someone in town sent me hate mail. Who? Why? Could Hunter have written this?

"Let me take that." Amos grabbed the letter and envelope. "I'm calling the police."

We waited in the marina store for the officer who showed up forty-five minutes later. "Sorry for the delay," he said. "Another one of them burglaries."

Amos showed him the letter. "My daughter got this, and it was mailed here. Has anyone else got this kind of thing?"

Henschel perused it, scratching his head with one hand. "Ugly. Real ugly." He shook his head. "Nobody's reported any such a thing before. Must be kids." He pulled a plastic bag out of his pocket and put the letter and envelope into it. "I'll take it as evidence. Check it for fingerprints. Can't do much with just this one letter, but if others start turning up, maybe we'll see a pattern."

Amos and I walked out with the police officer and followed him to the gate as he drove away. Amos locked the gate after him. The sun had almost set. I ran around the yard with the dog before feeding him. As I took him up into the boat, I reflected on the odd incidents that seemed to be directed at me. The prowler. The sawed buttress. Now the threatening letter. Only the letter could possibly be traced to Hunter, so who? And why?

I'm a newcomer. Is this what locals do to new people in town? What'll happen when I've been around longer and get to know more people?"

Chapter 21

I felt rattled as I sat in the cockpit. The sun was close to setting, but it would be light awhile yet. The frogs and cicadas were racheting up. This was usually a comfortable time of day for me. I needed that comfort. I heard Stu open the gate and drive his rattletrap through it and stop. His shoes crunched on the gravel as he got out of the car, shut the gate, and locked it.

Amos was probably working on his receipts in the office, still having only the barest notion of what danger he'd put me in. No one else was around. I idly listened to the chug of a boat plying its way up the river. It was the houseboat again on its usual rounds. I trained the binoculars on the deck and windows and tried to discern how many people were onboard. I counted three. Where did it go for the night? Some houseboats didn't need deep water. Hadn't I seen years ago a photo of one pulled up on the beach? They could nose into the shore and tie up alongside the bank and hide under the trees.

I checked my watch. Still early. I stepped down the ladder and walked briskly to the office. Poking my head in, I called to my dad. "Mind if I take your runabout out for a short while?"

Amos looked up from the pile of papers on his desk. "Guess it's okay. It's still light out there, but use your running lights. There's extra fuel onboard, and it's ready to go. Come back before it gets real dark."

"Okay." I ran down to the dock, untied the runabout, lowered the motor into the water, and pulled the start rope. For once, the motor sprang into life at the first pull of the rope. Not a given, I can tell you. I steered the runabout to the opposite shore under the overhanging trees, so it was practically invisible and headed upriver. I did not turn on the running lights.

Part of the houseboat was still visible as it rounded a bend. I followed, but my little craft couldn't go very fast, and I fell farther and farther behind. I rounded another bend in the river, and the behemoth had disappeared. At first I thought it outdistanced me, but the way ahead was a fairly straight course of the river. The houseboat was nowhere to be seen.

I studied the boat sheds I could see along the shore—only two, but they didn't look big enough to hide the houseboat, and the river side was open, so I could see they were empty. Then I searched the shore. Heavy branches hung out over the water with reeds and grasses growing on the banks. Birds had stopped singing, and it was eerily quiet. Chills ran down my spine as I felt I was being watched. I imagined a gun trained on my back.

As casually as I could while I controlled my panic, I slowly spun the boat around as if I had simply changed my mind and headed home.

Once I tied up the runabout at my dad's dock, climbed up into my own boat, and hugged Peedee, I felt better and laughed off as imagination and nerves the creepy sensation I'd felt on the river .

Where had the houseboat gone? Who owned it? What was it doing going up the river in the early evening? It seemed more like business than fun.

I microwaved a cup of milk to help me sleep, and my cell

rang. Simon.

Yes, I told him, he could come by around ten the next morning to put the name on my boat. His call reminded me I still had to paint the bottom and get the trawler registered. Tomorrow, I sighed.

***

Simon showed up at ten as he'd said, wearing the same paint-stained overalls over a T-shirt, but he'd exchanged the train engineer's cap for a floppy old fishing hat. His bushy white hair haloed underneath. He opened the hatch of the Subaru Forester and pulled out two vinyl strips. He spent half an hour lining up, measuring, and sticking the two strips of vinyl one above the other. "Little Peedee" and then underneath, "Richmond, VA."

He stood back with me to admire his work. I approved of it. The letters were plain, not at all remarkable. The name wasn't remarkable either. Nothing really clever about it. "All right then, luv?" Simon asked, squinting at his work.

"Just fine," I replied, holding Peedee's leash. He had his nose to the ground investigating a crawling insect.

Simon packed up his materials and took them back to the Forester. I followed him.

As he closed the back, he glanced at me. "Call me when you've got the registration numbers," he said.

I nodded. Next thing on my list for that morning. I waved goodbye and returned to the yard, taking another look at the name with satisfaction before climbing into the boat to pick up my laptop.

In Amos' office, I used the Wi-Fi to access the Internet and fill out the forms, paying for the registration online. I once again congratulated myself on the careful planning I'd put into this escape. Even though I had been in love with Hunter and planned a life with him, part of me didn't believe in the fairy tale. Before I married him, I bought a box at a private mail service and had my credit card bills and other mail sent there. During my lunch hour, I'd pick up my letters and pay bills. Nothing I received went home with me.

While I was in the marina office connected to the Internet, I changed my forwarding address with the postal service and requested all mail be sent to Amos' address.

As I closed the laptop, Amos walked in and nodded at me.

"Do you know anything about the houseboat that passes by every now and then?" I asked.

"Lot of boats come up the river," Amos said. "Especially now the weather is getting warmer."

"Sure. But I've been seeing this houseboat most evenings. Last night I followed it when I took the runabout out, and it seemed to disappear. It was in front of me, and then it wasn't."

Amos shrugged. "Any number of little inlets it could have gone up." He strode by me to his desk, not interested.

"Have you heard any more from Hunter?" I asked, dreading the response. I was pretty sure the black van blocking the road belonged to him.

"Nope. Got the feeling he'd be showing up any time, though." Amos raised an eyebrow at me as if daring me to object.

Amos would not protect me from Hunter. I could feel a panic attack coming on. I stumbled out of the office, closed my eyes, and leaned against the side of the building. The bleakness I'd felt as a child, alone and unprotected as the two adults I needed to lean on hurled fists and abuse at each other, weighed heavily on my spirit. There was no one I could call on for help then and no one now. For a moment, an overwhelming hatred blinded me. I felt such rage that it scared me. I took deep breaths and forced myself to calm down, get a grip.

As my vision returned, I saw Amos. He followed me out and stood staring at me in disbelief and maybe concern. No, it couldn't be concern. "Don't be silly," he said, his hands on his hips. "You're being overdramatic."

"No," I spat out. "I'm not. I'm serious." I banged my fist on the side of the building. "And I'm furious that you still think we're playing some kind of newlywed game."

"You two need to talk out your differences," he said as if to defend himself. "You can't discuss anything if you're separated."

I felt the urge to scream at him, but I couldn't trust myself to speak. I was still trying to steady my breathing.

I felt Amos watching me. His expression and his voice softened. "Here, you need to sit down," he said. He actually sounded concerned. "I know it's bad, but it can't be as bad as you're acting. He seems like a reasonable man to me." Amos helped me to the bench outside the store as I glared at him.

"You need to talk to him," Amos repeated, hardness returning to his words.

"Don't you understand?" I gasped "He will kill me. Didn't you hear anything I've been telling you about him?"

"Just a minute." Amos went into the office and returned with a bottle of water. "Are you crazy? I never heard of such a thing." He gave me the cold drink. "This'll cool you off."

"I told you he was a criminal with ties to the Mafia. Didn't you hear that at all?" I looked up at him with such hatred blazing in my eyes that Amos flinched.

"Why would you marry a criminal? Can't believe you would,

no sir," Amos said.

"Like you never beat Mom?" I retorted through clenched teeth. "Like you never hit me?" I took a deep breath. "You taught me what to expect, Amos, and I married someone even worse than you. You set me up. I tell you he will kill me."

Amos stared at the floor.

I got up. "I've got to get out of here fast."

"Wait a minute," said Amos. "Where are you going?"

"I don't know, but I can't stay here." I paced back and forth. "And I sure can't tell you."

"You can't go any place where he won't find you sometime." Amos blocked my way. "I'm not saying it's like you think, but I didn't raise no quitter. Anyways, you've got me and Stu here to protect you."

"I'll be afraid to go anywhere by myself." I felt perilously close to crying. I refused to let him see me cry. "Because of your pig head."

"Come on now, Mellie." He took my arm. I shook it off. "He can't stay around too long anyway. He has to work, doesn't he? Maybe you'll be able to talk out your problems while he's here."

I spoke through my teeth. "He is a criminal, Amos. He doesn't have to show up for work in an office. He works out of his home on his laptop. He can carry it anywhere and stay anywhere as long as he needs to."

Amos stared at me, pursing his lips. "You've got those papers you took safe, you said?"

"Yes."

"So he won't do anything to you until he gets those back."

"That is my hope, yes."

"So you fight him."

"Oh, sure," I said.

"If you don't, you'll be running all your life."

I didn't respond. I was pondering what Amos said. He was right. I'd be running all my life unless I did something about Hunter now. Could I depend on Amos or Stu to protect me? I didn't think so.

I had a few things to do. The shock dispelled somewhat, but I still fumed. I climbed into the boat, spent a moment cuddling the dog and wishing he were a pit bull. I found a large beach towel and draped it over the transom to cover the new name, securing the makeshift cover in place with duct tape, so it couldn't be lifted with a casual hand.

I was glad I'd signed up for the martial arts classes. I was relieved I'd paid extra for the special lesson. I carried the pepper spray everywhere. And I had the dog.

Chapter 22

The next morning, Peedee and I were playing on the dock when I heard the hated clattering noise of the loose chrome strip on Hunter's van. Its tires grated into the gravel as Hunter drove through the gate and stopped. I ran into the office and listened to the footsteps crunch, crunch, crunch as they approached the office and paused.

Amos didn't look up from writing in the ledger. I sank into a wooden chair against the side wall, panting with closed eyes, trying to gain control. I didn't want Hunter to see my fear . Amos glanced at me and then the door. "What's going on?"

I steadied myself with a deep breath. "Your guest has arrived."

"My guest?" Amos scratched his head, nodding as he understood. "I see. Well, aren't we ready for him? Let's get him in here and take a look at him." He walked to the door and opened it. I closed my eyes briefly. I'd only needed one quick peek to know I was right.

"Come on in," Amos was saying. "What can I do you for?"

Hunter dipped his head as he stepped through the door. He removed the baseball cap and grinned at Amos. "Hear my sweetheart is staying with you for awhile," he said, smiling as always. He shuffled his cap from hand to hand as if nervous. The jeans and flannel shirt almost matched the ones Amos was wearing.

Nice touch, Hunter.

"Sure do miss her." His voice had once seemed so charming, but now I could only think it smarmy. Oily, even, like the slick on water, but calculated to disarm.

Once again, Hunter amazed me with his shrewd manipulation. Matching the clothes Amos wore—how did he learn that? Next, he'd be mimicking Amos' movements and speech for added rapport.

I shrank in my chair as if I wanted to be invisible. Which I did. Where did he get those jeans and shirt? Quite a stretch from his usual conservative gray suit and tie. In fact, the ensemble was what had initially attracted me. He seemed so sophisticated, urbane, and cosmopolitan to me back then. He said he was a lawyer. My friends were impressed. Now he was dressed like a country bumpkin. Another good ol' boy. *What a phony*.

"How about it, sweetie?" Hunter asked, his words dripping with honey. "Ready to come back home now?"

I didn't reply as I sought a response that couldn't be twisted.

"Come on, sweetheart," Hunter said, shrugging at Amos as if to say, "You know how women are."

I took another deep breath to make sure my voice was steady and strong. "You need to go back home. I will be starting divorce proceedings."

Amos went toward the door. "I'll leave you two to sort this out."

"No!" I sprang from the chair and ran to him. "I'm staying with you. Do not leave me alone with him."

Amos hesitated.

Hunter smiled at his father-in-law, man to man. "Now, now, honey," he said. "You don't need to be afraid to be alone with me. We're married. I've never felt closer to anyone than you."

I gripped Amos' arm and looked at Hunter. "There is nothing to say, nothing to talk over, nothing to discuss. I want nothing to do with you. Leave. Now."

Hunter shrugged. "Women. You know how they are," he said to Amos. "You can't live with them and can't live without them."

I felt like sneering at the cliché.

He turned and walked back toward the door. "I think I'll go look around town. I'm staying at the motel down the road, so you know where to find me. It must have been a shock having me turn up. We can talk about this later, when you've had a chance to relax and be reasonable." He walked past Amos as I shrank against the back wall. He paused at the door.

"Amos, you know how lovers' spats are. Talk to her, will you? I love her so much." He shuffled his cap. "I'm willing to do anything to. . .to get her back."

I watched him leave in disbelief. What an act. Did he really make his voice crack at the end of his little speech?

Amos returned to his desk and gestured at the chair in front of it. I took it.

"He's right, you know—" Amos held up his hand as I started to interrupt. "You two need to talk things out, find your way through this. He looks like a good man, and he really loves you, Mellie. He's probably a better man than you deserve, being a lawyer and educated, not like me. I'd hate to see you make a big mistake." He steepled his hands and looked at me over them.

Still fuming at the outright brazenness of Hunter's charade, yet feeling inadequate to defend myself against Amos' prejudice, I remained silent. I remembered how his tantrums had terrified me when I was young. The fear of causing another one kept me silent. I still felt powerless and a long way from acquiring the strength to triumph against the angry abuse I'd suffered as a child or the physical abuse I'd endured as an adult. I still needed to fight the little girl regression I fell into when up against men like Amos and Hunter.

What would Hunter pull out of his bag of tricks next?

Chapter 23

As Amos and I stared at each other in impasse, Stu shambled into the office, shuffling his hat from hand to hand. "Boss," he began tentatively. "I got to go down to Richmond."

Amos tore his eyes away from me and grimaced at Stu. "Your mom again?"

"Yep." Stu glanced at me. "She's kind of frail and doesn't get around too good. She needs some help around the house, so she called me." He edged toward the door. "I'll only be a day or two."

Amos waved him away. Stu turned around to leave, a smile creeping across his face making me wonder what he was really up to. He closed the door gently behind him as if the charged atmosphere in the office might explode at a loud noise.

I followed him out in time to see Hunter's van disappear around a bend. He should have been long gone by now. Had Stu interrupted Hunter listening at the door? I debated whether to leave the safety of the marina office. "Can I borrow the pickup again?" I asked.

Amos handed me the keys. "Don't stay away long. I've got errands to run."

I drove the half-mile to the bike shop. I needed to talk to someone sane. Maybe Cal could help.

I parked the pickup behind Cal's store to hide it from Hunter and waved at Greg, who was testing a bike outside the shop as I walked in. Cal sat at the card table staring at the computer monitor and drumming his fingers on the table. He looked up as I closed the door behind me.

"What a relief," he said. "I couldn't figure out what to write next." He saw my face. "What's wrong?"

I shook my head and sat in the other chair. "Got a Coke somewhere?"

Cal leaned back to open the refrigerator behind him and took out two soft drinks. He twisted each of them open and handed one to me. "Want something stronger?" he asked. "Looks like you need it."

I shook my head. "Not going that route. I'll leave it for people like Amos," I wrinkled my nose in distaste. "You're one of the few people I know in this town, and you've helped me a lot." I took a long sip. "The bike is perfect, and you've even offered me a job."

Cal held up a hand. "Hey, it's what I do, finding people the right bike."

I nodded as I straightened a pile of papers on the table in front of me. "You offer a good service for this town. I'd like to take you up on that job offer, but first I've got to get rid of a nuisance."

"Two-legged?" Cal leaned back in his chair, watching me as he drank the Coke.

"My so-called husband. He's here." I tossed my head toward the back of the store. "That's why I'm driving the pickup. No matter what I say, Amos thinks this is some ordinary newlywed spat. It isn't."

"Okay," Cal drawled. "What is it?"

"He is a crook and an abuser, and if he can get me away from people I know, he will kill me." I saw the disbelief in Cal's face. "I am not making this up. He will try to kidnap me and take me away. I have papers that implicate him in criminal activities, and he wants them—and me—back. Those papers are the only bargaining chip I have, and they're in a safe place."

I saw Cal flick his eyes to the top drawer of his desk and answered the unspoken question. "Yes, a statement about what I'm telling you is in the envelope in your drawer."

Cal tipped his chair back, sipped his soft drink, and quietly looked at me. I couldn't tell what he was thinking. It was a bizarre story. He probably didn't believe me, thought I was crazy. I couldn't blame him, but I didn't trust Amos or Stu, so I hoped I could count on Cal for help.

"I am serious," I added. "I know we've only just met, and you don't really know me, but I need your help. I am not making this up. I am terrified. I thought I'd be safe here. I told him I was an orphan, and he knew I hated my father. This town would be the last place I would imagine he'd come to. I swear he didn't even know where Amos lived. I banked on that, and I was wrong."

Cal brought his chair down and sat up. "Do you want to hide out here?" he asked. "I have an apartment upstairs. Not much. Pretty rough, in fact, but he probably wouldn't think to look here, and I'd be around."

I thought a moment. The idea was tempting, but I'd have to leave Peedee behind. Anyway, I liked living alone on my boat. I liked being by the river and not having to answer to anyone. And I didn't want to enrage Hunter further, which would happen if he thought I was living with Cal, no matter how platonic the arrangement might be. I'd rather rely on the locked gate and Amos' protection, such as it was, and I had the pepper spray. Next

Monday, I started the self-defense course—if I lived that long. I looked at Cal.

"Thank you," I said. "I may take you up on it." I wouldn't though. I didn't want to endanger Cal. "Right now I'll go on as I've been doing and see what happens. Maybe Hunter will go away when he sees I'm not budging. All he has to do is give me a divorce, and he gets those papers back."

"Can't imagine why he'd want to stay married," said Cal. "To someone who didn't want him, I mean."

"Yeah." I nodded. "That's the way you'd feel if you were sane. Or kind. Or stable. Or honest. Hunter is none of those." I stared down at the drink in my hands. "Please don't tell anyone else about this."

Cal reached across and took one of my hands. "I won't. Let me know what you need, and I'll get it for you. You got my cell phone number?"

I shook my head and pulled out my phone.

Cal recited the numbers. "You stay put on your boat. Let me get any groceries or other stuff you need. Make sure someone else is around all the time, in case Hunter shows up and wants to try anything rough. If you feel threatened, call me."

"Thank you," I said, not quite willing to give up the distrust I'd lived with most of my life. "It's good to know you're here. Now I'd better get back to the marina in case Hunter is still roaming around."

"I'll see if the coast is clear first," said Cal, walking to the front display windows. "Uh oh," he said. "Does he drive a black van with tinted windows? New Jersey plates?"

I found myself short of breath. My heart pounded, and my ears buzzed. "He's out there?"

"Sure looks like it." Cal locked the door, walked back, and put his arm around me. "You still can stay here," he said.

"Oh, God." I willed myself to breathe. "He knows I'm here." I felt sick and leaned on the table, catching my breath. I paced the floor and wrung my hands. "You won't be safe either."

"I think he's only waiting. No one followed you here, did they?" He can't know you're here." Cal looked back at the door. "Let him try something. . ."

"I'm sorry I got you involved. I thought he'd gone back to his motel room." I chewed my fingernail. "How can I get back to the marina now?" I glanced at Cal. "Is there another way out? A back road to the marina?"

"Amos' truck is behind the store?" he asked.

"Yes."

"Good." He walked down a short hall to the back door, gesturing to me to follow. "You can sneak into my van, and I'll drive you back. He won't see you from where he's parked. Keep your head down until we're away from him."

A wave of relief flowed over me. "Oh, thank you, thank you. That's perfect."

I waited inside the door while Cal started the van, then I ran to it and crouched down in the seat as Cal drove us onto the road and headed toward the marina.

"Uh oh," he said. "He's following us."

"He can't know I'm in the van," I cried.

"Right. Maybe he's looking for possibilities." Cal smiled at me. "Is he the jealous type?"

I shuddered, remembering the fights we'd had when we were first married, and the slaps and punches I'd endured because of his jealousy. I soon learned not to look at or talk to any other man anywhere. At first I tried to think it meant Hunter loved me, but even as used to abuse as I was, I couldn't keep up the lie for long. I'd even looked up the topic online, and everything Hunter did was textbook behaviors. The abuser first separates the victim from family and friends. Check. He'd moved me away from New York to New Jersey and harassed me at work. Check. He'd hit me again and again. Check. Why wasn't that enough to make me run? Why did I stick around? What was I thinking?

"I get it," said Cal after a moment when I didn't reply. "You don't have to answer. He saw me somewhere and made a guess. Is he still behind us?"

"Yes," I said. "It doesn't matter. Just get me back to the marina. I'll stay in the office with Amos until he leaves."

We rounded a curve and moved over as a white panel truck sped past going the other way. "That looked like Stu driving," I said. "I thought he was going to Richmond."

"He probably had some errand to run first."

Cal dropped me off at the gate, and I ran into the office. Amos was sitting at his desk and glanced at me. "What's up?"

"Hunter's right behind me," I said, breathing hard, refusing to say again I was afraid of him.

"So who brought you home, then?" Amos asked.

"Cal." Thank goodness he was there.

"You mean you took a ride with Cal instead of with your own husband?" Amos sounded angry. "Hunter is your husband. Don't forget it. He had every right to. . ."

"To what? Hit me? Kill me?" Amos' words enraged me. "He has no right to anything from me. He lost that right three days after we married." I heard Hunter's footsteps on the gravel. He was coming in here.

"You're exactly like your mother. Overdramatizing every-thing." Amos frowned at me. I recognized contempt in his voice.

"Yeah," I said, matching the contempt I heard. "We're just supposed to take whatever you dish out. Is that it?" I hurled the words like poisoned darts. "My mother was right to walk out and leave you. Neither of us could live with it, but I was forced to." I bit my tongue to hold the tears back. I'd be damned if I'd let Amos see them.

Hunter walked in, and Amos stood as he picked up some pa-pers. "You two need to talk things out. I'm going into my apart-ment." He strode out of the office and disappeared into the back rooms.

"We have nothing to talk out," I said in a tight voice.

Hunter stepped forward, raising his hand as if to hit me.

I stepped back. "Don't you dare." I shifted my body slightly into position for self-defense, but not noticeably. Hunter would like a battle. He'd like the challenge of fighting me—and win-ning, bringing me to my knees. Yeah. He'd like it.

Hunter laughed. "Who was the man you were with?"

"None of your business." I watched his face turn ugly.

"You are my wife. It is my business. You are not going to run around town like a whore. What else has he been giving you?" he sneered. "You little tramp." He lifted his fist but glanced around and dropped it.

Because Amos would hear it and come back.

But if Amos weren't around, as he hadn't been around at the house in New Jersey, Hunter would not have dropped his fist.

I held my ground. As long as he stayed where he was, I could deal with him. "I want you to leave. Now. We have nothing to say to each other. Not any more."

He glared at me. "I want the papers you stole."

"You can have them as soon as we're divorced. And," I paused to glare back at him, "if something happens to me, they will go to the FBI and the IRS. They are in a safe place, ready to be mailed if something happens to me." I watched to see how he took that information.

Hunter's eyes narrowed, and his mouth tightened. He stared at me. Finally he said, "Don't be ridiculous. There's nothing in those papers to interest anybody but my clients, certainly not the government."

"Then you have nothing to worry about," I said. "Get out of here."

Hunter pushed his lips in and out. His smile a creepy vestige of the one I had once loved. I waited for his next move.

"You're nothing but a hick from a hick town," he muttered. "You don't understand business, and how it works."

I didn't respond. That was the best he could do?

Hunter turned to leave. "You haven't heard the last of this," he said. "You're not going to get away with it." He walked to Amos' apartment door and knocked. "You can come out now," he said.

Amos tentatively opened the door. "You two got things settled?"

I folded my arms and stared at Hunter. "He knows what he has to do."

Hunter looked at Amos and smiled. One man to another. "She always been this stubborn?"

Amos shrugged. "Like her mother."

"Sure do miss her at home. Wish she'd come back."

I stared at Hunter in disbelief as he assumed a sad, hangdog face. He'd even affected a southern accent. Just another good ol' boy, exactly like Amos, he seemed to be saying. The man was a chameleon.

"Hard when your woman leaves you." Amos glanced at me as he spoke.

I heard the subtext. Hard for him when my mother left, but I didn't blame her for that. She hadn't received any support from Amos either. He was an abuser, too. I did blame her for not taking me along. She'd left me to suffer Amos' abuse, learn how to live with it, and how to marry into it. A set-up. That's what it was. I was waiting for Amos to show his true colors. I didn't believe he'd changed.

"You can leave now," I said, pointing to the door.

"I guess I'll simply have to be persistent," said Hunter, on the way out. "I know I can get Mellie back." He sent a meaningful look to me. "I know it."

Amos didn't hear the threat in those words, but I did. As Hunter walked out the door, I shuddered. My cards were on the table. He knew what I wanted, and what he needed to do if he wanted those papers back.

"Could you hear what he said?" I asked. "In your room, I mean."

"Nope. Wasn't listening. Between husband and wife, I'd say." Amos walked to his desk and sat down, leaning back in the chair and looking up at me. "He seems like a good man to me. A good provider, being a lawyer and all."

"Then you should marry him. Anyway, I don't believe he's a lawyer."

"Did you ask him about the criminal business?" Amos asked. "Did you wait to hear his explanation? Did you even try to understand his side?"

I gritted my teeth in disbelief. Amos didn't have a clue. He understood nothing. Still seething, I asked in a dangerously quiet voice, "So you think I should ask a man who beats me if he has a legitimate reason for having a sheet of Social Security blanks and a stack of credit cards and passports with different names and a website selling ID cards with a link to a notorious drug-smuggling gang. . .you think I should ask him if he's a criminal?"

"You didn't tell me any of those things," Amos sputtered, raising his hands in front of his chest as if to buffer my words.

"You should have trusted me!" I yelled. "You should have believed me! I'm your daughter. What in hell is wrong with you? You persist in thinking I should go back to this man? He beat me! The beating alone should have been enough for you to want to protect me from him."

"Okay, but sometimes a woman doesn't know what's good for her," stammered Amos.

"Look at me. I am an adult. I work as an accountant. I make my own money and my own decisions. Why in hell would you think I or any woman for that matter wouldn't know what's good for herself? Especially if what you mean is I need to get a beating once in awhile to keep me in line." I threw up my hands. "You're hopeless. No wonder Mom left you. She should have taken me with her. You are a miserable excuse for a human being."

I heard Peedee barking, then a loud crash. Hunter's footsteps crunched on the gravel to his van, and the van door opened. I heard the familiar clattering of the loose chrome strip as Hunter backed his vehicle out of the gravel yard and turned onto the asphalt road. What did he break to make that crash? I headed for the door but paused with my hand on the knob. "By the way, I saw Stu driving a white panel truck out of town."

"Stu? He doesn't own a panel truck. Just his old rattletrap."
Amos scratched his head. "Must have been someone else."

I shook my head. "I don't think so." I walked out of the office
and to my boat. Peedee peered through a crack and hole in the
side. On the ground lay a concrete block. In the first wave of
shock, I laughed in horror. Not an iceberg and not the Titanic, but
sinkable all the same. I pulled Peedee out of the hole and held
him close as I walked back to Amos' office. "You've got to see
this," I called to him.

Under a cool facade, Hunter had left in a hot rage, controlling
it until he thought no one would see. Then he unleashed it by
bashing in my boat with a cinder block

Amos walked out and stared at my boat in disbelief. "Hunter
did it?"

I nodded. "And that's what he'll do to me. Thanks to you, he
knows where I am, and he'll stick around until he gets what he
wants. I am not safe here."

Chapter 24

I watched Amos stare at the hole before circling the boat. He came back to the hole, feeling around the edges and shaking his head. "Somebody . . . doesn't have to be Hunter . . . threw a concrete chunk at the Fiberglass hull." He nudged it with his shoe and ran his finger along the crack it made. "This wasn't an accident. Could have been the prowler or maybe kids." He whistled. "I'll call the police," he said, glancing at me. "You got insurance?"

"Of course." Minimal insurance. "Do you? My boat was propped in your yard by your employee. I came back to it once, and one of the buttresses was sawn through. Now the hull has a big hole in it. You're going to pay for repairing it, and I want my boat protected from further damage. This is all your fault, not mine."

Amos scratched his head. "I guess so, but nothing like this happened before you came." Amos walked back into the office.

"Great," I muttered. "He's saying it's really my fault, but something good may come of this. Maybe the police will arrest Hunter." I put Peedee down to run around the yard before climbing aboard to view the damage. The hole was over a bunk and above the waterline with cracks radiating from it.

After a few minutes, Amos returned with a large piece of scrap canvas and some duct tape. He glanced at me. "The police are coming."

"About time," I said.

Amos nodded. "So you think Hunter did it?"

I nodded. "I do. He walked out of the office in a rage, threw the concrete block, and left."

Amos was trying to give Hunter the benefit of a doubt. Unbelievable. He was still trying to defend the guy.

"I ran out when I heard the crash. Hunter's car was just leaving, and no one else was around." I put my hands on my hips. "That's enough for me."

We both looked up as the police car swung into the yard. I scrambled to get Peedee clear. This time, a different man got out of the car. He stepped forward to shake hands with Amos. "Police Chief Herbert Yost. So what's going on here?"

"Look at this, Chief." Amos led Yost around the boat to show him the hole. "Some no-good skunk did this."

"His name is Hunter McCann," I added. "He's staying at a nearby motel." I turned to Amos. "What's the name of it?"

Amos shrugged. "Way something. Don't remember."

The chief stared at the hole, arms crossed. "Wayfarer Motel. Up the road." He pursed his lips. "You get a picture of this?"

I pulled out my phone. "I will now." I snapped several photos of the boat and the damage. "I'll e-mail them to you."

Yost rubbed his chin. "So you saw this Hunter fellow pick up the block and throw it at the boat?"

"We didn't actually see him," I said. "We heard him."

The chief looked at Amos. "Did you see him?"

Amos shook his head. "I heard him, like Mellie said. Only one around. Then he skedaddled out of here in his black van."

"You need to go after him, Chief Yost. Arrest him," I said.

Yost walked to his car, reached inside, and pulled out a clip-board. "Well, now, you see," he began, "I don't think it'll work." He squinted at them. "If neither one of you actually saw him pick up the block and heave it at the boat."

"No one else was here," I said.

"You were in the office," Chief Yost said. "You didn't see anything or anyone. You got insurance?"

Amos nodded.

"I guess you need to have them take care of it, then, but I'll file a report on the vandalism." He pulled a pen out of his pocket and filled in the blanks on the form. After a few more questions for the report, I signed it, and the chief tipped his hat. "I'll see if I can find this Hunter guy and ask him about it, but he ain't going to admit to it. I can guarantee it." He glanced at me. "E-mail me those photos." He doffed his hat and retreated to his car. We watched him back out onto the road.

I glanced at Amos. "That was useless."

Amos nodded and frowned at me.

"What?" I asked.

"I'm not saying I'm wrong here," Amos said, "a man and his wife belong together." He spat on the gravel. "But whoever bashed in your boat is a no-good, rotten skunk."

I folded my arms. "Yeah. Hunter."

"So you say, but I can't believe it. I'll cover up the hole. You should be able to sleep in there despite the damage." He ripped the duct tape with his teeth as he held the canvas in place. I took one edge to help hold it while Amos taped it. When he finished, he rubbed his hands and stepped back to look at the temporary patch.

"It'll hold," I said. "I can live with it for awhile, but I want the hole repaired as soon as possible."

Amos nodded and walked back toward the office, leaving me staring after him. He knew who had bashed in my boat as well as I did. If I had been outside within range, Hunter would have thrown the block at me. The thought didn't scare me. It only made me angrier that Amos was still trying to defend Hunter.

I cuddled the puppy in my arms, still fuming about the hole in my boat and trying to control the panic building inside me. Hunter knew where I lived and how I lived. I could not move the boat with a hole in its side. How could I get to any jobs I picked up if Hunter could track me down as I bicycled alone and vulnerable on these country roads? My bicycle wasn't armored. I already received several more cleaning job offers, thanks to Ann's recommendation. How could I get to them if I didn't dare ride by myself?

I climbed the ladder into the boat, let the pup play in the cockpit, and used my hand to sweep into a pile the splinters of wood and fiberglass sprayed across my bunk. I pulled off the covers and took them and my pillow to the cockpit to shake out over the side. I'd vacuum up later. Amos came out of the office and walked to my boat. He stood at the foot of the ladder and looked up at me.

I folded my arms and stared down at him, still angry at his attitude. "What's up?"

"Put in a call to the insurance company." Amos said, running his hand across the canvas covering the hole. "They're sending someone out in a couple of days."

"Not sooner? The boat's a mess," I said.

Amos nodded. "Stu will be back tomorrow. I'll get him to order what we need to make repairs. I'll pay for it."

"You should. It happened in your yard," I said truculently.

"I know." Amos stared at the ground with shame on his face. "I should've listened to you."

I had to lean out farther and strain my ears to catch the last phrase, but I didn't have the nerve to ask him to repeat it. Amos turned and crunched the gravel back to the office. I watched him disappear through the door. I sat in the cockpit and marveled at Amos' last words. It amounted to an apology or as close to an admission and regret as Amos would get. Did that mean he would stop pushing me to go back to Hunter? Had the blinders dropped from Amos' eyes? I'd have to wait and see, but in the meantime I could cuddle Peedee.

I went to bed early and slept restlessly, waking in fear at every noise, worrying over how I could earn any money if I had to hide from Hunter on the road. I could still work for Norma, and I still had savings enough to disappear for a few weeks, but what then? I'd always live in fear he would attack me, kidnap me, torture me to get those papers back. What would he do to prevent my letter from reaching the authorities? Would he attack and kill or torture everyone I knew? I drifted asleep and woke sometime later caught in a nightmare.

I could anticipate what he might do. He laid the groundwork already by moving me to his house in New Jersey, away from my friends and anyone who knew and cared about me. I had, however unwillingly, acquiesced in his plan. The one good thing I did was to keep my job despite Hunter's urging me to quit. Now I had left the job, and even if Norma knew who to ask, which she did not, she wouldn't inquire about my whereabouts or well-being until it was way too late.

If Hunter kidnapped me, he could fabricate any kind of story to put Amos and my friends off, and he could force me to collaborate. Would Amos and Stu or even Cal try to push their way into seeing me? Try to get some kind of confirmation I was okay?

He could hide me somewhere. Lock me in chains. Beat me and torture me but keep me alive to answer queries by phone, mail, or e-mail. That's what he would do for awhile. Divorce was out of the question. He would never agree to my demands, because they were my requirements, not his. One day he'd kill me, and no one would know except the life insurance company.

Chapter 25

I spent the night alternately seething and trying to plan what to do next. I liked living on the boat in the marina. I liked Cal and bicycling instead of driving or waiting for a bus. I could make a good life here if I got rid of Hunter. What else could I do to protect myself?

I pondered the question in the boat's cockpit. The gate was closed and locked. Amos had retreated to his apartment behind the store, and his light was on. Several times I heard the clattering noise of Hunter's van as he drove it back and forth on the road.

He was playing a game of nerves, while he plotted how to eliminate me. I shook my head at the irony of two people, man and wife, planning each other's demise.

What I wanted from Hunter was a divorce and my own life back. I hoped the fake IDs and financial papers I held and the letter in Cal's safe would protect me against his reprisals. Since he'd tracked me down here, it was time to make sure he understood the situation.

After breakfast the next morning, I noticed Cal brought Amos' pickup truck back and parked it outside the gate.

Amos called me to the office. "I want to talk to you."

Another lecture, I thought. All about my duty to my husband and how I should go back to him. My father was a first-class jerk.

I followed Amos into the store. He gestured to one of the

chairs at the side of the counter. I sat on the edge, ready to bounce out. Amos took the other one.

"I've been thinking. . ." He rubbed his chin.

I waited, my mind rapidly sorting through the possibilities. I could just leave this marina and find another one farther down the coast or even elsewhere in town. Amos didn't need to know where. I'd grown to like this place, though, and I didn't want to leave.

I folded my arms and stared at Amos.

He shook his head, avoiding my eyes. "I never met Hunter before. Don't know him at all. But from what you say, he isn't a good man." He studied me with half-closed eyes. "I know things were pretty bad for you at home growing up." He sighed. "I wasn't much of a father."

"No, you weren't," I agreed.

Amos nodded. "I been thinking about your mother. Guess I can't really blame her for leaving me. I was hard to live with in those days."

"It was hell." I looked down at my hands, not wanting to listen, uncomfortable at the remorse in my father's voice. He should have done what he could to keep my mother, but he didn't.

"I do blame your mother," Amos continued, "for leaving you."

I couldn't speak. How dare he try to blame her. I refused to give in to tears, preferring rage, fighting down the anger, ready to scream at him, but his next words stopped me.

"So when Hunter called, I wanted to do something to help both of you. A wife belongs with her husband." He looked sternly at me. "Only I started listening, really listening, to what he was saying, and I got to tell you, now I've been thinking about it, he puts my back up." Amos stared off at the ceiling.

"How's that?" My anger subsided, and curiosity took over. Hunter usually made a good impression.

"I didn't like the way he talked about you."

"Really," I said with an audible sniff. I'd been listening to talk like that all my life.

"I know he was angry and all, but he acted like he owned you, like you were some kid who ran away." His eyes left the ceiling but now looked directly at me. "I heard what you said yesterday. I know you're a grown woman and need to be treated like one. I'm learning. Maybe I see why your mom ran away."

He paused and wiped a sleeve over his eyes, but he wasn't brushing off tears from thinking about my mom. It was sweat. The office was hot and stuffy. I waited in wonder. Amos being repentant? What would he say next?

"Hunter wasn't saying anything about loving you or missing you or any such thing. Then he called you a thief."

"He also called me a whore and a tramp," I said. I couldn't quite believe what I was hearing. Had Amos finally come around? "I showed you the bruises, didn't I? When I came? What kind of man beats his wife?"

"I said I heard you last night, but I didn't raise my girl to be a thief." Amos lifted an eyebrow as he looked at me.

"You didn't raise me at all," I retorted. "If you're wondering if I stole from him, then I'll say yes, I took some of his illegal documents, and they're in a safety deposit box here in town. He can have them back when we're divorced, and he renounces all association and all claims to me and has not initiated any contact whatsoever for one year."

Amos nodded. "Are you afraid of him, honey?"

Honey? Where did that come from? "You're damn right I'm afraid of him. He'll kill me if he gets the chance. You don't know him like I do. He doesn't let anyone go unless it's by his choice. He's a criminal, tied in with the mafia or some other gang of crooks, and they're not so forgiving, either."

"Seems like you poked a hornet's nest taking those papers." Amos shook his head. "He can't let you go with those over his head."

"But I needed something to hold against him to get what I want. You're probably right, now that I think about it, but it's done." I got up and pulled a Coke out of the bait refrigerator. "Put this on the tab," I said as I opened it and took a swig. "Anyway, I gave letters to a couple of friends about those documents. Wrote on them, "To be opened in case of my death.""

I sat and took another swig. "What worries me is what you said to Hunter. Because of you, he found out I was here. If I don't go with him willingly, he'll try to kidnap me."

Amos looked at me. "I'm not your enemy," he said. "Yes, I told him you're here because he's your husband, but now I've told you he got my back up. I didn't tell him anything about what you're doing or about your boat, but you're his wife, and when you go back to him, you need to insist on being treated right."

When I go back to him? I spluttered the first angry words of a reply, but then Stu entered. He glanced from Amos to me and tipped his hat at me. "Hot out there." Stu walked to the refrigerator and took a bottle of water.

Amos looked back to me and wagged his finger. "I acted like a genuine concerned father . . ." He narrowed his eyes at me. ". . . which I am."

I forced my mouth to close. Amos had heard what I'd said to

him—and changed his mind halfway. Miracle of miracles. He still thought I should go back to Hunter eventually, but he'd shifted some of his views. He even sounded somewhat reasonable, and he did listen. He wasn't at all like I remembered him. He wasn't drinking, and that alone was intriguingly different. Maybe I wanted to get to know him better. What a surprise.

Chapter 26

The hole was repaired, and I spent the rest of the morning painting the hull of my boat. As I finished, I glanced at my watch. I'd forgotten lunch. I let Peedee out for a quick run around, then took him to Amos' office. There was a time when I wouldn't trust any animal to Amos, but he'd changed so much I found myself reassessing him at every step. Now he was fussing over little Peedee. He'd even bought some treats and was handing one to the dog, who was happily wagging his tail.

"Can you watch him for awhile?" I asked. "I want to buy some things in town. And, thanks to you, I need to drive the truck. Hunter could attack me on the bicycle."

"Sure. This little fellow and I are good friends, aren't we, buddy?" Amos watched the puppy wriggle and squeal. "You go on."

I found the keys under the seat where Cal left them and drove to the café for lunch. I savored the breeze in my hair and the freedom of cruising down the one-lane road. As I'd hoped, Cal was seated alone in one of the booths. He looked up surprised as he saw me enter and motioned to the empty seat.

"You didn't bike here, did you?"

"I took the truck. No sign of Hunter."

Cal picked up his cup of coffee and waved it. "Good. Creepy the way he's following you."

"Terrifying is a better word," I said, signaling the server who arrived with a menu. I waved it aside. "Vegetable soup and a grilled cheese, please."

She nodded and passed on to the next table.

Cal eyed me as he sipped his coffee. "So what are you going to do now?"

I studied my hands, debating what I could tell him. He was hiding the letter I gave him. What did he really think of my story? Was he merely humoring me? I'd told him the truth as much as I dared. Who has people hunting to kill them? He'd been supportive so far, but did he think I was making it up or a nutcase or worse? I didn't want to come across as needy. Or afraid. Or whiny.

Cal didn't question my fear of Hunter. He'd even hidden me in his van and driven me back to the marina. He'd also never rolled his eyes at me or shown any other ridicule of the sort I'd endured from Amos and Hunter.

We'd need to keep our distance while Hunter was around. I didn't really believe Hunter would be jealous, although he'd act like it. He wouldn't want me to be telling my story or gaining interest or support from anyone who would thwart his plans. Even now, I might have put Cal in danger. Should I warn him? At least, I should distance myself.

"I'll be pretty busy the next week or so," I added. "Won't be able to drop by."

"Whenever you can." Cal finished his soup and started on his sandwich.

I ducked the urge to explain, and Cal didn't ask, which was fine. "Anything happening in the bike world?" I asked, looking up as the server delivered my lunch.

Cal laughed. "Always something happening. Especially now it's spring. We'll be running guided bike trips all summer on Saturdays starting in June." He snapped his fingers. "Say, if you need a job, I could sure use someone on Saturdays to run the shop while I do the trips."

I waited for the soup to cool as I thought about the offer. Hunter should be gone by then. "You'd need to show me how to change a tire and do minor repairs."

"Sure. Everyone should know how, anyway." He laid aside his napkin and put his elbows on the table. "So what do you say?"

"I would love to do it." I shook my head. "But not for a couple of weeks. I have a problem to get rid of first." A problem to get rid of. Yes, indeed.

"I won't need someone till the first trip in three weeks." He glanced at the bill and pulled out his wallet. "Plenty of time to teach you what you need to know." He slid out of the booth. "Got to go. Talk to you later."

I nodded. Would I still be alive in three weeks?

After lunch, I stopped by the Food Lion and bought enough groceries, so I could hole up in my boat for as long as needed.

As I drove out of the parking lot, I glanced at the rearview mirror and gasped. Following me out of the lot, too close, was the black van. All the side windows were tinted exactly like Hunter's, and the sun visor was down, so I couldn't see the driver, but I knew who it was. He was watching me. Of course.

What should I do? Would he try to run me off the road on the half-mile home? Could I lose him in town? No. This wasn't a big city with alleys and stoplights and streets. The town ranged along the one road with side streets leading off but no place to hide.

I needed to get to the marina behind the locked gate. It was only half a mile ahead. I drove down the stretch of lonely one-lane road, keeping an eye on the rear-view mirror. The van followed, too close. There was no other traffic. Would he try to ram me? Pass me and push me off the road? I gripped the steering wheel. If I drove into the marina yard, he'd follow. I wouldn't be able to get through the gate, jump out, and lock the padlock in front of him to block him. If I were lucky, Amos or Stu would be outside to protect me.

I approached the marina and slowed. The van behind me matched my pace. I swallowed, and my hands trembled. "Oh no . . . oh no . . . oh no," I muttered to myself. Ahead, the marina gate was open, but no one stood in the yard. I sped up and passed the marina. The van did likewise. He was toying with me. It was time for me to get some backbone. I gritted my teeth and drove up to the motel where Hunter was staying. I pulled to the side of the road and crossed my fingers. Hunter drove in behind me and parked in a slot at one of the units. *He thinks I'm going to talk with him. He thinks I'm a fool.*

I waited for him to step out of his van, then I made a quick turn on the road and raced back to the marina, through the gate, and sprang out of the truck to lock the gate.

I disappeared into the office.

Amos glanced at me. "What's going on?"

I shook my head, panting, and collapsed into a chair. I listened for the clattering noise, wondering what Hunter would do.

A few minutes later, I heard the telltale clattering and Hunter lean on his horn. Peedee lifted his head from the floor and barked in response.

"What's that?" asked Amos.

I shrugged. "Hunter. He'll go away after awhile."

Amos got up. "I'm not going to stand for it."

"Don't go out there," I pleaded. "He's dangerous. He might have a gun."

"Just let him try something." Amos walked out the door, leaving it open. I crept to the threshold to listen.

"We're closed," Amos said. "The gate's locked.'

I heard Hunter say something in response.

"You're gonna hafta leave," said Amos. "Don't want to call the police on you."

More mumbled words from Hunter. I heard the van back up and Amos' shoes crunching on the gravel back to the store.

He walked in and grimaced at me. "Not a problem," he said.

I picked up Peedee and hugged him, relieved to be back behind the locked gates, relieved that Amos hadn't invited Hunter in to "talk it out." I walked back to my boat and climbed the ladder. Did I make the right choice in keeping it propped up on land? I was close to Amos and the office, but if it were in the water I could make a quick escape if necessary. The best plan depended on Hunter's strategy. How would he attack next?

Chapter 27

I woke in a cold sweat, pulled together clothes, towel, and soap, and clutched Peedee as I struggled down the ladder to wash up at the boater's shower behind the office. I set Peedee free to run around the yard and checked the gate lock. It was secure. I saw no sign of Hunter's van parked on the road, waiting.

After the shower, I brought Peedee back up to the cockpit to feed him and fixed a quick breakfast for myself, all the while pondering my situation. What could I do to protect myself? More self-defense lessons, which I badly needed, were still days away, but now I would be afraid to bicycle into town for them—unless I rode in with Amos when he was going that way. I'd have to go with him for groceries anyway. I could call Cal and explain the situation. He said he'd help, but it would put him in danger.

How could I get to my cleaning jobs? I threw a treat at Peedee and listened as Stu's rattletrap came down the road and stopped at the gate. He opened it, drove in, and left it open for the day's customers. And Hunter.

I followed Peedee to the docks. Seeing Amos' runabout gave me an idea. If he'd let me use the boat, I could get to the houses by water, since they all backed onto the river. Hunter never showed any interest in boats or the water. I remembered our honeymoon when he'd sneered at the idea I might even have a watercraft. That blissful time seemed so long ago now. It belonged to a different Melanie.

I walked into the office and found Amos slumped at his desk. "I have several jobs in the development up the river," I said. "I can't take my bike. Not now. I'd like to use the runabout."

Amos looked up. "The runabout? Sure. Take it. No problem."

"Good." I left as Stu walked in, banging the door behind him. As I stepped out of the office, I saw once again the houseboat going down the river. This time, it seemed low in the water as if heavily loaded. I looked back at Amos and Stu. "The houseboat is passing the marina again. I've seen it a lot," I said. "Who owns it? What's it doing? Where does it go?"

Stu was quick to reply. "Lots of 'em on the river," he said, frowning at me. "People out having a good time, that's all." His eyes narrowed as he grinned at me. "Why would you want to know?"

"Just curious." Stu never did act friendly, but now he seemed to be laughing at me, but I persisted. "So neither of you knows who owns it, and where it comes from?"

Amos shook his head. "Doesn't stop here for fuel or dockage. I got enough to worry about."

"Probably has a slip in one of them fancy marinas down river," added Stu. "Too rich for our blood." He stared at me. "None of your business." His words sounded like a warning.

I slid by him—he had come too close—but paused at the door. "By the way," I said, "thought I saw you driving a white panel truck. Is that what you took to Richmond?"

Stu glanced at Amos. "All I got is my old Chevy. Don't have a panel truck, white or otherwise."

"Really? Sure looked like you."

"It wasn't." Stu walked to the refrigerator and found an apple.

"I'll go check the pumps," he said as he ambled out.

I walked back to my boat wondering why Stu was telling me to back off. I was just curious, but now I was even more so. It sure looked like Stu driving the white panel truck. He lied about it—but why?

I could feel Stu's antagonism toward me. There again, why? I'd done nothing to cause it unless he shared Amos' prejudices. Another misogynist. Stu was warning me off speculating about that houseboat. It didn't look like any rich man's toy, stripped to bare bones—no elaborate fittings or bright work, no signs of leisurely accoutrements, not even any deck chairs, and no one lounging on the deck waving to those onshore. It went up and down the river at odd times just about every day. None of it made any sense.

After lunch, I stowed my cleaning supplies in the little runabout, put fuel in the tank, added extra in a canister, and put-putted up river to the development. I was to meet Ann at her house, and she was to let me into the house next to hers. As I tied up at the dock, she watched me from the back deck of her house.

"Glad to see you," she called. "I've been e-mailing my friends. We've got a bunch of houses for you—enough to keep you busy all season."

I climbed the steps and followed her to the house next door, cutting through the narrow patch of woods that separated the two houses. Ann opened the door, and both of us surveyed the living room in front of us. The furniture was tossed around and arranged oddly. I raised an eyebrow.

"Their son brought his friends down from college over spring break," said Ann. "I guess this is the mess they left."

"Looks like vandalism."

We walked into the kitchen. I winced at the dishes in the sink. "Where's the toaster?" I asked. "And the microwave?"

"Can't believe they wouldn't have those appliances. I'll call them." Ann made a note.

We moved to the living room. No television, but some people liked to keep their television out of the main family areas. We investigated the entire house. No television. No computers. No radios.

We looked at each other. "Another hit," I said.

"I'll call the owners to make sure and then the police." Ann walked out the front door.

I waited until the police came again. It was Officer Henschel. Ann followed him in. He looked around and made notes of what he found. To my relief, since I'd have to clean up afterwards, he decided not to dust for fingerprints. "Same guys,' he said. "They wear gloves."

Ann continued to note missing items and record Henschel's comments. "I'll get back to the owners," she told him. "What do you need?"

"Descriptions, model and serial numbers of whatever is missing. We'll try to track the stuff. No promises." Henschel walked to the front door. "I'll go talk to the so-called security guards."

After he left, Ann turned to me. "So how long will it take you to straighten this place up?" she asked.

I made a quick guess. "I should be able to do the basics in three hours, which will give me a good idea of what is needed. I can stay longer next time if necessary." As I looked at the chaotic mix of furniture, I added, "I'll keep an eye out for anything we thought was missing. "

"It's so close to my house, naturally they'd rip into it, too, while they were at it." Ann turned to leave. "Drop by when you're finished. I'll pay you for your hours," she said as she left.

I set to work. I found the vacuum in a closet off the kitchen, but as I pulled it out, I glanced at the back door. Out of curiosity, I tried the knob. It opened. It was unlocked.

Did the owners or the college kids forget to lock the back door?

I pondered the question as I vacuumed and dusted and then cleaned the kitchen and bathrooms. Three hours passed quickly. I enjoyed the work. Physical exertion felt fresh and good, and the results gave me pleasure.

I closed up the house, walked back to Ann's, and knocked on the door.

Ann opened it. "All finished?" she asked, stepping aside and waving me in.

I followed her into the living room. "Except I'm a little worried about a couple of things." I hesitated. "Did you know the back door was unlocked?"

Ann frowned at me. "Unlocked?"

I nodded. "The college kids could have left it that way or the burglars did. I didn't see any signs that they broke in. They took everything they could sell easily.

"Let me call the owners again and report." Ann crossed to the phone. "Have a seat." She waved at the sofa as she tapped in a number. "Hello, Helen?"

I sat and listened to the one-sided conversation.

"Yes, I did. All spic and span, but she says your back door was unlocked." Ann listened, raising an eyebrow at me. "I see. All right. I'll tell the police you're putting together the list." She hung up.

I got up to leave. "I guess you won't need me now, and the police know where I live if they have any questions."

Ann followed me to the door. "Wait till I give that security guard a piece of my mind," she said.

Chapter 28

I again slept restlessly, waking up once after a vivid nightmare. How could I live a normal life with Hunter lurking nearby, ready to force me back to New Jersey or worse? I was convinced the papers in my safety deposit box kept me alive so far. Amos and the locked gate helped. How long could Hunter stay away from his work? Could he really do everything online? In New Jersey, he'd go out frequently to do whatever he needed to do. Didn't he have to use the machinery in the basement? He must be accountable to someone, even if he was a crook. Could I survive until he left? What would be his next ploy?

I thought about it for awhile, concluding that Hunter would want to keep tabs on me. To do so, he'd come back to the marina and apologize, no doubt blaming his actions on my stubbornness. I could hear him now, commiserating with Amos. Then he'd offer to pay and help out around the yard.

The next time I went into town, I'd mail the letter with the safety deposit key to Norma. I held off so far, because I was afraid the postmark would give away my whereabouts, which would somehow make its way to Hunter. Not an issue now.

I woke early, dressed, and carried Peedee down the ladder for his morning play and poop time around the yard. I wanted to see Cal, continue the self-defense lessons, and buy groceries. The town was too small for a cab service, and I felt too vulnerable on my bike. I could ask Amos for the pickup, but I didn't want to rely on him or give him any reason to hand out advice.

I walked to the gate and stared down the road. Thick, thorny multiflora rose bushes encroached on each side most of the way to town. I couldn't count on finding a deer trail and running into the woods and hiding when I heard or saw the van coming. There had to be some other way.

Peedee jumped up on me, wagging his tail. He wanted to play. I threw him a stick to chase and played that game for awhile, ruminating on the problem. I heard Stu's rattletrap polluting its way toward the marina. It was seven-thirty. I picked up Peedee and carried him as I climbed the ladder, setting him in the cockpit and stepping down to the galley to fix breakfast for the two of us. As I casually glanced at the pile of clothes on the unused bunk, I hit on an idea. Maybe a disguise would work. Hunter barely noticed my clothes. He probably wouldn't remember any outfit I wore. I could dress in an old pair of jeans, put my hair up under a cap, carry a fishing rod, and take long strides. Anyone who saw me would think I was a country boy going fishing.

I loved the idea. I owned an old pair of jeans. I dug through the pile of clothes until I found them. They needed a few alterations. I pulled a knife out of a kitchen drawer, ripped at the knee and the bottom hems to make them ragged. I looked for a shirt. Nothing I found would conceal my "womanly figure." The phrase made me laugh, but I could borrow one of Amos' shirts. Big and floppy enough for sure. I also searched for the pair of old sneakers I'd brought for wading.

I finished breakfast and took Peedee to stay with Amos in the office. Then I plunked into the armchair. "We need to talk," I said.

Amos sat in the other chair, working on papers. "Talk," he said, glancing up.

"Hunter's going to come here and apologize," I began.

"Nah." Amos shook his head. "Not after what he done with your boat."

I folded my arms. "He'll say I drove him to it by my stubbornness. He couldn't help himself."

Amos scratched his head. "I've felt the same way myself, you know."

"He'll count on it." I watched Amos. Would he accept what I said or deflect it because I was a woman?

"You can't know what he'll do," said Amos.

I can make good guesses. "Next he'll offer to pay for the damage and help out around the yard."

"He should do that, yep." Amos sat back in the chair and gazed at the ceiling. "I could use the money and the help."

"I'm asking you to refuse his money and his help. Tell him to get out."

"You don't mean it, honey. I don't like him much, either, but there's no real harm in the man."

I spoke through gritted teeth. "He will kill me."

Amos slapped the arm of the chair in irritation and stood to pace behind the counter. "You've been watching too much television," he said.

"All right," I said. I'd have to let Amos see the truth for himself. A stubborn old man. "Can I borrow an old shirt for painting? And an old ball cap?"

"Sure," he said. "Glad to help you with those."

By nine o'clock that morning, I changed into a country boy out for a day of fishing, carrying a bucket that held good jeans and a clean shirt. I watched for a chance to leave the yard when Amos and Stu would be busy elsewhere and not see me. I didn't trust either one not to betray me to Hunter. Stu was malicious enough to do it, and despite everything, Amos still believed Hunter and I could "work things out." What a laugh. Despite my bashed-in boat and everything I'd told him, Amos identified with Hunter, seeing my "poor" husband as another victimized man whose wife ran out on him.

My chance came when Stu threw his cigarette butt into the can under the oak tree and walked to the gas pumps at the end of the dock. Amos was still in the office. I darted down the ladder and stayed in the cover of the other propped-up boats in the yard as I ran to the gate and slipped out. I looked both ways to make sure I didn't see a black van and walked as much like a boy as I could manage to town.

Cal was unlocking the door of his store as I approached. "Not open yet," he called as he stepped inside, closing it in my face.

I rapped on the wood. "Cal, it's me, Melanie."

Cal opened the door and peered out. "Melanie?" He opened it wider and pulled me in. "What's going on?"

I explained. "I needed to get away from the marina. I've got things to do."

Cal nodded. "Yeah, I ran into your self-defense instructor. He was asking about you."

"That, too." I took the bucket with me into the restroom. "Just a minute." I changed into the good jeans and shirt and dropped my old clothes into the bucket, setting it down behind the counter. I looked at Cal. "Okay?"

"Sure," he said. "Now what?"

I poured out a cup of coffee from the stand behind the counter, walked to the rocking chair, and plopped into it. "Need to catch my breath before I take care of my errands."

Cal sat beside me. "What's been happening?"

I filled him in. "So you see, I have to be careful not to get caught alone with Hunter. He is mean, vindictive, and desperate. I am supposed to be his victim." I gazed at Cal with narrowed eyes. "But I'm not."

Cal nodded, a slight smile playing around his lips. "No, you are not."

"Can you give me a ride back to the marina when I'm through here?"

"Sure. No problem." He stood and walked to the collection of bikes near the front door. "Got to get these out for display." He stopped and glanced at me. "Do you need a ride while you're in town?"

I shook my head. "I'm all right here. Enough people and stores around I can duck into. He won't try anything with witnesses around."

"Okay, then." Cal picked up a bike and carried it out to the sidewalk. I watched him a moment, then took my cup to the sink behind the counter, washed it, and set it on the small table.

I waved at Cal as I went along the street to the karate school, hoping for a few self-defense lessons. I mailed the letter to Norma on the way.

***

That afternoon, Cal drove me back to the marina still in my "good" clothes with the old ones in the bucket. He helped me carry the groceries to the boat ladder and glanced at the glistening white paint covering the repaired hole. "Your dad did a good job," he said, nodding at the hull.

I glanced at the patch. "I have to thank Hunter for the hole, but Amos did get it fixed. Even after that performance and whatever he says, Amos still thinks I should go back to Hunter."

Cal gave me a lopsided smile. "And you don't agree."

I put my hands on my hips. "That's right."

"Good." Cal walked back toward his truck, turning to wave at me at the gate. "Be glad to pick you up and take you wherever." He passed through the gate and climbed into his truck. "See you," he called.

I stored the groceries away in the galley and strolled to the marina office. Peedee was sleeping in the corner but sprang up when he saw me. He ran to me, wagging his tail.

Amos glanced up. "Hunter's been looking for you."

I froze. "When?"

"Earlier today. Wanted to take you to lunch." He rested his chin on his hand and tapped a pencil on the desk with the other. "And you were right. He apologized, paid me for the damage, cash, and offered to help out here, but I said I didn't need any help."

I folded my arms. "I told you what he'd say."

Amos nodded. "So what are you going to do about him?"

"Next time you see him, tell him to go home, and I want a divorce."

Amos went back to his papers. "Okay."

Swallowing my disbelief, I said, "Good." I turned as Stu set the butt can outside the door and walked in.

"What else you need, boss?" he asked, his thumbs stuck in his pockets.

"You seen that houseboat yet?" I asked.

"Not today," Stu said indifferently.

"It usually comes by in the late afternoon. I don't think it belongs to one of the wealthy landowners around here," I said. "It's stripped down, no deck chairs. Not built for fun."

Stu opened the bait refrigerator and perused its contents. "Maybe it's a work boat, out robbing crab pots."

I considered this possibility. Stu might have hit on the right idea. Made sense, I supposed. "How big a problem are crab pot robbers down here?"

"Big," said Stu. Amos nodded.

"Could they be fishing, too?" I asked.

"Could be," said Stu.

Amos shrugged.

Chapter 29

When evening came, I sat in the cockpit and watched the sunset, Peedee dozing at my feet. Hunter stopped by, but I refused to talk with him. Amos closed the office, forcing Hunter out of the yard, and locked the gate. I wanted to laugh at the chagrin on Hunter's face as the gate was shut in his face, but I didn't dare. He'd get really vindictive. Unable to enter the yard or find anyone sympathetic with his plight, he left.

Still, I gritted my teeth at the van's repetitive clattering as Hunter drove up and down the road. His form of harassment. Why didn't he get that strip of chrome fixed? It had to be nerve-wracking for him, too, but I was glad he didn't. Even though the familiar clacking chilled me, it also warned me of his presence like the rattles of a poisonous snake.

I heard the van again early the next morning, and when Stu opened the gate for customers, Hunter drove in and parked. He stepped out of the van. "Melanie," he called.

I stared down at him from the cockpit. Peedee growled. "Go home," I said. "Give me a divorce."

"You don't want a divorce," Hunter whined. "Makes you look bad. Running away like this makes you a coward. People already think you're no good."

I met these arguments indifferently, wondering what he'd try next. I'd been right, though. He was spreading rumors about me in town. That could hurt me as I tried to find work here, especially if he spread word I was a thief or worse. I'd find it hard to find any job, unless Cal and maybe the karate master or the server in the diner came to my defense. I could talk to the police chief, too, and Officer Henschel. I turned away from Hunter and stepped down into the galley.

I assumed that Hunter's colleagues, whoever they were, and their spouses thought the worst of me. Certainly they did, but I hadn't met any of them and didn't care. At first, I thought Hunter had been shy about introducing me. What a laugh. They were all crooks. Their perspective was warped. I'd have to do some heavy soul-searching if I met their approval.

Whatever Hunter did—spread rumors, bash my boat—didn't matter. What counted was I was out of the house I shared with him and no longer under his control. Except not totally, yet. He was still controlling my life to some extent. Though not, I hoped, for long.

Hunter walked around my boat. "Too bad about the hole in the side," he said as if he'd had nothing to do with it. "Could have been worse," he added.

I refused to engage.

"Why don't I climb up, and we can sit down and have a chat about all this like adults." He put a foot on the bottom rung. "You're acting like a child."

"You stay down there," I said, "or I'm calling Amos and the police. I'll charge you with harassment, trespassing, and assault if I have to."

Hunter paused, his foot still on the ladder and looked up at me with anger in his eyes and a smile on his lips.

"Get out," I said.

Hunter turned. He crunched across the gravel to his van. I heard him start the engine and drive out of the parking area. He was gone, but he'd be back. What then?

I tried to relax and think. I was a sitting duck for harassment here. I needed to get away for awhile to figure this thing out. If Hunter thought I'd left for good, he'd leave, too. I was considering Richmond or Washington when the phone rang. Ann.

"I have three house cleanings lined up for you," she said. "Starting tomorrow morning."

I smiled. Of course I was available. "Sure. Maybe I should give you ten percent as my agent."

Ann laughed. "You do a good job, and you're reliable, and we sympathize. I've told my friends and neighbors about you, and they're all hot to have you get their houses ready for the summer. You're in the right place, right time, that's all."

"A lucky break." I said as an idea formed. A possibility. I called Cal later and talked it over with him. He agreed it might work.

"By the way," I added, "if you hear any rumors about me, please scotch them fast. The next thing Hunter might pull is to spread lies saying I'm a thief or worse. Please don't believe him."

"Don't worry. My sister endured the same kind of harassment when she divorced her husband. He wasn't an abuser, though, just a jerk. I know you're a nice person, one of the good ones."

I felt tears well up. How long had it been since anyone, ever, thought I was a good person, a nice one. "Thank you," I managed to whisper.

"Only the truth." Cal paused. "Don't forget. I'm here if you need me."

How comforting this conversation was. My heart and my step

were lighter as I walked to the office to talk to Amos about taking care of the dog for awhile. I watched Amos with Peedee, and my fears about how Amos would treat the little guy dissipated. "I need to get away from Hunter," I said. "He's harassing me, but if I'm not here, he'll leave."

Amos pushed out his chin and frowned. "You think leaving might do it, huh?"

"Hope so. Can you take care of Peedee while I'm gone?" Peedee looked up at the sound of his name.

Amos reached down to pet the puppy. "Yeah, I can. When are you going?"

"I have a job to do tomorrow morning, then I'll be leaving from there. I'll probably go up to Washington. I met someone in town who'll give me a ride." I knew Amos had a better under-standing of Hunter now, but I still didn't trust him not to leak the information to the wrong people. Like Stu, for instance. In fact, I hoped Hunter would hear the gossip and leave for Washington to hunt for me.

"You gonna be all right?"

"Hope so," I said and headed for the door.

"Wait. What if I need to contact you?" He stared down at his hands. "About your boat, say."

I thought about the years when there was no contact at all. "I'll call you."

The next morning, I donned my fisher boy outfit, put clean clothes in the bucket along with cleaning supplies, and trekked to Cal's. He opened the door to me and waited while I changed into my usual clothes.

"Take me to the grocery store first," I said. "I hope you don't mind."

"Not at all. I need a few things myself." Cal drove the couple of blocks to the Food Lion. I ducked as I saw Hunter's van patrolling the street.

Next, Cal drove me and my supplies to Ann's house. The gate guard didn't bother to sign me in. He beckoned us through the gate and waved us on.

I stared back at the guard until we lost sight of him around a curve. "Stop here," I said.

"Here?" Cal braked where I said, at a thick patch of woods between two houses.

"I'm going to hide the food supplies. I don't want Ann to know anything about what I'm doing."

Cal nodded. "Okay." He carried one of the bags into the woods with me.

I followed Cal back to the truck.

"Are you sure about this?" Cal asked.

"No, but it's the best plan I can think of," I said. "Let's move on."

"You've got my phone number?" Cal glanced at me.

"My phone's all charged. I'll be careful." I pointed ahead. "That's the house, just ahead on the right."

Cal pulled over. "Be careful," he said. "Call me if you need help. Any time."

I leaned in and pecked him on the cheek. "Thank you."

Ann was waiting for me and opened the door before I knocked. "We're going to a different place, three houses down from me but still on the river. I'm wondering what we'll find."

"I hope it will be okay," I said, even though the security guard set-up they had in this development seemed to be useless, frequent patrols or not.

We walked past the three houses and on to the fourth. Ann opened the front door with a key on a ring. We held our breath. Everything looked okay. The living room had a mounted television. The kitchen featured a microwave, a radio, and a small television. I looked at Ann and grinned with a thumbs up.

"Haven't hit this place," I said.

"What a relief. I'll phone the owners when I get home." Ann headed for the front door.

"Why don't you peek into the houses between your place and this one," I suggested. "Maybe the burglars are working their way through this row along the river." The implications of that statement suddenly hit me like a stomach punch. This house could be next on their list. My safety plan burst like a bubble. I could call Cal and have him pick me up, or I could find a way to protect myself if the burglars did show up. They probably would not. They must know the security patrol had increased its surveillance, and the marine patrol had been notified.

Ann paused with her hand on the doorknob. "I'll do that. Good idea." She left, and I watched her stop at each house and peer in the windows but couldn't figure out from her reaction what she saw. Everything must have been all right, though, because neither the security guard nor the police showed up. That meant the burglars might go to the next house from the one they robbed last. I was a couple of houses away.

I set to work. Again, the job was simply a matter of vacuuming, dusting, and cleaning the bathrooms and kitchen. No clutter. No dirty laundry. Three hours max.

While I worked, I reviewed the possibilities. I still liked the idea of camping out in the house for a few days, but I needed to protect myself. How to do so effectively was the problem, but

Ann would be three houses away, and I had my cell phone. Worse came to worse, I could call the police. I finished the job and walked back to Ann's to collect my money.

"You locked up?" she asked.

"Yes, I did," I lied and gave her the key. "I'm going to start on the next house later this afternoon, and the third house tomorrow."

"Good." I'll pay you for those houses now, too." She stepped into the kitchen and picked up a couple of house keys. "Here are the keys. I have to get back to Richmond tonight, so be sure to lock everything when you leave. The security patrol has been reamed out for negligence, so they should be diligent, but who knows?"

"I'm sure everything will be okay," I said and walked out the door toward the next house on my work list. So Ann needed to leave, but it was a spur of the moment decision. No one else, like the burglars, would know she wasn't home.

Ann never asked about my transportation arrangements, assuming I still used my bicycle, although this time Ann must have seen Cal drop me off. She probably thought Cal would be picking me up, too.

I walked past the house I just cleaned and darted into the patch of woods immediately beyond. I snuck quietly through the trees to pick up my groceries, then tracked back to the rear of the house, entering it through the kitchen door I'd left open.

I'd never done anything sneaky and without permission before, and my stomach was doing flip-flops. What if the owners arrived unexpectedly? What if Ann walked in to check on things? How would I ever explain what I was doing here? It seemed like such a great idea last night. I didn't have a car to take me to

Richmond. My boat was disabled. There was no bus or train service here. I might have prevailed upon Amos or Cal or even Ann to drive me someplace, but would they keep mum or blab? I could even have asked Ann to take me to Richmond with her and drop me off at a motel. Why didn't I?

I hadn't expected she would be leaving, but the big reason was the money. Anyway, if the burglars would stay away, it shouldn't be too hard to lie low here. It was a large house, designed to impress with an expansive living room, den with floor-to-ceiling shelves filled with books, and a formal dining room with an oval oak table and sideboard and crystal chandelier. The kitchen was huge, too, with granite countertops, all-electric appliances, and a breakfast nook with wide windows looking onto a landscaped garden. The kitchen opened into the dark walnut-paneled family room with fireplace. Not too shabby for a summer place.

I walked into the den, which they probably called the library, picked a light mystery from the shelves and took it into the kitchen to read while I ate lunch. I happened to glance out the front window and saw Ann leave in her white BMW. That left all the houses on this side of the street empty except for where I was. Still, I didn't dare turn on a light, a television, or a radio for fear the security patrol would notice.

After lunch, I spent three hours at the next house. It hadn't been robbed, and I left it in white-glove shape before returning to the first house for the night. I'd clean the third house in the morning.

I tied a couple of small tin pans to the kitchen door and two large serving spoons to the front door as simple burglar alarms. All I needed was a minute or two to escape if any invaders showed up, but what I really wanted was to sleep without worry, something I hadn't done in a long, long time. I liked being totally alone but safe with the security guard on patrol a scream away.

I used the microwave to heat a bowl of soup for supper, then drifted off to sleep on the living room couch.

Chapter 30

The next morning I cleaned the third house, but after that job with nothing to do, I returned to the place I was staying, prepared to wait out a boringly quiet afternoon. I didn't want to use anything that might be an extra expense for the owners of the house or alert the security guard, so I didn't turn on the television or turn up the heat. The day was so warm I didn't miss the heater, and the house remained comfortable. I finished the mystery I was reading and found a stash of others in one of the upstairs bedrooms.

I settled down in the living room with a book. From there, I could see the street and watch for any cars. Only a few came along, interspersed occasionally with the security patrol. After awhile, I nosed around in the kitchen and found a deck of cards. Playing solitaire kept me amused for another hour.

The day dragged on. I was regretting this move and debating whether I should return to the marina and depend on Amos, Stu, and Cal for protection. Cal was a better bet than either Amos or Stu. I distrusted both of them—Amos for pigheadedness and Stu for unreliability and, I suspected, a mean streak meant to do me harm. Stu didn't like me, but why would he have any reason to hurt me? He didn't even know me. It made no sense. I dismissed the idea.

How long would I need to stay here before Hunter left for

Washington to hunt for me, or better yet, went home? He must have business to take care of back in New Jersey. I couldn't stay here more than a couple of days. I sank onto the couch. What would Hunter do next?

He'd probably drive into town, cozy up to the regulars, and pump them for information. I froze. Would he recognize me as Sierra, the name I used on my notices posted around town? Had I ever used that name with him? Mentioned it at all? I searched my memory. I told him once in our early days together how I'd wished my name was Sierra. Would he remember it? Would it lead him to this neighborhood? If he found me, how could I protect myself? There was no one here, and no one knew where I was except Cal.

Maybe this wasn't such a good idea after all. Maybe I should go to Richmond. Maybe I should have left with Ann.

I froze as I heard the clattering noise of the van's loose chrome strip. It couldn't be. I peered out the front window to see Hunter's black van cruise slowly past. How did he get through the security guard? He had no business here and knew nobody in the neighborhood. There was no way he could know I was here, so how did he get in?

He did have his laptop. He could easily track down the owners of the houses. In his business suit, driving his van, he could talk his way into Fort Knox and probably snowed the security guard with some bullshit about analyzing a house's market value or whatever. He'd get in.

I watched him pass and drive on toward the cul-de-sac. He'd be back, and then I hoped he'd leave. There was no clue anywhere outside I was hiding in the house. He was on a fishing expedition, and I was the fish.

I didn't breathe easier until he drove back and headed toward the gate to exit the development. He didn't find anything here. He couldn't have. He might hang on in town another day or so, but then he'd be gone.

That night, I found a couple of sheets and a pillow case in the linen closet and made up the bed in one of the upstairs bedrooms. I lay on the mattress, staring into the dark, unable to sleep. The illuminated numbers on the clock never seemed to move. How could I stand another day and night of this nothingness?

Despite restless tossing and turning, I must have slept because I was suddenly awakened by a noise downstairs. My heart stopped. Hunter? Did he figure out where I was hiding?

I crept out of bed, tiptoed to the bedroom door, and looked out. I heard a window slide open. A window. I'd booby-trapped the doors, but not the windows. Why use the windows when the doors would be so much easier?

The noise seemed to come from the kitchen. There was a window next to the back door. I heard laughter. They'd probably found my booby trap, a tip-off for them that someone was in the house. They wouldn't want to risk trouble, not with the security guard on the alert. I expected them to leave.

Even so, I shrank away from the bedroom door. Where could I hide in case they came in? I softly stepped aside to peer out the window overlooking the back yard and the dock. I could make out the outlines of a huge hulk resting at the dock and the moving shapes below on the path to the kitchen door. The moon was only half full, but as my eyes grew accustomed to the darkness, I could see the shapes were two men, their bodies and faces shadowed. Creeping behind them on the dock were three other men.

At least it wasn't Hunter. He would work alone. As I had this thought, a second one surfaced. Wouldn't the burglars stay away for awhile? Their thefts were reported, and extra patrols roamed the neighborhood. These guys were brash and overconfident, it seemed to me. They came by boat, as I suspected, which is how they escaped the security guard roaming the street.

I must get out before they came up the stairs. Where could I hide? What could I do? My eyes darted around the room and rested on the smoke alarm. All I had to do was alert the roaming security guard.

But then he'd search the house—and find me.

Anyway, I had no matches to trip the smoke alarm.

I opened the window, slowly and carefully, wincing at the squeaks it made. No screens, so I leaned out. All the men were inside the house now, and I had to get out. Then I looked down and saw that this window was over the flat roof that covered the stoop at the kitchen door.

I tiptoed to the bed and straightened the covers, throwing the extra sheet and blanket I'd used underneath. It looked slightly sloppy, but no one would suspect anyone had been sleeping on it. I didn't think I'd left any telltale signs downstairs either. I slipped out the window onto the small roof, crouching to close the window behind me. I huddled low against the wall in the darkness, hoping I'd look like a part of the house, so no one on the ground would spot me.

From this vantage point, I heard the men rummage through the house and then watched them stream in and out carrying the microwave, a laptop, television, and miscellaneous other electronics and goods down to the hulk at the dock. My eyes now accustomed to the darkness and with the help of the half moon, I recognized the hulk as a houseboat, probably the same one motoring up and down the river in front of the marina. I hadn't paid attention to the noise of the engine on the river, even as it approached the dock, nor had I heard the men below secure the boat there. They must have muffled the engine, but maybe I was used to the racket of the powerboats trying to make a speedway out of the river. The men tramped back and forth quietly, talking only in whispers punctuated by bursts of laughter.

I strained my eyes in the darkness to make out the features of the men as they carried their booty from the house to the boat and returned for more.

I recognized only one of them. Stu. A cigarette hung from his lips, the red glow at the tip reminding me of Rudolph.

Stu. Suddenly that white panel truck made sense. Of course. They had to have a truck to take things to their fence or whoever was buying the stolen goods. That person could be in Washington or Richmond or even Baltimore, all cities less than four hours away. Probably the police in Richmond had a unit calling around to the pawnshops there. Did they have any kind of reciprocal agreement with the police in Washington or Baltimore?

Another thought crawled through my mind. Was Amos involved in this? Both Amos and Stu together? Or had Stu found an additional way to supplement his income?

Chapter 31

I huddled on the tiny roof and mulled over the possibilities, watching Stu. As the moon emerged from behind a cloud, it shone full on my face. I found myself staring directly into Stu's eyes.

I hunkered down, knowing it was too late. Stu spotted me. I was trapped on this roof, but I might have a chance if I could get into the bedroom and dodge them when they came up the stairs after me. I knew it was a vain hope, but it was my only recourse. I'd break a leg if I tried to jump after they ran into the house. I crawled back through the window and ran for the master bedroom, barely closing the door behind me when I heard the pack running up the stairs.

My ear to the door, I listened as they slammed into the other bedroom, then I peeked out, found the hall clear, and ran downstairs. Behind me, the men cursed and crowded out of the bedroom.

"There she is," one shouted, galvanizing all of them to run after me. I raced for the front door, wrestled it open, and careened into Stu's open arms.

"Gotcha," he said as I fought to free myself. My arms were pinned to my sides, and his heavy work boots crunched my toes to the floor. Before I could devise any kind of defensive tactic, the other men surrounded us. I tried banging my head into his nose, but he turned his face away as he twisted my arm behind my back. I felt an excruciating pain.

"You're breaking my arm," I gasped.

Stu kept up the pressure. "Then behave," he said.

I nodded. Stu loosened his grip.

"She the owner of this place?" asked one of the other men. He wore a ball cap and seemed familiar. Then I remembered seeing him in the diner, chatting with Officer Henschel.

With Stu's reinforcements surrounding me, he stepped back. "Nah, she's hiding out." He snickered. "Hiding from her hubby."

"What are we going do with her?" asked another. "I don't want no trouble."

I watched Stu's eyes turn crafty. They knew I'd go to the police first thing, tell all I knew, and describe the lot of them. Could I talk them into letting me go? Probably not, and I didn't like the look in Stu's eyes. My clever dodge of Hunter landed me in the middle of a home invasion—avoiding one snake to fall into a nest of vipers.

"She's my boss's kid," said Stu. "Didn't know she existed until she came nosing around. Her and me's gonna have a little talk."

I saw him sizing up the situation and wondered what he planned. He'd let go of me and shoved me into the middle of the group. I looked for an opening to make a dash out of the house and into the woods. Could I trip any of them? Distract them? I stared through the living room window and focused on a spot outside the house.

This made the others nervous, and they turned to see what I was looking at. I broke through their ranks and ran for the door. They caught me as I fumbled with the knob. Anyway, it was locked, but through the window I saw the security patrol car coming down the road. About time. They must have been too far away to hear the shouts or had the radio on loud. I reached for the booby trap pans hanging from the knob and opened my mouth to scream.

"No, you don't," Stu said, clamping his hand over my mouth and pulling me away. "Get me a rag, somebody," he whispered. One of the men brought a dish towel from the kitchen. "Shove it in her mouth," Stu said. "And get me something to tie her up with."

My heart sank. There were too many of them to fight. Self-defense training or not. Now I couldn't even talk my way out of this fix. It probably wouldn't have worked anyway.

"We got to get out of here," whispered one of the men. Another one brought in a length of clothes line. "Don't reckon they need this here," he said and chuckled. "They got a dryer."

"All right. You all stay here while I tie this little lady up," said Stu, winding the clothesline around my wrists. "Then you skedaddle with the boat. Go down the river a ways, out of this development, and I'll run along the shore to meet you. Wait for me."

He tied an efficient square knot. Then he wound the rope around my ankles, again tying it off with a knot. He looked up at the men and nodded. "Go," he said. "This little lady and me, we're gonna have ourselves a little talk." He laughed. "Only I'm gonna do the talking."

"I don't want no part of this," said one of the men. "Robbing is one thing. Don't mind taking stuff off rich people. You be careful what you do." He hesitated, then turned and followed the others out the back door. He stopped and looked back at Stu.

"We're outa here, and we don't know nothin' about this lady."

I watched them leave, not bothering to try to wriggle out of my bonds with Stu watching. What would he do now? I turned my head to stare at him, putting all my contempt into my eyes.

Stu sat on the arm of a chair. "Not so smart now, are you, miss?" He stood and poked the toe of his boot at my knee. "Now what am I going to do with you?" He snickered again. I hated the sound, but I heard more than anger or bullying in his tone. Resentment was there as well. Resentment? At me? Why?

Stu wandered aimlessly around the room. "You're one interfering little bitch," he muttered. "You got no call to come to your dad's business, messing up what I've been working for. His marina gonna be mine when Amos goes. I got plans."

He brought his face down close to mine. "And you know the first thing I'm gonna do?" He took the cigarette out of his mouth and waved it in front of me. "I'm kicking the old coffee can, butts and all, into the river."

I turned my face away from the glowing ember. I couldn't believe what I was hearing. Stu thought he would get the marina when my dad died. Maybe there was a will made up or promise made. When I came to the marina, like some kind of prodigal kid, I became a rival contender for the property. Amos had a lot of years left. He could remarry or sell it. I couldn't imagine he'd leave it to me in any case.

Stu waved his fist in front of my nose. "Mine, you hear? And sooner rather than later." Then he repeated, "I got plans."

Did I hear him right? Sooner rather than later? It sounded like his plans included getting rid of Amos. Murder? Stu was the one who'd sawn through the boat buttress. Probably sent the threatening letter. Running me down on the road was no accident.

Stu sat in an armchair and stared at me with lips pulsing in and out. His legs were splayed and his hands rested on his thighs. "Let's see," he mumbled, "what am I going to do with you?"

Oh, brother! All this time, I had blindly accepted the situation at the marina at face value. My dad owned it. Period. I never considered that I was the only legitimate heir, which meant I could inherit the marina unless Amos made other provisions. Or that Stu, thinking there were no close relatives, thought he had a good chance of owning it if he could work Amos around to the idea.

I shook my head. I had enough problems dodging Hunter, and now I faced this new wrinkle. I looked up at Stu to see a calculating glance appear as he watched me. If I stood in the way of his inheriting the marina, then he would think he needed to get rid of me. It's what he was working out now. How was he going to get rid of me? I didn't expect he'd be subtle, hatching some plot to discredit me to my dad but leave me alive. No, Stu would do the uncomplicated thing.

I felt chilled, and my body trembled. I tried to hide my fear, but I was vulnerable enough. I thought of my dad. If Stu got rid of me, he'd soon do the same to Amos once he'd wangled the marina out of him. I needed somehow to get out of this and away from Stu to protect Amos. I glared at the handyman-thief, unable to speak because of the towel they'd stuffed in my mouth. It desiccated my mouth and tongue. I longed to pull it out and would have begged if I'd been able to.

I watched him chew on his knuckle as he stared at me, obviously trying too hard to imagine what to do. Maybe it was beyond his brain capacity. Maybe he'd give up the idea and just leave. I watched him, hope buried deep in my heart as the rational part of myself thought it unlikely.

Finally, Stu seemed to come to a decision. "Got it, little lady. Keep my hands clean, too."

He walked to me and leaned down. "I'll just hide you and leave it up to fate." He laughed. "The owners won't be back for three or four weeks, but I'll come back sooner than that and take care of. . ." He glanced down at me. ". . .the remains. Course maybe you'll get free. You got a chance this way." He twisted his mouth. "Maybe."

I focused all my energy into a glare as I leaned away from him.

He snapped his fingers. "I got a better idea. Yes, sir. I don't have to do the dirty work. I'll just be helping a young couple get back together."

I froze. What did he mean?

"Your hubby would sure like to see you again," Stu said. "Maybe I'll help him."

I flinched. He grabbed my hands and dragged me to the closet, pushing me in among the outdoor boots and vacuum cleaner. I sneezed, gagging on the towel stuffed in my mouth. I felt a panic attack coming on. I must not panic. I breathed slowly through my nose, willing myself to stay calm. I was not going to let that rat-faced bastard win.

Stu smirked at me as he closed the closet door. I heard his boots pound the floor, the sound diminishing as he walked away. Straining my ears, I heard the back door close softly. Did he really leave? I waited.

I couldn't see my watch. I could only estimate the time passing. When I figured I'd heard nothing in half an hour, I tested the rope, trying to stretch it at my wrists. If only he'd made the mistake of tying a granny knot, but he was too much of a sailor for that. My wrists were tied together behind my back, so I couldn't bite and chew at the knot. Stu tied my ankles together and pulled the end of the clothesline and my ankles up to bring them close to my wrists, forcing me into a huddled position.

The ropes allowed a little play in them, so maybe I could keep working them looser and looser. If I could get out of the closet, maybe I could crawl to the front door, open it, and fall out where someone in the security patrol, would see me.

I looked up at the closet doorknob. It seemed so high. If I could manage a kneeling position from the way I was tied, then maybe I could use my head to turn the knob. Maybe.

I wriggled around to adjust my body. The towel in my mouth was choking me. If only I could get it out. I pushed it with my tongue. That wasn't too hard, since the towel wasn't taped or bound across my mouth. I only had to work it awhile to push it out, although my mouth was so dry the towel stuck to my tongue and the roof of my mouth. Eventually, I worked the towel out and was able to moisten my mouth with saliva.

Now I could yell if only someone would come to the door. Little hope of that. I needed to get out of the closet. I twisted my body in the tiny space hemmed in by vacuum cleaner and boots, trying to adjust myself to an upright position on my knees.

After a long, painful struggle, I managed it. I rested my head on the door. If I stretched my body, my head could reach the doorknob. After several failed attempts, I was able to push my forehead against the knob and attempt to twist it. Again and again, I stretched myself up to twist the knob, but each time, my forehead slipped off, and I fell backwards in frustration. My legs ached. I couldn't bear the pain. The closet was stuffy and hot.

But I couldn't rest. Stu or those men might be back any time. Stu might have already told Hunter. Whoever came back to check on me, they mustn't find me here, trussed up like a pot roast ready to be cooked.

Groaning, I raised myself again. This time, my forehead, beady with sweat, stuck to the doorknob and turned it. Not enough to open the door, but enough to give me hope. I tried again, pressing harder this time, and the knob turned. The door opened, and I fell out of the closet.

I lay on the floor, eyes closed, panting as I savored the fresh cool air. I'd hit my shoulder and arm as I tumbled free, but what a relief to be out of the closet. I opened my eyes and worked my hands, twisting my wrists. There was a little more give in the rope. What else was possible? I scanned the room. What might help?

If I could make it to the kitchen, which seemed miles away, I could open a drawer with my mouth and maybe get a knife. I glanced at the front door. Or should I try to open the front door the way I got out of the closet? I eyed the door for a minute but shook my head. Probably locked, and that I couldn't fix with a sweaty forehead. Whatever, I couldn't afford the time to make a mistake.

I tried moving toward the kitchen like a caterpillar, scrunching my body and then releasing it in a forward creep. I could manage only a foot or so at a time before I needed to rest and readjust my body.

The night brightened into day. The kitchen seemed miles away. I forced myself to quell the fear of Stu returning and finding me. Or worse, Hunter breaking in. I used the panic to keep me moving.

It was full daylight, and the sun streamed into the window when I arrived at the kitchen drawers. Which one might hold knives? I painfully raised myself on my knees, picked a drawer at random, swallowed the drawer pull in my mouth and drew back. The effort toppled me to the floor, but the drawer was open. I raised myself up as high as I could to look into it. I sighed with relief. It did contain sharp knives. If only I could reach in, but my hands were still tied behind me. I couldn't raise myself high enough to retrieve one of the knives with my mouth and sank back down.

I would have to pull the drawer onto the floor. I hesitated because of the noise it would create, but it was foolish to worry about the clatter. The burglars were nowhere close, and if the noise attracted a security guard, then good.

I struggled up again, took the knob with my teeth and pulled the drawer out and onto the floor. It crashed and spilled out knives and flatware. I lay down and rested. The next challenge would be to grasp a knife and saw at the clothesline.

I waited a moment, gaining strength, and then felt around the floor with my fingers until they located a steak knife. It was awkward to hold, but I found the rope securing my ankles to my wrists and sawed it apart in less than a minute.

It took more grappling and positioning to use the knife to cut one of the lines around my wrists. This loosened the rope, and I slid my hands out of it. In another minute, I was free of all the ropes and stretching my legs and arms.

I was exhausted from the effort and the fear. Now I must get out of this house.

Chapter 32

I picked up the knives and flatware, replaced the drawer, and delved into my bag of groceries, pulling out a banana. It would have to be good enough. I was hungry and bone tired after a night of no sleep, and I desperately needed to get out of here. Stu might be back. Stu's buddies might have second thoughts about leaving me here, and Hunter might come sniffing around.

Stu was ready to commit murder. He knew I'd run to the police the first chance I got, and then Stu's gang of house robbers would be out of business. The hitch for him was his fellow robbers wanted no part of murder.

Would Stu try to sidestep murder himself by alerting Hunter to my whereabouts and letting Hunter take care of me? That would eliminate Stu's problem, but it was risky unless Stu was aware of some reason to think Hunter was as eager as Stu to get rid of me. He knew I hated Hunter and hid from him, but did he think it was a simple domestic argument? How much did Stu know about Hunter as a criminal?

What was Hunter doing now? Did he swallow the story I planted about going to Washington, or was he scouting for my hiding place? He might come to the conclusion I did about how these empty houses would be fine as a hideout. I'd seen him drive through the neighborhood, but he couldn't know I was here. He was just guessing.

I looked out the back door. There was no boat traffic on the river. Stu and his buddies were long gone. They would think they had plenty of time to take care of me. I didn't trust any of them to save me. None of them would risk his own life to claim any knowledge or show any remorse about what Stu did to me, so no one would come back and free me. All of them knew I'd blab to the police.

Stu wasn't a bright dollar. He'd only hinted at telling Hunter about me. Maybe Stu wouldn't speak to Hunter, if he did at all, until much later when he'd had time to consider such a plan. The security guard wouldn't let any of Stu's scruffy crew in by the road unless they came up with a good reason, and the houseboat would be too conspicuous at the dock in the daytime. The guard would ask questions, find out who they were, tell them to leave.

I needed to get out of here, but I didn't want to go back to my boat until Hunter was gone. I could stay with Cal, but I'd have to stay hidden in his apartment. For how long? It would be awkward and stifling. Not an appealing idea. I'd missed the chance to go to Richmond with Ann. Could I ask Cal to drive me there?

I could hide in a different house and wait for Ann to return, but I didn't really know her well. Could I trust her to protect me? Would she be willing to drive me away from here? Maybe not, but I might call the police, which would be okay but not ideal. Stu and his buddies would be arrested, but Hunter would still be loose.

As I mulled the possibilities, the realization of how narrowly I escaped death floated like a dark cloud over my spirits. I rubbed the rope burns on my wrists and ankles. I couldn't rest yet. I needed to get out of here. I heard a runabout on the river. Glancing out the window, I saw Amos' boat. Peering hard, I recognized

Hunter at the wheel. He was scanning the shoreline and examining each house he passed. I stepped back from the window, chilled to the bone. He was out there now looking for me. I should have gone to Richmond with Ann.

Hunter couldn't know I was here unless Stu told him. Then he'd know I was in one of the houses. He might even know which one. I watched Hunter steer the boat past my hiding place and around a curve. Hunter didn't know I was here, but he was searching likely places, looking for some sign to tell him where I was.

I entered Cal's number on my cell phone. No response. I tried again, leaving a message this time. Cal was probably at the diner for breakfast.

A glance at the clock showed it was almost nine. I worked all night to get out of the closet and cut off the clothesline. I stood at the back door watching for Hunter to pass by on his return to the marina. When he did, I'd run to the woods and keep trying to reach Cal. I heard a noise in the living room. My stomach dropped.

Oh, no. Did Hunter have enough time to beach the boat and get here? I glanced at my watch. If it was a security guard, how would I explain my presence? I ought to be able to get away with no one knowing I'd spent the night in this house. Opening the back door with the pots and pans hanging from it would give me away. The window would make noise if I opened it. What if it was the owner? Hunter couldn't already know I was here.

I stepped into the pantry, silently closed the pantry door, and stood against the back shelves in the darkness, hoping whoever it was would go away. But then I heard the floorboards creak and soft footsteps. They came into the kitchen and stopped.

I cringed as far into the recesses of the pantry as I could.

The door opened. "Come out, come out, wherever you are. . ." sang a taunting voice. Hunter stood, a menacing silhouette against the lighted kitchen. "Now what have we here?"

He held the door open wide and pointed a gun at me. "Out," he said, smiling as he always did and gesturing with the weapon. "Now."

I emerged from my obviously poor hiding place, seeing no other choice. I eyed the gun as I passed, but trying to hit it out of his hand would be foolhardy. I'd have to play along. "How'd you know?" I asked.

Hunter laughed. "Pays to have friends like Stu. Plus a window was left open upstairs. Every other house was shut tight. I got in and saw those." He waved the barrel at the ropes still on the floor.

I hadn't taken care of that one little detail. "How'd you get in?"

"Easy. The front door was unlocked."

I closed my eyes in disgust with myself. Stu didn't bother to lock it. I hadn't paid any attention to details like that while I was being tied up and gagged.

Hunter saw my chagrin and laughed again. "The pans made a cute little burglar alarm, but I opened the door slow and careful—wasn't sure what I'd find—and there your little booby trap was." Hunter grinned at me. "Being a considerate chap, I didn't want to wake the neighbors, so I took the pans down and laid them aside." He waved the gun. "Quiet as a mouse."

"Stu told you."

That rat. He probably told Hunter everything I did. Maybe Hunter paid him him for information all along, and now Dad's crooked employee found someone to do his dirty work. I suffered no illusions about what Stu and Hunter both wanted.

Hunter grinned. "Stu and me, we have an agreement when it comes to you, my sweetheart. But I don't think Stu is as bright as he thinks he is. I didn't trust his story about tying you up and leaving you in the closet. Seems I was right."

"What are you going to do?" I asked, feeling my wrists hurt. I kept my eyes on them to avoid looking at Hunter's insane smile. "If I disappear, the papers I took go straight to the FBI."

"Maybe so," he drawled, "maybe not. We're going to take a little ride down the river. You should like it," he said with a cruel twist, "seeing as how you like boats so much."

I didn't respond. What was he planning? I told myself I was a survivor, and I'd get out of this. Meanwhile, I looked for any way to escape. I'd have to delay, delay, delay. Maybe a security guard would notice us. Maybe Cal would come by.

"Come on. Let's go," said Hunter, grabbing my arm with one hand, keeping the gun handy in the other. He pulled me into the living room and stopped.

"Wait a minute." He stood still, turning the muzzle on me as his eyes darted around the room. "Your purse." He said. "We're going to need it." He dragged me into the living room. I saw my purse, available to the world, on the coffee table. Hunter picked it up. "Now we're ready."

He pushed me through the living room and kitchen to the rear door, peered out the window in the top half, quietly opened the door, and dragged me out.

"I'm aiming this gun at you, so don't try anything," he said. "Go on down to the boat."

"Where are you taking me?" I asked. What was he planning? Would he try to drown me? "You know I can't swim." It was a lie, but I'd be thrilled to have him throw me overboard.

Hunter snorted. "And birds can't fly."

We made our way to the water, and Hunter pulled me over to the bushes at the side of the yard where he'd hidden the boat. That's why I failed to see him come back. "Pull the boat closer and step into it," ordered Hunter. "At the back. You're gonna drive."

I complied, looking for a chance to knock him overboard. Hunter didn't know boats, and I did, but Hunter kept his distance. I watched him step in, awkward and clumsy. He'd never grown up around boats. Could I use that to my advantage?

"All right. Start the motor and get us moving downriver toward your dad's place." Hunter settled back in his seat. "Remember, I got a gun on you."

Hope leaped into my mind. Could we be going to the marina? Just as quickly, the hope died. He wouldn't risk going there. He must have some other plan. I maneuvered us along the shoreline. He was facing me. Maybe I could steer us under a low branch and hit his head or distract him.

He turned in his seat to watch both me and the water ahead. He motioned with the gun. "Get away from the shore."

I steered toward the middle of the river. "You kill me, and a lot of people will be hunting for you," I reminded him again. "Two people you don't know have letters with instructions on what to do if I disappear or am found dead."

"Maybe so." He laughed. "Or you could simply disappear. Maybe I'll have an alibi. One way or another, I don't care."

I shrugged off his words. He was trying to appear unconcerned about the papers I held, but he was here, wasn't he? Threatening me. He was worried, all right.

What was he planning to do? "Are we going back to the marina?"

"You wish. You'll see." He lolled in his seat. "Meanwhile, I'll take it easy, and let you do all the work."

"Okay," I said, my mind furiously seeking some escape. I didn't dare jump overboard or try any fancy maneuvers with that gun aimed at me. Maybe someone on shore would see him menacing me with a weapon and call the police. I stared at the houses as we passed. Most of them empty. No one was watching us.

As we reached the bend near the marina, Hunter waved the gun at me. "Pull over to the shore here."

I looked where he pointed and saw Hunter's van. My spirits drooped. We weren't going back to Dad's place at all. He was going to drive me somewhere else. This was bad. Worse than I'd thought.

I steered the runabout to shore and beached it.

"Out," said Hunter. He followed me onto land.

The van was parked off the road and hidden behind some bushes. No one passing on the road would notice the black vehicle or either of us.

He waved the gun toward the back of the van. "Over here."

I couldn't see any way out. I complied. I walked to the van's rear doors. Was he going to tie me and hide me in the back?

Hunter opened the rear doors, and I saw a roll of heavy duty tape. My heart sank even lower. Duct tape.

"Put your hands behind your back," Hunter ordered. He proceeded to secure my wrists together, then my ankles, and final indignity, he slapped a length of tape over my mouth. He pulled out a burlap bag and covered my head and upper body, drawing

Eileen Haavik McIntire

the string tight to close the bag at my ankles.

"That ought to hold you." He chuckled, then he lifted me and dropped me into the van like he'd plunked me on the floor when he first carried me over the threshold of his house. I felt the bruises, but nothing was broken.

"See you later," he said.

Chapter 33

It didn't seem fair, I thought, after the struggle to get free in the house. Now I was duct-taped and bagged like a sack of potatoes and thrown into the back of the van. Caught and bound by two different people in one day. I was never so popular in high school. I couldn't even laugh at my own joke, but the irony of the situation helped me control the panic.

It took Stu and five of his buddies to capture and tie me last time. Now I was only up against Hunter. And his gun. I knew some self-defense tactics. Norma and Cal had those letters. I'd escaped from one impossible situation. It gave me confidence I could escape this one.

The burlap bag was dark and smelly as if it once held rotten onions, but loosely woven so I could breathe, and I could see through the fibers with a little effort. I twisted my head to look for any way to push a tail light out. Sometimes trunks had mechanisms to open the lid if someone were trapped inside. Or so I'd heard. Did vans have something similar? Hunter outdid himself with the bag. The damn bag. I doubted I could wriggle my body around in this confined space to take advantage of any way to get free of the bag and signal for help.

I decided to close my eyes, rest, and go over in my mind the self-defense strategies I'd learned from that first introductory lesson. I reminded myself how I was a survivor. I would find a way out of this predicament. Meanwhile, I wondered where Hunter was taking me. I listened for tell-tale sounds or bumps. In the movies, the victim heard clocks striking or trains whistling. So far, I hadn't heard much except traffic on a smooth road. I felt we were going fast, so maybe a cop would stop him. Then I could bang on the van floor with my feet to draw his attention. Even if the car stopped at a light, I could do that. I hoped for stops.

The car sped along—Hunter seemed to be going very fast, which buoyed my hopes. The police were always looking for speeders in these small towns. I wriggled around, but no position was comfortable or improved my situation for defense. I couldn't get my hands placed so I could read my watch. I lost track of time. I felt overcome with drowsiness and then panicked as I realized the drowsiness could be from carbon monoxide fumes. I could do nothing about it. I tried taking deep breaths through my nose to calm myself, but the danger of choking on the dust and suffocating made me stop. I was helpless. If I were to survive, I needed to be rested and prepared. And I would survive. Hunter was a crook and therefore not very bright. Whether that bit of logic worked or not, I was pretty intelligent, and I could outsmart him.

Sometime later, I felt the road change and become bumpy. So we were off the highway now. It wasn't a driveway, though, because we took a long time twisting and turning and bumping along a dirt or gravel road. Finally, the car came to a stop. I heard the front door open and Hunter get out. He slammed it shut. He was whistling. Fear raced through my body as I turned my face in the direction of the van's rear doors.

But he didn't open it for ages. I heard his footsteps on dirt and leaves and then fade away until a door to a building opened.

Checking out the situation, I supposed. Where were we? I couldn't hear any sounds of cars or people. We must be somewhere in the remote countryside. I was alone. Hunter had made sure there would be no rescue.

Eventually, I heard him come around to the rear of the van and open the doors. He pulled me out and stood me on my feet, still encased in the sack. I felt pins and needles in my legs. He untied the string on the bag and pulled it off over my head. He stared at me grimly for a moment. I glanced at my surroundings. We were parked in front of a cabin in the woods. A dirt road wound back through the trees, but formed a dead end at the cabin. There would be no through traffic here.

"Move," said Hunter, prodding me on the back. He held my purse in his other hand.

He forced me to hop to the door and pushed me in. I fell to the floor, biting back the tears as my elbow hit a wooden chair. I lay there, eyes closed, moving my fingers and feet to make sure nothing was broken. I refused to open my eyes to see Hunter's triumphant grin.

"Not so high and mighty now, are you?" he said. "You're right where I want you. If you'd been a decent wife, none of this would have happened. Now I've got to deal with you." He stared down at me, fists closed as if he wanted to hit me but still, as always, smiling. "Remember this. You deserve what you're going to get."

He wandered into the kitchen. While he rummaged through the cabinets, I surveyed my surroundings. The cabin was rustic with rough wooden floors, no carpet, and wood walls once painted white. A burgundy sofa, overstuffed plaid armchair, and wooden rocking chair furnished the living area. Stairs went up one side to what were probably bedrooms upstairs. I supposed it was some kind of vacation cabin Hunter rented.

When he came back, he had a bottle of Jim Beam and a small glass. He sat in the armchair, legs splayed, and poured the whiskey into the glass. He took a long swig as he sat back and eyed me. "You and me," he said, "we got a problem in our relationship." He pointed at me with the glass. "And we're going to work it out right here."

What a jerk, I thought.

Hunter took another long swig. He picked up my purse and rummaged through it to find my wallet. He saw me staring at him and winked. Rats. Ann had just paid me. He found the cash and pulled it out. "Pay day," he said, waving the money at me. He stuffed it back in the purse. "I'll get this later."

He riffled through my credit and other cards until he found my New York driver's license. "Bingo." He pulled it out and put it in his pocket, then he leaned over to rip the tape off my mouth. Again, I stifled the tears.

"Don't think you can yell and get help," he said. "We're miles from anywhere." He seized a hank of my hair and pulled my head up. "Where are the papers?" he said.

"What papers?" I asked, knowing he'd hit me.

He slapped me hard across the face. "Where are the papers?"

I squeezed my eyes shut. *I'm used to this from him. He can't hurt me anymore than he already has.* I stared down at the floor, trying to think of some way to buy time. Maybe I could faint. I dismissed that idea. It would give Hunter license to slap me even more. I was helpless. He could torture me any way he wished.

I glanced around the room for anything that might help. I must not buy into the helplessness of my situation. I was a survivor, and I would survive. But how?

I saw nothing in the room to help me, but as my mind focused on escape, I realized I needed to convince Hunter to go away. I could do nothing with him two feet away, staring at me. I waited for him to hit me again. It didn't take long.

"I can hit you all night," he said. "In fact, it's punishment you deserve." This time he gave my hair an extra yank while he slapped my face one way and the other.

Reeling from the pain, holding back the tears, I moaned aloud. He wanted weak. I'd give him weak. "Don't hit me again," I cried. "Please don't hit me again."

"Tell me where those papers are." The cold menace in his tone chilled me.

"All right," I gasped. "All right." I panted for breath and leaned away from him as if in abject fear. I was afraid. Terrified. But I gathered my wits about me. "In my purse." I stopped as if in too much pain to continue.

Hunter glanced at the bag on the floor beside me. Then he picked it up and opened it. "Here's your purse," he said contemptuously. "No papers I can see."

"The key," I said. "Bank. Safety deposit box. The papers are in there."

I watched him as he shook the purse out over the table. Some change, a comb, and a small stainless steel key fell out. He seized it. "This one?"

I nodded. Actually, the key opened the steel fireproof safe I kept stowed under the bunk in my boat.

"Where's the bank?"

I pretended to have trouble with a dry mouth as I thought what to tell him. I could say it was in New Jersey near his house.

That would send him up there, but what would he do with me in the meantime? If I said it was at the bank in town near the marina, would the lie buy me time while allowing him to check it and think he could come back if it didn't work? I decided on the latter option. I wanted him to leave, but I also needed him to be unsure enough to think he might have to come back and torture me some more. I wanted him to leave me here alone and alive.

I swallowed. "The bank in town. Citizens Bank on Main Street." I closed my eyes as if I were too exhausted to say more. I didn't tell him anything else about the letters to be opened on my death. They should remain my insurance to be used only when necessary. If he thought about them, he'd stay and torture me to find out who had them. I'd put Cal and Norma in danger.

Hunter looked from the key to me and back again. I could imagine his brain clicking. He had the key, but he couldn't open the box without me. Would he risk freeing me to go with him to retrieve the papers? I waited. He told people he was a lawyer. Let him pull something out of his "legal" bag of tricks.

He went out to his car and returned with his briefcase, opened it, shuffled through the papers, and pulled out one. I read the title at the top. "Power of Attorney." Could he force me to sign the paper, and use it to get to the box? But it had to be notarized, didn't it? He'd have to take me to a notary. In that case, why not simply take me to the bank?

"I'm going to release your hands, so you can sign this paper," he said.

I decided to act as if traumatized by shock and not ask questions. I did as he asked, still wondering how he was going to make that nonnotarized piece of paper work. How secure was a notarized signature? How easy was it to get? Being a lawyer, he probably was a notary himself. Being a crook, he probably had all the answers. Would the bank accept such a statement?

I still acted shocked as he rewound the tape around my wrists.

He put the paper in his briefcase, brandishing my driver's license in front of me before throwing it into the briefcase, too. He bent over me to check my bonds, then went out to his van. He came back with the roll of duct tape and placed another strip across my mouth and wound some more around my wrists and ankles.

He stood, hands on hips, and appraised the situation with a smile. "That ought to hold you," he said, nodding. He saluted me as he opened the door and stepped out. "I'll be back," he said. "Don't think anyone's going to rescue you. They aren't. You'll still be right here when I come back." His smile bared teeth that looked wolf-like to me as I lay on the floor.

"If I get the papers, maybe I won't come back," he added, prodding me with his toe. "You'd like that, wouldn't you?" He snickered.

I heard him lock the cabin door on the outside. A minute later, he started the motor, and I heard the familiar clatter as the van bounced down the dirt road. I was glad to hear the clattering fade as Hunter drove away.

I took a deep breath through my nose. Now to get to work. *I will survive. I will survive.* I repeated this mantra to myself. I had already been twisting my wrists behind my back, weakening and stretching the bond, but not enough, and it still held. He hadn't secured me to any furniture, so I could wriggle my way across the floor. If I didn't hurt so much, I'd laugh. The situation was ludicrous. Captured and trussed twice by different people in twenty-four hours. How did I get to be so important?

I didn't have time to spare. I needed to free myself quickly, get out, and find help even though I didn't know where I was.

The cabin didn't have a fireplace, but an unlit pellet stove stood in the corner. I couldn't see anything there that would help. In fact, nothing in the sparse living room looked usable for my purpose.

I wriggled toward the kitchen and remembered the home economics classes I so disdained in high school. The problem was they didn't teach you anything really useful like getting out of rope or duct tape bonds. With my mouth taped shut, I couldn't push myself up and grab a drawer pull with my teeth to open it as I'd done before. What then?

I needed something to rip the binding on my wrists. What? I noticed a loose piece of quarter-round trim at the base of the wall. Those were secured by nails, weren't they? I wriggled to the slack section and bounced around to back up to it, so I could pull it away from the wall with my hands to expose a nail. I punctured the tape with the nail again and again around my wrists as I worked them back and forth.

It didn't take long to rip the tape apart and free my wrists. I carefully pulled the piece off my mouth. That hurt. I ached all over. I reached up to the kitchen drawers, opening them one after another until I found one with a knife. I picked it up and slashed at the tape around my ankles.

In a moment, I was free. I stumbled into the living room and sat in the armchair for a few minutes to quiet my nerves. I wasn't worried about the locked door. Once I calmed myself, I went back to the kitchen, pulled a heavy pot out of a cabinet, and broke the kitchen window.

I retrieved my purse and wallet and climbed out of the window, then took stock of my surroundings. The cabin sat on the edge of a meadow, but in the distance I could see low mountains. I was probably in western Virginia or West Virginia. I could see no signs of habitation that way, and the dirt road ended at the cabin. I began walking, listening for cars, especially the van's clattering chrome strip. I heard nothing but bird songs and insect buzzing. The spring growth on each side of the lane would be easy to hide behind if I did hear a car. I checked my watch. Three p.m. I should have several hours of daylight left and probably all night until noon tomorrow before Hunter returned.

Chapter 34

I kept walking. The rutted dirt road ended at a two-lane paved highway after a mile or so. By this time it was late afternoon. The sun was going down in the sky to my left, so I turned right, hoping to be going east and a more likely direction toward civilization. The woods on both sides of the asphalt were so dense I couldn't get a sense of the terrain except it was hilly. Hunter drove west from the marina toward the mountains rather than stay in the flatter tidewater country, but did he go as far as West Virginia?

I felt hot and dirty and tired, but I was free. I wanted to remain that way. Once I heard a car and hid behind thick roadside bushes. It was a red pickup driven by a man in a ball cap with a shotgun hanging on a rack inside the rear window.

I kept walking, hoping to reach a house where I might find help, but I wasn't about to follow some other long dirt drive to another abandoned cabin. When I heard another car coming, I hid again in the brush, peering through leafy branches at the car and driver. A young couple this time, both wearing cowboy hats, but Hunter could have called for help and brought in buddies. How did he know about the cabin in the woods? I couldn't afford to risk hitchhiking, but until Hunter came back—and I knew he hadn't so far—I was safe and free.

My feet were killing me. Thank goodness I was wearing running shoes, but my socks were damp, and I could feel them forming blisters on my heels. I wanted a long hot shower and a good meal. I forced myself to trudge forward, step by step, and eventually I came to a small development of modest white frame houses. I could see cars parked in front and lights on inside. Scanning the set-up, I decided that the chance of Hunter knowing any of these people was infinitesimal. I picked a house on a back street, smoothed my hair, brushed off and straightened my clothes, and resolutely stepped forward to knock on the front door.

I heard steps inside approaching. The door opened, and a woman wearing an apron peered out at me. "Yes?"

Suddenly I was tongue-tied. I hadn't thought about what kind of story to tell. What would she buy? "I'm sorry to bother you," I stammered, "but, uh, my car battery is dead, and I need to get to a town where I can find a motel for the night."

"Your battery is dead? My husband can go with you and jump it." She turned as if to get him.

I reached out to restrain her. "Oh, no. I don't want that," I pleaded. "I just need to use your phone, or maybe you could call me a cab. Would a cab come out here?"

The woman's glance gave me the once-over, pursing her lips. I could see she was trying to place me. She must have decided I was escaping a bad date or boyfriend and didn't have any money because she nodded. "A taxi from town would be too expensive."

I looked down at my dirty T-shirt and jeans. "I fell a couple of times walking so far on the side of the road," I said. I decided to play into her scenario. "My boyfriend and I drove out this way for a picnic. . . " I mustered up a few tears. "I didn't think he'd try anything, but he did, and he's got my car. Now I need to go home. Please, I need to find a motel for tonight. My parents can come for me tomorrow."

The woman's glance softened. "All right then. Come on into the kitchen with me. Rest a bit. My name's Edna. What's yours?"

Panic struck me. I couldn't give them my real name. Hunter would be looking for me. "Uh, my name is Anna, Anna Mitchell, and I'm from, uh, Richmond."

"Your parents live in Richmond? Quite a drive."

I nodded. "It's getting dark, and they don't like to drive at night. Tomorrow will be fine for them to pick me up."

"I can understand," Edna said, leading me into the kitchen. "Grab yourself a seat and rest yourself. You look frazzled." I gratefully sank into a hard kitchen chair. It felt wonderful. My story was full of holes, but she bought it. Or said she did. A kind woman.

Edna took a pitcher out of the refrigerator and poured me a glass. "Here's some iced tea. Relax. I'll have supper ready in a few minutes."

I looked around at the homey kitchen with red and white curtains in the window over the sink, the aroma of roast chicken coming from the oven, something bubbling in a pot on the stove. I was starving and it all smelled so delicious. When I was small, and my mother still lived with us, our house smelled like this sometimes.

"I walked a really long way, Edna. I got lost. I'll get it all sorted out in the morning."

"You must be hungry. You can join us for supper, and then Sam will take you into Martinsburg."

"Oh. Thank you." Martinsburg? Where was Martinsburg? I didn't dare ask.

Two hours later, I profusely thanked this helpful couple as they dropped me off at a Holiday Inn in Martinsburg, which I learned from the road signs was in West Virginia. It was off Interstate 81, wherever that was, and there were other motels and restaurants, so I stood at the door of the Holiday Inn, waved goodbye, and once they were out of sight, I walked to a different motel three blocks away.

Edna and her husband Sam were a pleasant couple and generous to me, but they would talk and innocently tell Hunter if he fabricated some story about his missing wife. It was safer to stay in a different motel and leave in the morning. Thank goodness he had not stolen my credit cards or even my cash, only my driver's license, which was bad enough, since I couldn't rent a car.

Why didn't he take my credit cards and cash? He was a criminal. He could make my credit cards work for him. Such tricks were his business. The answer came to me. Of course. He didn't take them because he'd be back. Then he'd take care of all the details, and he'd probably destroy the cards and driver's license, leaving no connections to him in case my body was found.

I registered under my own name because the motel night clerk required identification but accepted my credit card as ID, especially when I paid cash. I signed the registration card, then asked the young African-American man for a map of Martinsburg. He produced one from under the counter. "Anything else, miss?"

I pondered how to get back to the marina. What was available in Martinsburg if you couldn't rent a car?

"Is there a bus service through here? My car is in the shop." I suddenly realized I was listening to a train whistle. A train.

He pursed his lips. "We have public transportation, ma'am. Be glad to call you a cab, though." He reached again under the desk. "We have AMTRAK and the MARC commuter train. They leave from the downtown station. The MARC train goes into Union Station in D.C. Here's the schedule." He handed me a brochure. "We also have a shuttle to take you over there."

"Thanks." I turned away with glee. Trains. I could get a train out of Martinsburg to Washington, and from there I could go anywhere, like maybe Richmond. I ought to be able to find a ride from Richmond to the northern neck of Virginia and the marina. Maybe Cal could pick me up. He said he made trips to Richmond. Meanwhile, I was extremely tired.

I picked up a Coke and potato chips at the motel vending machines and took them to my room for a snack. I felt exhausted but was too wired to go to bed. I knew that even as tired as I was, I'd have a hard time sleeping, and one thing was gnawing at me. I needed to take care of it before I'd be able to sleep. I'd seen a computer in the lobby designated for motel guests. I walked down and accessed it.

I logged onto the Internet and typed in "New York Driver's License, Lost or Stolen."

I filled out the form to report a stolen driver's license to the police and requested a replacement.

Let Hunter deal with that.

Chapter 35

The next morning, I woke early—rested, optimistic, and pleased with myself. I was held captive twice and escaped each time through my own ingenuity and efforts. I didn't even need to use my self-defense tactics—not that I knew much yet. I scarfed up the complimentary breakfast in the lobby and sipped a cup of tea. I studied the MARC rail schedule, noting the times the commuter train departed for Washington. In D.C., I could catch a train to Richmond. I'd worry about how to get from Richmond to the marina later.

The next train left Martinsburg at eight. The clock behind the counter said seven-fifteen. I took my cup of tea to the reception desk. "I need the shuttle to get to the railroad station for the eight o'clock departure," I said. "I'll get my things and be right down."

I hurried back to the room, brushed my teeth with toothbrush and paste from the motel's complimentary toiletries bag and ran back downstairs. Hunter couldn't have reached the bank yesterday before closing time. He'd have to go in after nine today. I didn't know how long he would take trying to get into the safety deposit box with the wrong key, but once he discovered he couldn't, he'd race back to the cabin. That would take at least three hours no matter how fast he drove. In three hours, I'd be on the way to Richmond.

The shuttle waited at the door for me. The drive took about ten minutes, so I arrived at the station in plenty of time to buy a ticket. I kept a wary eye out for Hunter's van but didn't see it. I was still safe.

All the way to Washington on the two-hour trip, I debated with myself about the best course of action. I could stay in the D.C. area for a week or so, until Hunter gave up and left to return to New Jersey. He was impulsive and impatient and probably wouldn't want to wait around long. He'd be back, but I knew what I was dealing with. By that time so would Amos and the police .

I should never have tried to hide from Hunter or to bargain with him. It was too dangerous a game. I didn't need his permission for a divorce. We weren't married a year yet, and I didn't want anything from him—no alimony, no settlement. Just a quick, simple divorce.

What I worried about now were the repercussions from him or his criminal connections. Would he let his felonious buddies know about how I'd stolen his papers? Wouldn't their loss put him at risk, too? He seemed to work alone, and with his ego, he wouldn't think he'd need help, especially help that might consider him too risky to live.

I could charge him with kidnapping, assault, and robbery, but he'd soon be out on bail with even more of a grudge and reason to get rid of me. Too many people were killed by those they'd filed restraining orders against.

I escaped twice after being kidnapped, tied up, and abandoned. I was not to be messed with. And I was not going to live my life in hiding. Somehow I needed to eliminate Hunter in a way to let me live my way and not in hiding from him or any of his criminal associates in a witness protection program.

I could easily bury myself in Washington, D.C., so Hunter would never find me, but Richmond would be less expensive and closer to the marina. Cal and Amos occasionally drove to Richmond—Cal to visit his mother, Amos to pick up supplies. Then there was Ann who seemed to drive back and forth frequently. Ann's cell phone number was in my phone. I could stay in Richmond until one or the other came in, or Ann headed back. Whatever happened, the police were going to learn about Stu and the robbers and what they did to me.

The other option would be to somehow get to the marina myself, but there was no bus service to Dad's area from either Washington or Richmond. A cab was way too expensive. And other than Ann in Richmond, I knew no one who lived in either city. How far would it be to bicycle? The idea brightened my spirits. A bike ride might be long and difficult, but it would be possible. I could disguise myself so if by some chance Hunter drove by, he wouldn't recognize me. Anyway, he'd never expect me to get to Washington or Richmond, much less find a way back to the marina on a bicycle. Not in a million years.

I was still debating the options when the train pulled into Washington's Union Station. I followed the crowd of commuters off the train and left them as they scrambled for the Metro. In Union Station, I called several budget motels outside the city, one in Arlington and two in Silver Spring. The rates quoted confirmed my suspicion the Washington area was too expensive. I couldn't afford a decent motel here, but Richmond was only two or three hours away. I walked to the Amtrak window and bought a ticket for the Main Street Station in Richmond.

Chapter 36

By mid-afternoon, I stepped off the train in Richmond and hailed a cab, asking for the nearest Holiday Inn. I got a room there and then walked to a shopping area to buy a few new clothes. I'd been wearing the same grubby outfit for three days, but it seemed like a week.

I picked up a pizza on the way back to the motel, and even though it was only late afternoon, I went to my room and settled in for the night.

I sat on the bed and called Cal, telling him about Stu and the robbers and the abduction by Hunter. Cal barely spoke during my recital. When I came to the end, he didn't respond at once.

I waited. It was a bizarre story. Who would believe it? Cal probably didn't and now thought I was a nut case. It was only my word, after all. I was a newcomer in town. Even Amos, my own father, didn't believe me half the time. Probably Cal didn't, either. The longer the silence grew, the more I fretted.

"You know," said Cal at last, "the police are probably already onto this gang. They've got the serial numbers on all those electronics Stu and his buddies stole. They must be running those numbers through the pawn shops. But your testimony will put those guys behind bars for sure."

He paused, and I sank down on the bed in relief. Cal believed me, and he was right. Stu and his buddies weren't too bright.

They were bound to make mistakes leading the police to them.

"Good work, Melanie," added Cal. "So you're at the Holiday Inn in downtown Richmond?"

For a moment, I couldn't speak as tears of relief sprang to my eyes. I was glad to be on the phone, so Cal wouldn't see me cry. Anyway, it was a natural response to all the stress. Later, I'd have to figure out why I didn't have a whopper panic attack either time I was caught, tied up, and left alone to die or to be killed later.

"Melanie?"

"Yes, yes. I'm in Richmond. I hesitated, but the train ride had convinced me biking to the marina would require more endurance and time than I possessed, and I couldn't think of any other way to do it without a driver's license. "Could you pick me up here when you come into Richmond the next time? There's no bus service out to the northern neck. I can wait several days until it's convenient for you."

"Don't worry about it," said Cal. "You get a good night's sleep. I'll come by your motel in Richmond tomorrow afternoon to pick you up. Be good to have you back home."

A great weight lifted off my shoulders. I breathed a sigh of relief. "It would be wonderful."

"By the way, I haven't seen Hunter's van around here the last couple of days. Maybe he's gone home."

Gone home so soon? I didn't think so. He was out on the road searching for me.

"Thanks," I said.

"See you tomorrow then." Cal rang off.

I hung up the phone and sat on the edge of the bed, feeling thankful. At least one friend supported me. I glanced at the phone, picked up the receiver, and kissed it.

Chapter 37

I watched the flat farmlands, freshened by a spring rain, speed by as Cal drove north from Richmond to the bridge across the Rappahannock on our way to the northern neck of Virginia. White dogwood blossoms were sprinkled like fairy dust across the woods along the roadside, and dandelions were already spreading across the fields. I breathed a sigh of relief to be alive to enjoy the scenery and sank farther back against the hard cushions in Cal's van.

I turned my head to watch him driving efficiently down the two-lane road. "Thanks," I said.

He glanced at me and winked. "I like Richmond. Needed a break. Glad to help out a friend." He turned his eyes back to the road. "So what are you going to do now?"

I stared out the windshield, pushing my lips in and out. "Somehow I've got to get rid of Hunter."

"You need to get the police on his case," Cal said. "Get him arrested."

"Yes, I know, but. . . "

I could feel Cal's eyes on me. "But what?"

"He won't stay in jail long, you know," I said. "Then what?"

"I've still got your letter," Cal said. "File for divorce now."

I shrugged. "It's more complicated." He'd still be out there somewhere, waiting to kill me.

"What? I can't believe this." Cal banged on the steering wheel. "He kidnapped you, tied you up, beat you, and left you to die. You're going to let him get away with it all?"

"He's a lawyer, he says, and a drug dealer, and he deals in fake IDs," I said. "I've got proof. I also think he's a murderer. He kidnapped and assaulted me, but he is a killer mixed up with other dangerous people."

"Talk to the FBI. Give them your proof. Put him away."

"I'll be dead and discredited before that happens." I folded my arms, still looking straight ahead. "If he doesn't kill me, his friends will. Or I could be squirreled away in a witness protection program and lose everything I value in life."

"I don't think I should take you back to the marina," said Cal, shaking his head. "What's to prevent Hunter kidnapping you again or worse?"

"Me," I said, "and those incriminating papers. That's why I need a plan to use what I have to get what I want."

Cal glanced at me. "Exactly what do you want?"

I smiled at him. "Hunter out of my life and no threat."

Cal shook his head. "Good luck with it," He put his hand on mine. "Let me know how I can help."

I smiled at him, thinking what a great guy he was. Maybe I'd broken the curse of being attracted to the bad ones. I marveled at the thought. Cal seemed to be a genuinely nice man. I was attracted to him, and I liked him. He seemed to like me, too. I sat back and pondered this miracle. Had I actually found a nice guy with no issues? Unlike my other boyfriends, Cal had friends in town—a lot of them. It also spoke well for him.

Maybe I had turned a corner. I was never attracted to Stu at all. Stu would have been a target for the old me, the me who sought out the abusers and the manipulators. Amos seemed changed, too. Not enough to make me want to call him "Dad." I smiled at the thought of him sneaking out at night to go dancing. He was gradually winning back some of my love, but I still didn't trust him, though. Would he believe me when I told him what Hunter did yesterday? I couldn't quite put much faith in that yet.

I glanced at Cal with affection. I couldn't tell him what I was really thinking. I didn't want him involved, and I didn't want him hurt. I was going to have to fight this battle myself. It was Hunter against me, and only one of us would win.

Cal pulled into the marina parking area. Hunter's van was missing and so was Stu's rattletrap, but Amos' pickup was still there.

"Want me to go in with you?" Cal asked as he opened the door.

I shook my head. I picked up my purse and my bag of clothes and stepped out. The crunch of my shoes on the gravel seemed oddly welcoming. So did the smell of seaweed and river. I waved goodbye to Cal as he backed up and headed out the gate. Then I walked into the office.

Peedee squealed and wriggled his little body as he ran to me. I stooped and hugged him, murmuring loving words. Then I looked at Amos, sitting at his desk and frowning at me. "About time you got back here," he said. He threw me a large manila envelope.

I caught it and read the return address. My mail box service. Credit card bills, I thought, but maybe also a letter from Corinne's mother.

I glanced at Amos, stiffened my back, and folded my arms.

There was a time when his tone of voice would have terrified me or turned me to stone. After all I'd been through with Stu and Hunter, I was in no mood to play the vulnerable little girl. Knowing how unjust Amos was in his criticism now made me want to laugh. I narrowed my eyes and curled my lips. "Would you like to hear what happened to me?" I did not hide my sarcasm or distaste. I welcomed his attempt to cut me down.

"Go ahead. Where you been these last few days?" Amos stood and folded his arms in a mirror of mine. His attitude was confrontational and skeptical. "Just like a woman to skip out."

"Really," I said sarcastically. A showdown, I thought. "First, I have to call the police. Where is Stu anyway?"

Amos glared at me. "I don't know. He didn't show up yesterday or today. Why do you want to know?"

"In a minute." I picked up the phone and dialed 9-1-1. This wasn't an emergency, exactly, but it was the best way to get the police. "Police Department, please," I said to the dispatcher. "I want to report a robbery." I tapped my foot as I waited. "Police? I have information about the robberies at the new development. I stayed later than usual to finish a cleaning job there. . ." Would they buy the slight equivocation?

I explained what happened and brought in Stu's involvement, keeping an eye on Amos. What would he think about this?

"Yes, sir, the assistant dock master at the marina was one of the burglars. He's also one of the men who tied me up and left me in the closet. I would have died if I hadn't gotten free." I listened a moment, then said, "Thank you. No, Stu isn't here right now. No, I don't know where he is, but I think they took the stolen goods to some contact in Richmond."

I hung up the phone and turned to face Amos, who was staring at me with his mouth open. "You sure about all that?" Amos asked at last as he walked back to his desk and sat. "You're not making it all up to get rid of Stu, are you?"

"Why would I make any of this up?" I sat in the chair facing his. "Why would I want to get rid of Stu?" Peedee jumped into my lap. I put my arms around the pup and cuddled him as I watched Amos stare back at me, pursing his lips, ready to judge and condemn.

"You know I was going to leave this marina to Stu. Maybe you're making all this up about him because you want it and are trying to get Stu out of the way."

I reared back in disbelief. "You really think I would do something like that?" I shook my head and laughed. "I simply can't believe you would think so little of me, your own daughter." I added, because I knew it would sting, "You have no understanding of people, do you? You can't even tell a good person from a bad one." I shook my head. "Could be because you're a bad one. Maybe that's the kind of thing you would do. That's probably how you got this marina in the first place."

"Now you wait a minute. . ." Amos blustered. "This marina is mine. I bought it with my own money fair and square." He glared at me.

I glared back, but suddenly, Amos' attitude came into sharp focus. He couldn't tell a good person from a bad one, and the motives of all women were colored by his own prejudice and grudges. That's why he sided with Hunter. With Stu, too, of course. I looked at my father with new eyes. He wasn't all-powerful. He was merely a fallible, dysfunctional human being. Who made mistakes. Big mistakes.

The realization made me laugh out loud. I laughed some more

as I thought of the irony in Amos' defense of Stu. "You think I wanted Stu out of the way, so I could get this marina?" The stress I had dammed inside me since I'd married Hunter burst into a cascade of giggles and than outright hilarity. It was a few minutes before I was able to talk. "Did you know that Stu tried to get rid of me, so he would be certain to get the marina?"

"Stu couldn't know anything about that," said Amos.

"Of course he knew," I countered, smiling at Amos. "That's why he was staying around here. He must have been the one who sawed the buttress under my boat. He wanted to get rid of the competition."

Amos shook his head. "I can't believe he'd do such a thing."

I rolled my eyes as I stood and leaned toward Amos, ridiculing him in disdain. "Of course not. I'm your daughter and would lie about everything. Isn't that what you think?" I went back to the chair. "Let's get rid of one idea right now. I don't want your marina. I'll even sign a paper renouncing all claim. How about that?"

Amos stared at me. "But Stu? He wouldn't do what you're saying."

"You don't think so?" I waved my hand impatiently. "It doesn't matter what you think. The police will take care of Stu. I'm sure there's tons of evidence now that the law knows where to look." I hugged the dog. "I've got a bigger problem."

Amos sat back in his chair. "What do you mean?"

"Hunter."

"You're still harping on him? You need to go back and be a good wife to him. You married him, said your vows." He stabbed his finger at me. "It's a promise you made."

"Yeah, I made my bed, et cetera. Is that it? But my vows

didn't include being married to a criminal, being beaten, and getting killed for it."

Amos rolled his eyes now. "Aren't you being a bit overdramatic? Nobody's out to kill you."

I folded my arms. "Stu and his buddies almost did." I paused for the next thrust. "You always say I'm being melodramatic. I say you're being stupid and obtuse. Hunter will be here soon to finish the job Stu botched. The only reason Hunter hasn't killed me before this is because he wants the proof I have." I shook my head cynically at Amos with an ironic smile. "Would you like to keep your own bullheaded wrong ideas or hear the rest of the story? I am not lying about any of this."

Amos shrugged as if he were indulging me in a fantasy. I knew what he was thinking, but it didn't matter. He could help me or not. I had his measure now, and it was a lot smaller than I'd thought.

"I am not making this up," I repeated. I told him about Hunter tying me up and leaving me in the cabin, how I escaped and made it to Richmond, how Cal drove there and picked me up to bring me home. Then I added in a fit of spite, "I didn't trust you to help."

Amos stared down at his hands, shaking his head as I spoke. When I finished, he was silent for a long time. Then he looked up. "You swear you're not making this up?" he asked at last. "It's hard to believe."

"Yet it happened. You can ask Cal."

I waited for Amos to disparage the story and his own flesh and blood in the process. Would he support me as family or persist in believing I was a liar?

"If your story is true," Amos said, his disbelief apparent in the emphasis on "if," "you need to call the police again." He stopped. "Or I guess the FBI, since you say Hunter took you to West Virginia and tied you up there."

I shook my head. "Not yet. He's been back to the cabin by now and found me gone. He'll clean up every shred of evidence. Probably already done that. Even if they do arrest him, he'll be out in a day or two—and gunning for me. He'll always be there waiting in the shadows, looking for the opportunity to get rid of me."

When I saw Hunter again, I'd remind him yet again about the letters I'd given to two different people. Despite his casual attitude, the letters worried him. I knew they did. Two different people he didn't know could expose him to the FBI if I disappeared or was killed. I was not under his control or subject to his punishment unless he again captured me. I must make sure he did not. But I needed a better plan.

I sat back in the chair and studied Amos. Maybe I'd made a dent in his pigheadedness. I never expected he'd treat me as a beloved daughter. The thought was ludicrous. He'd never done it, but was there anything in his psyche to support and protect me? *All right, Amos. Which will it be?* I waited.

Amos stared down at his hands, frowning and saying nothing for a long minute. He heaved a heavy sigh. "I'm so damn tired," he said, turning away from me. He seemed to be staring blankly at the wall. He sighed again and glanced back at me. "I think you're telling the truth. I guess you're right about Stu. Him and his damn cigarettes." He frowned. "I keep this place clean. Nice. Real nice. Stu would have it covered in cigarette butts in half a minute. Never did like the man." He drummed his fingers on the desk for a moment. Then he looked at me. "You wouldn't make up all that stuff you told the police."

I sat back and folded my arms. "No, I wouldn't."

He rubbed his hand against his forehead. "I don't know anything anymore. I've been all wrong." He sighed again. "Wrong about everything. It's all too much." He reached for a napkin and swiped it across his eyes, looking away from me again.

Was he crying? I sat stunned in the chair. I didn't know what to do. I'd never seen Amos like this before. Ever. He'd been blustery, angry, hot-headed, drunk, and out of control. Was he now dealing with remorse? Could that be?

I couldn't cope. I tiptoed out of the office, taking Peedee with me. I climbed the ladder into my boat, watched the sunset, and thought about Amos.

Chapter 38

I woke the next morning still puzzling over Amos' reaction. The vengeful part of me was glad to see him shaken in his unshakeable attitudes. The other part felt pity and maybe a little compassion for a man forced to reverse his long-held assumptions. He had once overwhelmed me with his parental authority. He no longer had that power, and I now saw his flaws and vulnerability, his weakness. How would we reshape our relationship as two equal adults?

I had a bigger problem. Hunter could show up any time, but would he risk it? For all he knew, I reported him to the law and instituted legal proceedings against him, and the police were ready to arrest him. Hunter's wiser course would be to stay hidden, see what I did. Why didn't he simply divorce me and be done with it? Odds were he was afraid of his criminal connections, whatever they were. He was more vulnerable to their punishment for his mistakes. Marrying me and leaving incriminating evidence around was a big one.

At this point, divorce or no divorce, Hunter would try to destroy my credibility as he sought a way to kill me that would appear accidental. How would he do it? If he were hiding out, would he pay someone to find me, maybe drug me into acting irrational and crazy? Give me some kind of truth serum to find out where the safe deposit key was? Or tell who had the letters?

He would always haunt me, unless I found some way to stop him. What were the possibilities? What did I know about him that might be useful? I spotted the manila envelope on the galley table. I ripped it open and shuffled through the junk mail until I came to a letter addressed to me. I tore it open.

The letter was handwritten on plain copy paper, no address and no date at the top. It began with questions for which I could offer no answers. Where was Corinne? What happened to her? I had explained I was Hunter's wife, so the next questions were about how such a thing could be when Corinne was Hunter's wife. Corinne would have called her mother, probably come back home, if there were a divorce. Where was Corinne? The anguish came through in every word and confirmed my worst fear. Hunter killed Corinne and no doubt collected her life insurance settlement. If I stayed with Hunter, I would be next.

Hunter knew how to navigate the legal system. He possessed some kind of law education—maybe a degree. I stopped. That's what he'd told me. In his office, he displayed a diploma and some sort of certificate from the New Jersey Bar Association. Forged? Yes, probably. How come I didn't realize earlier he was such a liar? The clues were all there.

He was a fraud and a crook involved in bogus identifications, counterfeiting, and drug dealing. People like him also indulged in murkier crimes like human trafficking. Maybe he'd tapped out the insurance fraud racket and used his wives in other ways. Could Corinne have become one of his victims in sex trafficking? Hunter and his "colleagues" were all bad, bad people. Thugs and murderers.

Hunter harbored grudges and was vengeful and abusive. Staying with him, thinking I was at fault, seemed so stupid now. I should have left at the first slap. No, when he told me, told me, not asked me, about moving to New Jersey. No, before that, when we were dating, and I saw how he treated servers in restaurants. It was a major tip-off. I ignored everything I didn't want to see.

I could give no comfort to Corinne's mother, but I could try to find out what happened to her daughter. When Hunter was gone, I would give the evidence I had to the FBI, and I would tell them about Corinne's disappearance. They might not care to look into her case, but he probably faked the papers to declare her dead to collect her life insurance. They would investigate.

Divorce now seemed too mild and naive. I'd always known the stakes were high. It was foolish of me to think that hoarding incriminating papers might protect me. Even the letters held by Norma and Cal might not be enough. So now what?

I brewed a cup of hot tea and sat in the cockpit as the mist rose on the river at dusk. By the time I went to bed, I pulled together the makings of a plan to do the job.

The next morning over breakfast, I worked through the details. I needed to learn a few things first.

The country boy disguise served me well for getting into town. I needed a different disguise now for another purpose. I took my laptop to the marina store to use the Wi-Fi. I surfed the web for a new outfit, one that suited my plan. Thank goodness I had my credit cards, including the one I'd hidden on the boat. I hadn't successfully survived life in New York for nothing.

I found what I was looking for, made my purchases, and paid extra for one-day delivery. I would soon have two disguises to give me a measure of freedom. In a spirit of atonement, Amos agreed to let me use the pickup whenever I needed it.

***

I hadn't seen Hunter's van lurking nor heard it pass by. What was he going to do next? He couldn't know my decision to hold off contacting the police or the FBI. I was sure he hadn't given up and gone home. Not with my evidence hanging over his head. He was planning something. Since I didn't see him around, I dressed in my disguise as a teenaged boy going fishing and walked into town but kept a wary eye out for a black van.

I stopped at Cal's bike shop first. Cal was fixing a tire and nodded at me as I entered. Cal's helper Greg was standing beside him watching.

"Cool outfit," he said.

Cal glanced at me. "Seen any sign of him?"

"No. Doesn't mean he's given up."

"I'm sure not." He attached an air pump to the tire. "So what are you going to do now?"

I shook my head. "I'm making a plan."

Cal inflated the tire. "He's a criminal. You be careful dealing with him."

"Yeah." I retreated into the restroom to change back into jeans and a flowered blouse, folding my disguise and tucking it away under the counter for the return trip to the marina. I waved to Cal as I left to walk down Main Street to the karate school. I hoped one of the instructors would make time for some instruction since most of the kids would be in school. I was right. The owner was pleased to give me a lesson. Afterward, he said, "You come back regular time, every week, okay?" I waved and nodded as I left.

Next, I stopped at the police office located in a brick building across from the diner. I walked back to the chief's office down a hall painted an institutional green but marred here and there by penciled graffiti. Past a bulletin board covered with layers of wanted posters and employment notices, Chief Yost sat at his desk, chair tilted, gazing out the window. He turned at my knock.

"Hello there, young lady," he said. "We got them all."

Got them all? It took me a few seconds to realize he meant Stu and the burglars.

"That's good to know," I said. "What about the stuff they stole?"

He gestured to the other chair. "Have a seat. We've been running the descriptions and serial numbers through our pawn shop database connections. Some of the stuff is turning up."

"I'm glad," I said, sitting.

"We've got to thank you for the tip about them. I understand you saw them in action. When you have time in the next day or two, we'll need your statement."

I nodded. "I do some work for the owners," I said, hoping he wouldn't start asking questions yet. "By the way, could you tell me about the general crime rates here? Like, what about murders? Drugs? Thefts?"

Chief Yost grinned at me. "Hey, those house burglaries are the biggest crimes we've had around here for years. No murders in quite awhile. We mostly have minor stuff."

"I guess that's due to the low population and all. It is pretty rural. . ."

"Sure. We're about the safest place you can live in Virginia, except now we've got gangs moving in here. The Bloods and a couple of those other gangs. Their infiltration and activities are what we've got to watch out for."

"Gangs?" I asked. Exactly what I wanted to hear. "Aren't they mostly high school stuff?"

He laughed. "National networks, some of them. Their own tattoos, hand signals, colors, you name it. Whole families in the gangs. They're into drugs, human trafficking, prostitution. Vicious and ugly, the stuff they do." He tipped the chair back once again. "Any despicable crime you can name."

I raised an eyebrow. "What about ID fraud? Counterfeiting?"

"They could get into that, too." He shrugged. "Probably use a lot of fake IDs."

I tapped my finger on the chair arm. "Tell me about the gangs coming in."

"We're keeping an eye on the first of them, you know." The police leaned forward in his chair. "We've got a drug problem here like anywhere else. Why are you asking?"

My questions were making the chief hostile and defensive. I sat back and fluttered my hand. "Yeah. Drugs are everywhere. Must be really hard to control them"

He snorted. "We're on top of the problem so far, but there's always a new wrinkle. We're seeing some gang violence we never saw before."

"So how do you keep an eye on the gangs?"

"How come you're so interested?" Yost twisted in his seat. "Planning to go after them, too, like you did the burglars?"

I laughed and fluttered my hands again. "Nothing like that. Just wondered, that's all. Thought I should keep my eyes open. Tough customers come into the marina now and then."

"I guess so. We brought in someone on a traffic charge a week ago. My detective here got suspicious and asked him if he had any tattoos. The perp said no, no tattoos, then my guy pointed to one on his arm and asked him to take off his shirt. Would you believe it? There was the tattoo of a Korean hit man on his back."

Yost pounded his fist on the desk. "A Korean hit man. That's what this guy was, and he was way out here in the country, nowhere near any big city."

"Omigod, and he was in town? Here?" I asked. Maybe I didn't want to pursue the idea germinating in my mind.

Yost narrowed his eyes and nodded. "It's what we're dealing with, ma'am. You'd best stay out of anything to do with gangs, if that's what you're thinking."

I rose. "Not at all, Chief Yost. Thank you for the information, though." I headed for the door. "Let me know if I can help put Stu and his thugs away. I'll write a statement. Do you think I'll need to testify in court?"

"Don't worry," he said. "With all our evidence and confessions, we may not need it."

"Thank you. Oh, and I'd appreciate it if you could keep an eye on the marina. Chase off any suspicious strangers loitering around. You know how it is."

"Sure. Be glad to. I'll tell my officers to patrol it regularly." Chief Yost rose and walked with me down the hall to the door. He waved as I headed for the sidewalk.

I felt his eyes watching me, but my mind was elsewhere. Gangs, I thought. Gangs. They were territorial, weren't they?

Chapter 39

I walked back to Cal's bike shop to find him sitting at the computer with a Coke and a package of tortilla chips. Greg stood behind the counter, sipping a bottle of water. I retrieved my bag of clothes from behind the counter and took a chair next to Cal.

"Know anything about gang members in this county?" I asked, reaching for a chip.

Cal shuddered. "Please, don't scare me."

"No, really. Do you know any?"

Cal stopped typing and rested his chin on his hand. "Don't gangs go around on motorcycles? Can't see them riding bicycles, can you?"

I laughed as the image came to mind. "Not really."

Cal's shop was on the main drag of town. Would he be vulnerable to shakedowns from a gang? I'd never smelled even a whiff of illegal drugs or noted anything criminal from Cal or his shop. Bicycles tended to draw a wholesome crowd, I'd always thought, and this was such a bucolic area. Gangs typically gathered in poor neighborhoods in big cities, didn't they?

"I'm serious. The police say gangs are coming in here, selling drugs and whatever else they do," I said.

He whistled. "I've never seen anything like it around here. I'll keep an eye out from now on, though."

I nodded, thoughtfully. "They have special hand signals and

tattoos, wear certain colors, stuff like that."

"Why are you so interested? You have enough problems with Hunter, don't you?"

I stared at the road through the plate glass window in front of the store. Yes, I did have enough problems with Hunter, but my plan was taking shape. A dangerous idea, but it might work. It could work. I turned back to Cal. "So how would someone find out where to get drugs in this town?"

Greg had been listening to this interchange and finally spoke up. "I know a couple of guys in the Bloods," Greg said thoughtfully. "I don't mess with them. Kids want drugs . . ." He cocked an eyebrow. "They go to those guys."

"Where do ordinary kids find those gang members?" I asked.

"Easy. Outside school. Any day. I see them dealing, but I'm not into it. I got things I wanna do."

I studied Greg for a moment.

Cal stood and regarded me. "Now wait a minute. Don't tell me you've got a drug habit. You don't want to get messed up with those people. I don't want you killed."

"Of course I don't have a drug habit." I rose and faced him eye to eye. "I don't want me killed, either. Don't worry, I'll be careful, and I won't be buying drugs."

Cal grabbed my sleeve. "Hold on. Let the police handle Hunter. Or call the FBI. You should've done it in the first place."

I pulled my arm away. "As soon as he was out on bail, he'd kill me—and he'd get away with it. I refuse to hide away the rest of my life. I want to live my own life the way I choose." I looked Cal straight in the eye. "I thought I could blackmail him with those fraudulent IDs and offshore accounts into giving me a divorce and leaving me alone. I was wrong." I turned back to the windows and frowned. Speaking more to myself than to Cal, I said, "Now I've got to come up with a more permanent solution."

I picked up the bag of clothes and retreated into the restroom. After a moment, I was back in my country boy disguise and studied myself in the mirror. "I'm pretty good at disguise, aren't I?" I asked, smiling at my reflection.

Cal had returned to the table. "You're serious, aren't you?"

I nodded. "I am, but I'll be very careful, and I won't have to do much other than plant a few seeds." I turned to Greg. "Could I pick you up tomorrow after school? I need you to point out someone who sells drugs."

"Whoa. You don't want to mess with those guys," Greg said.

"I'm not. I'm just going to give them a tip."

Cal groaned and shook his head. "I don't like the sound of this."

I patted his arm. "It should be perfectly safe."

"All right," Cal said. "But call me if you need help."

"Thank you," I swallowed the sudden surge of gratefulness before it brought tears to my eyes. I wasn't at all sure how to pull off the plan that was developing in my mind, but Greg was helping, and it was good to know I could rely on Cal even though I didn't want him involved. I didn't want Greg hurt either.

"So where is the high school?" I asked Greg.

He gave me the directions, and we agreed I would meet him out in front when classes let out the next day. I expected Hunter to show up by then.

I walked out the door with a wave and headed back to the marina, making my strides long and lanky. No cars passed me, but I examined the multiflora rose hedge for escape routes each step of the way. I half-expected Hunter to cruise the road looking for me.

Maybe he wouldn't expect me to return to the marina, but wherever he was, I could bet he eradicated all traces of me in the cabin in the woods. If he caught me again, I would not escape.

No one was out in the yard at the marina, so I climbed into the boat and changed out of the country boy outfit and back to my jeans and blouse. Peedee must have heard me come into the yard. He was barking and squealing inside the store. I walked there, opened the door, and stooped to let Peedee jump up on me in greeting. I saw Amos watching us play, and for once he wasn't scowling. In fact, he was grinning, and I might go as far as to say it was with fondness. Imagine. I caught myself before I asked him why.

"Anything happen while I was gone?" I asked, meaning, "Has Hunter been by?"

"Nothing."

I paused for a moment, wanting to ask about Hunter but not wanting to spoil the moment with any flak from Amos. "I'll take Peedee out for a run then," I said, opening the door and following Peedee out into the yard. I raced him to the gate and closed it before the little pup could run into the road. Then I saw a county patrol car, creeping along as if the driver were looking for something. It was Officer Henschel. I waved him to stop.

"What do you need, ma'am?" he asked, rolling down his window.

"Are you looking for someone, Officer?" Perhaps a warrant was issued for Hunter's arrest. I hoped.

"Lost dog." He tipped his hat. "Don't worry."

"Hope you find him." I smiled at him and waved at the marina. "I live there, but I'm so new in town. Are there places I should stay away from? Dangerous places?"

"No, ma'am. This is a pretty safe area. We do have our petty thefts and such. Just don't get mixed up with drugs or criminals, and you'll be okay."

I tittered and fluttered my hands. "Of course not. Just wanted to know where to stay away from. You know, in case there are gangs and shoot-outs."

"Sure, I guess." He pursed his lips. "They show up around the high school, in the bars, outside the convenience stores. Just don't buy illegal drugs. Stay away from any dealing. That's my advice."

"Okay. Will do," I stepped back and let him drive down the road. I stared at the car for a minute, then walked back to the store. My act was pretty lame, but Henschel confirmed what Greg had already said. My plan was going to work.

Later that afternoon, I returned to the marina store with another request. "I need a receipt for what I've paid so far for my boat slip. Call it a slip rental or better, apartment rental."

Amos looked up from reading the newspaper. "Why?"

"Driver's license. They need proof I live here." I saw the question in Amos' eyes. "Hunter took mine when he abducted me. Anyway, I need a Virginia license. Might as well get it now."

"Sure." He walked to his desk. I saw his stooped shoulders, his slow steps, and I realized he was an old man. The thought saddened me. I watched him scrawl the words on the receipt book. He ripped it out and gave it to me. Then he reached under the counter and pulled out a couple of packages. "Came by UPS. They're for you."

"Thanks," I said and watched him for a moment before I turned to leave, but I stopped halfway to the door. "By the way, are you hiring a replacement for Stu?"

Amos sighed. "I guess so. Haven't thought about it yet."

I crossed my fingers and took a deep breath. "How about hiring me for the job?"

Amos sat up startled. "You!"

"Why not? I can take care of everything Stu did. You can teach me what I need to know. I don't smoke, and I'll keep it as clean and neat as you would."

Amos nodded and pursed his lips. "I guess so. I'll think on it."

"Okay, then," I said as I walked out, Peedee following. "Just remember helping out here doesn't mean I want your marina."

Behind me, the sun was setting, and the croaking of the frogs escalated with the dusk. I climbed up the ladder, Peedee in my arms, and set him on his feet in the cockpit. As the last rays of the sun disappeared, I heard the familiar chrome clatter before I saw the black van. I watched it from my boat as it slowly passed. The driver rolled down his window and waved at me. Hunter. A brazen gesture. He was back. And he was smiling.

Chapter 40

That night, I opened the packages as second thoughts crowded my mind. This idea was ridiculous. So crazy it would never work, but if it did. . .

I pulled a black, straight-haired wig out of one of the packages and fluffed it by shaking. I turned it around dubiously and stretched the elastic headband, then gingerly tugged it on over my own hair, tucking in the stray blonde strands. I crossed to the mirror on the door of the head and studied the effect. Good enough, I thought. I can pull this off. Peedee barked in agreement.

The other package contained a pair of skinny jeans and a frilly, low-cut, flowered blouse. Not my usual style, but I wriggled into the outfit, Peedee watching every move. At the bottom of the package were a pair of high-heeled cork sandals to complete the ensemble. I went back to the mirror and added sunglasses. I couldn't recognize myself, and Peedee reared back until he sniffed my hand.

The next morning, I puttered around the yard in my usual jeans and T-shirt, seeking chores to pass the time and quell my nervousness. I picked up trash and Stu's butt can and tossed them in the dumpster, wiped down the gas pump, and threw sticks for Peedee to chase. Amos remained inside the store.

After lunch, I poked my head in. "Mind if I borrow the pickup? I have a few errands in town."

Amos barely looked up. He reached into the desk, pulled out a set of keys, and threw them over to me. "You sure? You don't have a driver's license yet, do you?"

I caught the keys. "I'll be careful." Back in my boat, I tugged on the skinny jeans and the frilly blouse, leaving the shoes and wig in the bag. Amos was still in the store, so I scurried down the ladder and into the truck before he could spot me in this outfit.

I drove to the high school, circled it and the middle school next door, then I went along the main street of town, passing the bars and glancing into the alleys. Where and how would you buy drugs or fraudulent IDs? Would I recognize a gang when I saw it? What if a group of teenagers I thought were a gang were really a group of teenaged boys and girls looking for fun or mischief? How would you connect with a gang? I hoped Greg knew, since he was a student, but I ought to be able to wing it.

At two-thirty, I parked in the line of cars across from the high school, donned the black, long-haired wig and the shoes, and watched the teenagers pour out of the school and disperse, usually in groups of twos and threes.

Then I spotted Greg and waved at him. He loped toward me as I scanned the crowd of kids, looking for teenagers with tattoos or in groups dressed in similar bandannas or colors. Most of them seemed to be wearing the same kind of jeans and nondescript shirts, T-shirts, or sweatshirts. Even the girls.

I remembered my own teenage years and the agony of dressing, hoping I wasn't going to stand out or embarrass myself in some way. I was lost in painful memories until a teenager rapped on the truck as he walked by. I turned to see who it was and saw him join three others. They all raised their hands in a "V" signal. A gang signal? They were all wearing black bandannas around their heads. They must be in a gang. And they were white. Not black. Not Hispanic. So much for the stereotype. Maybe they were kids being kids.

I saw two older boys, no, these were tough-looking men shouldering backpacks. They didn't come out of the high school. They'd been waiting on the corner. They acted the part of teenagers themselves, but there was something calculated about them. This must be what gang leadership looked like.

I mustn't forget they were dangerous.

Greg ran to the pickup and did a double-take when he saw my black wig. "Ms. Fletcher?" he asked.

"Hi. Don't mind the outfit," I said. "Disguise."

He climbed in.

"What now?" he asked.

I surveyed the area. Girls and boys were still coming out of the high school and walking in various directions. "Point out the drug dealers."

"Okay." He glanced at the various groups of teenagers before he subtly pointed to the men I'd already noticed waiting on the corner. "They don't go to our school, but they hang around with some of the kids. They've got the drugs, all right."

"Good." As I started to slide out of the pickup, Greg stopped me.

"Let me go instead."

"Not on your life," I said. "I don't want you identified in any way with this. . . this caper." The word lent a whimsical air for Greg's benefit to what I was trying to do, even though I was aiming for deadly consequences.

I walked quickly to catch up with the men Greg indicated. As I approached, I slowed and assumed a nonchalant, flirtatious attitude, an acting job I'd never be able to pull off if I weren't so deadly serious about stopping Hunter.

The gang sauntered along to a corner, indulging in horseplay along the way. The two older men joined them as if their meeting were accidental.

I took a deep breath to calm myself. I had nothing to fear. Nothing to fear. I repeated the mantra in my head. Nothing to fear. I was terrified and peeked behind me to see if other people were around. They were, but no one paid attention to me. Get a grip, I told myself. I waved at Greg.

I stopped at the corner and smiled at the group. "Hi, guys," I said.

One of the teens hung his arm arrogantly around my shoulder. "Hello, baby," he said.

I stiffened. A real smart ass. Play it cool. I peeked behind me. Three teenagers were heading my way but too far back to pick up on what was happening and would have no idea what to do even if they did.

"How's about comin' home with me?" he asked, looking at the other teens with a special glance at the older men. "We can play house." The teenaged satellites laughed nervously.

I shook his arm off. "Not today." I conjured up a smile I hoped was provocative but disinterested. "But maybe I can help you boys out. I've got a secret."

The older men hung back, but the smart ass who seemed to be the leader of this gang of teenaged thugs said, "Yeah? How's that?"

I wondered who the older men were. Why would they want to hang around with teenagers unless they were some kind of Fagan characters or undercover cops. They worried me, but I had to go through with this little charade. Casting my eyes about as if I were afraid I'd be overheard, I said in a low voice, "I heard about a new guy who's dealing in this town. Good stuff. He can fix you up real good."

I glanced around again, still acting a bit fearful, stupid, and restless. I hoped I wasn't overdoing it. "He's selling cheap, so you'll start coming to him."

"So where is this dude?" the leader wanted to know. I caught the meaningful look he shot at the older men.

"Don't tell anyone it came from me," I said, acting hesitant, so they'd have to push.

"No, no. We won't." The leader said. The other teenagers were silent. I could see them figuring things out in their little minds. They knew what was going to happen, all right.

"Okay, if you're sure," I drawled. "He's over at the motel on the river. You know the one I mean. The Wayfarer. It's not too far to walk, and believe me, he's got primo stuff, and it's worth it." I smiled at all of them flirtatiously and glanced furtively around again. Then I whispered, "Careful who you tell. Don't let him get caught."

One of the older men studied me with narrowed eyes, and the teens all stared as if they didn't quite believe their ears. A short, squat teen with greasy hair and an even shorter, oilier girl hanging on his arm looked up at me and spoke first. "Sweet. You better go tell—"

"Wait a minute," the older man interrupted. "How will we recognize this dude? Good stuff, you say?"

"The best," I said. *Don't blow it now.* "He can also fix you up with IDs to get you into any bar in town. Tell him, uh, Chantelle sent you. He's cheaper than anywheres else 'cause he's just started setting up here in town. Give him time, and he'll probably have jobs for you, too."

A current seemed to run through the boys. The leader waved them down. "How do we connect with this dude?" he asked.

"Easy. Like I said, he's staying at the Wayfarer down near the marina, but he doesn't want anyone to come to his room while he's setting up here." I manufactured a giggle. "Catch him at his van in the parking lot. A black van. The only one there. Can't miss him." I made a show of looking at my watch. "Oops. Gotta go. I fluttered my hand. "Don't forget, boys. He's good for whatever you need, and it's all good stuff."

I turned away from them, feeling their eyes on my back as I walked away. I crossed the street and turned left. Swallowing my panic, I waved at them and kept my pace slow and regular as if I weren't shaking in every fiber. After that, I didn't look back, but I didn't hear them following me. I expected they were watching me in stunned silence until I turned a corner, and then I risked a peek. They weren't following me.

I practically ran to the pickup. Most of the students were gone along with their rides. Greg pushed the door open for me. I didn't see anyone around to notice me get into the red pickup. It was a common make, style, and color. Probably hundreds around the area and more when the summer crowd came in. I pulled off the wig and started the engine. Nothing now to connect a black-haired floozy with the pickup truck or the truck with the marina.

I asked Greg to keep his head down until we got to Cal's place and dropped him off with my thanks.

He shook his head. "Just hope whatever you're doing works, ma'am," he said as he closed the door.

When I got back to the boat, I stepped out of the jeans and

sandals and hid the outfit in a plastic bag. Dressed in my usual working clothes, I sat on the end of the dock, trembling with my arm around Peedee and watched a branch with spring leaves drift down the river.

This afternoon's adventure was one I'd have to keep to myself. I never wanted to repeat it. The question was—did it work?

Chapter 41

I awoke early next morning after a restless night of worry and fear. Peedee slept beside me and lifted his head as I stretched. "Ready for a walk?" I asked, pulling on my clothes. I threw on a navy sweatshirt against the morning chill. Outside, fog floated over the river and into the yard. I carried Peedee down and set him on the gravel. He sniffed around, did his business, and while I picked it up, he looked at me for the next entertainment. I threw a stick toward the water for him to chase.

The river surface lay flat and undisturbed. Fog smothered the fish splashes and bird songs so an unnatural quiet lay over the marina. I walked to the end of the dock and watched a gull circle. Peedee lay down beside me. No boats plied the river. On the other side at the forked top of a dead tree, an osprey had built its nest and sat on top. It's mate circled overhead. The silence soothed me. I sat with feet dangling over the edge and tried to relax, willing the serenity to gather all the tension in my body and disperse it into the mist.

Whatever Amos thought, however he might try to diminish me or treat me dismissively, I had proven myself to be strong, resilient, inventive, and able to prevail against obstacles. I was, I thought proudly, a tough adversary.

I sat by the river a long time, stroking little Peedee lying beside me and feeling the peace and quiet, but my nerves were stretched tight with worry. Had my plan succeeded?

When I returned to my boat, I heard Amos stirring in the store. I climbed the ladder up into the Peedee's cockpit to eat breakfast. The other Peedee stayed on the ground, sniffing his way around the perimeter. Eventually, he pawed at the door of the store and Amos let him in.

I thought about Amos. He no longer possessed the power that tyrannized me when I was young, and I refused to let him control me now. This went double for any man I decided to date. Whatever else Hunter was, criminal and abuser, he'd been a good teacher. What I learned in dealing with him would stay with me the rest of my life.

I watched Amos come out of the store and open the gate for business. A short while later, a police car pulled up. Chief Yost eased out of the front seat and walked directly to my boat. "Ms. Fletcher?" he called up to me, waving as I leaned out. He climbed up the ladder but stayed on it, leaning in with his elbows on the gunwales. "You been here since last night?" he asked.

"Of course, Chief." I said, my stomach turning over. I knew why he was here.

"I've got bad news for you," he said, assuming a mournful face. "I know it might be hard on you, even if it looks to me like you were separated, begging your pardon, ma'am." He pulled out a handkerchief and wiped his face. "I mean I'm real sorry."

I folded my arms. "What is it, Chief?"

"Your husband, ma'am. This Mr. McCann, I mean. Took us awhile to find out you was married to him. Different last name and all."

I waited.

"He's been shot, ma'am. Killed." He wiped his face again.

"These gangs coming in. They're territorial, you know. Somebody told them he was dealing. Selling in their territory, I mean, you know. I told you about the gangs the other day, remember?"

"I remember. So they thought he was dealing drugs in their territory?"

"Looks like it, ma'am."

"Terrible thing." I shook my head.

"Gangs are coming in everywhere." The chief shifted his feet on the ladder. "We'll get 'em, though, ma'am. Don't you worry." He stepped back down to the ground.

I leaned over. "I'm sure you will, Chief Yost. Thank you for telling me." I watched him trudge to his car.

I picked up Peedee and carried him down the ladder, not sure how I felt. Hunter was dead. An abuser, a criminal, and a murderer was dead. I felt a sense of disconnect. It would take a while to overcome the oppression and fear-induced stress and to fully realize I was free of a terrifying beast. I wasted no time mourning him.

I supposed his death meant I now owned the black van. The first thing I'd do was rip that chrome strip off. Then maybe I'd take a sledge hammer to the whole ugly vehicle. That would feel good. Then I never wanted to see it again.

The store was open, but Amos wasn't there. Tantalizing aromas of coffee and bacon issued from his apartment behind the store. I heard him fussing with something and rapped on the door.

"Come on in," he called. He was frying eggs and glanced my way when I entered. Peedee ran to him and sat at his feet, angling for a treat. "Care for some breakfast?"

I surveyed the close quarters. I'd never been in here before. The galley kitchen took up half of one side of the living room. A table and chairs formed a dining nook in front of the kitchen. A bed took up a quarter of the room opposite. The only other furniture was a gray sofa and matching armchair. Amos made quite a homey place here. I sat at the kitchen table.

"Sure."

"What'd the police want?"

I reached for the pitcher of juice and poured myself a glass. "Hunter is dead."

Amos stopped, spatula in hand, and turned to stare at me. "What?"

"He got caught in a gang shoot-out. They thought he was dealing and invading their territory." I shrugged. "He was a terrible man."

I felt Amos' eyes on me. I sipped the juice.

"I was wrong," he said. "I should have listened to you."

My mouth flew open.

Amos nodded. "I was wrong," he repeated. "I am right proud of you, honey." I could see he was blinking back the tears. "You are tough and smart, and you bounce back. You got a job here if you want it. Learn the business. Take over when I'm gone. Set you up, it will. And I won't be telling you what to do." He paused. "Unless you ask."

"Dad!" I said and got up to hug him. He put his arms around me and held me tight. He was trying not to cry. So was I.

Cal visited in the afternoon to watch my boat return to the water. "I'm staying aboard," I said. "Peedee can jump on it from the dock now." I looked over at the growing pup splashing happily at the water's edge.

"How are you doing?" Cal asked.

"Fine," I said. I wondered if I'd feel any remorse, and so far there was none. If I hadn't set Hunter up for the gang, he would eventually have killed me. He couldn't afford to let me live. So I felt only relief. I did have one more task to be done regarding Hunter, and that was to find out what happened to Corinne. Now I could turn over all the evidence involving his criminal dealings to the police, the FBI, and whoever else might be able to help. That is, after I hired a good lawyer.

There was also the matter of Hunter's life insurance policy naming me as beneficiary. I needed to decide if I wanted anything from Hunter, even to profit from his death.

Cal smiled down at me. I looked in his eyes and my heart hammered. I liked Cal, which worried me. What would I find out about him when I got to know him better? My instincts and judgment were terrible. It would be a long time before I could trust my internal selection mechanism. Had I learned anything staying here with Amos? With my dad?

Cal saw my hesitation. "You know, we haven't actually gone on a real date yet."

"That's true," I said. "I like you, but I'm afraid. . ." Do I want to start now? Am I ready? I've always chosen the bad guys. What if Cal turned into an abuser or a nuisance? Could I handle that?

"You're afraid I'll turn into a monster like Hunter," he said.

That was it in a nutshell. How could I explain my doubts and hesitation without hurting Cal's feelings?

"Don't worry," Cal said. "I understand."

I studied him. "Do you?" I doubted it.

Cal folded his arms and smiled at me. "I do, and I'm only suggesting we go get dinner at the diner in town. Think you could handle that?"

Just dinner at the diner in town. "No other agenda?" I asked.

"None. Not one." He winked. "The next time we go out, you'll have to ask me. I'll wait."

One step at a time. This was not going to be a spontaneous, spur of the moment love affair. I refuse to follow that route again. It will take a long time getting to know Cal and his family and his friends. Maybe he'll wait until I'm ready. Maybe not. Going to the diner with him would begin to change our relationship. Maybe.

But if I don't take the first step, I'll never grow, and my selection mechanism will never change.

"Okay," I said, overruling my doubts. "You've got a deal."

THE END

See Eileen Haavik McIntire's website

SecretPanels.Net

Murder, mystery and mayhem
for the reader.

If you liked *The Two-Sided Set-Up*,
please write a review
on Amazon.com.
I'd love to hear your comments.
E-mail me at eileenmcintire@aol.com.

Other books by
Eileen Haavik McIntire

The 90s Club Series: Cozy Mysteries

Nancy Dickenson and the 90-year-old residents of Whisperwood
Retirement Center uncover theft and murder at Whisperwood.
They turn up clues like tricks in a bridge game and risk their lives
to catch the murderers.

The 90s Club & the Hidden Staircase.
ISBN 978-0-9834049-3-4.
"With plenty of humor and its own original. tale...a must for readers of
cozy mysteries.": *Midwest Book Review.*

The 90s Club & the Whispering Statue.
ISBN 978-0-9834049-7-2
> "A fun read...nostalgia and...social commentary, wrapped up in
> an engaging mystery novel." *Foreword Reviews*

The 90s Club & the Secret of the Old Clock
ISBN 978-0-9614519-0-5
"An impressively well-crafted and thoroughly entertaining mystery
that plays fair with the reader. "*Midwest Book Review*

The Shadow Series:
Historical Adventures

Shadow of the Rock
ISBN 978-0-9834049-0-3
Two women, 200 years apart, seek their past and their
future on journeys that will link the old world with the
new and change the map of Florida.
"A riveting tale of time and humanity, highly recommended."
Midwest Book Review
"A bold adventure...Chapters move quickly in a mixture
of danger, excitement, and pure enjoyment..." *Fore-
word Reviews*

In Rembrandt's Shadow
978-0-9614519-5-0
It's 1616 in the Spanish Netherlands, Saul Levi
Morteira rows ashore at night to rescue a family from
the ravages of the Inquisition and take them to tolerant,
egalitarian Amsterdam. In gratitude, the family asks
Rembrandt to paint Morteira's portrait as a gift to him.
Thus begins the provenance of the painting hidden in
the Holocaust and found by Josh and Sara in *Shadow of
the Rock*. They now seek its rightful owner.

From Summit Crossroads Press

**Practical, easy to read, and recommended books
for parents by Dr. Roger McIntire.**

Teenagers & Parents:
12 Steps to a Better Relationship

This new and revised version of *Teenagers &Parents* adds tips
and strategies for dealing with the growing obsession and
danger of cell phones, computers, and social media. What's the
parents' best strategy for protecting their child from the preda-
tors that lurk on social media—and in the malls, playgrounds,
and schools? ISBN 978-0-9614519-4-3

Staying Cool and In Control

What should you say to your kids at supper and how should
you say it? This is a practical guide that begins with the basics
and proceeds to school problems, bad habits, and good habits,
for Mom, Dad, and the kids. From eating problems to problems
with cell phones, Dr. Roger McIntire presents dialogues and
examples that can smooth the family airways and strengthen
family relationships. Parental strategies and solutions fill every
chapter of this complete guide.
ISBN 978-0-9834049-8-9

Grandma, Can We Talk?

These tips for Grampa and Grandma on getting along with and
helping the grandkids will help make conversation with the
grandkids enjoyable for everyone.
ISBN 978-0-9991565-0-6.

Summit Crossroads Press Also Publishes

The First Person History Series

On My Own: Decoding the Conspiracy of Silence
By Erika Schulhof Rybeck. Erika enjoyed a magical childhood
in Austria before the Nazis came. She escaped by Kinder-
transport to Scotland where she grew up in a convent boarding
school. The book is a tribute to her parents and the story of
how she found out what happened to her parents and family.
ISBN 978-0-9834049-9-6

Return to the Shtetl by Dorothy Sucher.
This is the author's story of traveling alone to Russia and
Belarus in 1992 to search for information about her grandpar-
ents. She kept a journal and took many photographs. She paints
a vivid and moving picture of the state of Belarus at the time,
not long after the Chernobyl explosion, with writing that will
capture the reader.

The Twentieth Century Through My Eyes by Isadore
Seeman. This is the autobiography, written at age 99, of a man
who lived through and played a part in the tumultuous events
of the twentieth century. As a community and national leader
in public health and social welfare, he helped shape the nature
of those services in ways that affect all of us.
ISBN 978-0-9614519-3-6.

CPSIA information can be obtained
at www.ICGtesting.com
Printed in the USA
LVHW03s0509021018
592106LV00007BA/907/P